BILBURY GRANGE

Other books by Vernon Coleman

The Medicine Men (1975)
Paper Doctors (1976)
Everything You Want To Know About
  Ageing (1976)
Stress Control (1978)
The Home Pharmacy (1980)
Aspirin or Ambulance (1980)
Face Values (1981)
Guilt (1982)
The Good Medicine Guide (1982)
Stress And Your Stomach (1983)
Bodypower (1983)
An A to Z Of Women's Problems
  (1984)
Bodysense (1984)
Taking Care Of Your Skin (1984)
Life Without Tranquillisers (1985)
Diabetes (1985)
Arthritis (1985)
Eczema and Dermatitis (1985)
The Story Of Medicine (1985, 1998)
Natural Pain Control (1986)
Mindpower (1986)
Addicts and Addictions (1986)
Dr Vernon Coleman's Guide To
  Alternative Medicine (1988)
Stress Management Techniques (1988)
Overcoming Stress (1988)
Know Yourself (1988)
The Health Scandal (1988)
The 20 Minute Health Check (1989)
Sex For Everyone (1989)
Mind Over Body (1989)
Eat Green Lose Weight (1990)
Why Animal Experiments Must Stop
  (1991)
The Drugs Myth (1992)
Why Doctors Do More Harm Than
  Good (1993)
Stress and Relaxation (1993)
Complete Guide to Sex (1993)
How to Conquer Backache (1993)
How to Conquer Arthritis (1993)
Betrayal of Trust (1994)
Know Your Drugs (1994, 1997)
Food for Thought (1994)
The Traditional Home Doctor (1994)
I Hope Your Penis Shrivels Up (1994)
People Watching (1995)
Relief from IBS (1995)
The Parent's Handbook (1995)
Oral Sex: Bad Taste And Hard To
  Swallow? (1995)
Why Is Pubic Hair Curly? (1995)
Men in Dresses (1996)
Power over Cancer (1996)
Crossdressing (1996)
How To Get The Best Out Of
  Prescription Drugs (1996)
How To Get The Best Out of
  Alternative Medicine (1996)

How To Conquer Arthritis (1996)
High Blood Pressure (1996)
How To Stop Your Doctor Killing You
  (1996)
How To Overcome Toxic Stress
  (1990,1996,2000)
Fighting For Animals (1996)
Alice & Other Friends (1996)
Dr Coleman's Fast Action Health
  Secrets (1997)
Dr Vernon Coleman's Guide to
  Vitamins and Minerals (1997)
Spiritpower (1997, 2000)
Other People's Problems (1998)
How To Publish Your Own Book
  (1999)
How To Relax and Overcome Stress
  (1999)
Animal Rights – Human Wrongs
  (1999)
Superbody (1999)
The 101 Sexiest, Craziest, Most
  Outrageous Agony Column Questions
  (and Answers) of All Time (1999)

novels
The Village Cricket Tour (1990)
The Man Who Inherited a Golf
  Course (1995)
The Bilbury Chronicles (1992)
Bilbury Grange (1993)
Mrs Caldicot's Cabbage War (1993)
Bilbury Revels (1994)
Deadline (1994)
Bilbury Country (1996)
Second Innings (1999)
Around the Wicket (2000)

short stories
Bilbury Pie (1995)

on cricket
Thomas Winsden's Cricketing
  Almanack (1983)
Diary Of A Cricket Lover (1984)

as Edward Vernon.
Practice Makes Perfect (1977)
Practise What You Preach (1978)
Getting Into Practice (1979)
Aphrodisiacs – An Owner's Manual
  (1983)
Aphrodisiacs – An Owner's Manual
  (Turbo Edition) (1984)
The Complete Guide To Life (1984)

as Marc Charbonnier
Tunnel (novel 1980)

with Dr Alan C Turin
No More Headaches (1981)

with Alice
Alice's Diary (1989)
Alice's Adventures (1992)

BILBURY GRANGE

Vernon Coleman

Chilton Designs

First published in the United Kingdom, 1993,
by Chilton Designs Publishers,
Publishing House, Trinity Place, Barnstaple, Devon, EX32 9HJ, England.
Copyright Vernon Coleman 1993

Reprinted 2000

The village of Bilbury does not exist. And neither do any of the characters in this book. Neither the village nor the characters are based on any existing village or individuals. All characters in this publication are fictitious and any resemblance to real persons, living or dead, is purely coincidental.

ISBN: 0 9503527 7 2

Printed in Great Britain by J. W. Arrowsmith, Bristol

CHAPTER ONE

The two roofers seemed quite unconcerned about the fact that there was a gale blowing. They both wore dark green oilskins and had their hoods up. They stood, balanced in a small gulley in between the wet and slippery slates of two of the peaks of our multifaceted roof, and pointed at something I couldn't see. One of them cupped his hands around his mouth and shouted down to me. But the wind took his words long before they reached me and I couldn't hear a thing he was saying. The taller and stouter of the two, the one with the droopy moustache and straggly beard, knelt down on the edge of the roof and peered down. I felt dizzy just looking up but he seemed quite unconcerned.

'Climb up!' he shouted. 'I'll hold the ladder for you.' He must have noticed the look of apprehension on my face. 'It's perfectly safe!' he yelled. 'As safe as houses.' He laughed, though the joke came out so fluently that it clearly wasn't new.

I swallowed hard, pulled the zip on my green oiled coat right up to my chin, pulled my cloth cap down firmly onto my head and started to climb the ladder. It was difficult to believe it was May. I could feel the wind tugging at me as I climbed upwards and the rain, lashing against my hands and my face, was sharp enough to sting. The higher up I climbed the worse the wind got and I shivered involuntarily, though whether through fear or the cold I wasn't sure.

'Your nails have all rusted through,' shouted the taller roofer when I reached the top of the ladder. 'It's the salt in the sea air. Come on up and I'll show you.' He was crouching down with one foot resting on guttering which was, I

1

noticed, clogged solid with last autumn's dead leaves.

'I am up!' I shouted. 'This is as high as I'm going.' Owning a big house had seemed a wonderful idea a few weeks ago but the attraction was rapidly beginning to pall.

'Please yourself!' shouted the roofer with a vague shrug of his shoulders. He stopped, as though he'd suddenly thought of something. 'You're not frightened are you?'

'Of course I am!' I yelled back. 'I'm terrified.'

'But you're still on the ladder!' laughed the roofer. He held out a hand. 'Come on, I'll give you a hand up.' I stayed where I was, with my hands gripping the top of the ladder as though my life depended on it, which I suppose it did. The rain had found a way in between my neck and the collar of my coat and it was trickling down my back. Every few seconds the wind would howl a little louder and blow a little stronger and I wasn't sure whether it was my imagination but I was convinced that the ladder had moved at least twice. I realised that from where I was perched I could see the sea and I wondered if estate agents would count it as a 'sea view'. The roofer reached down, unhooked my fingers from around the top of the ladder and took hold of my right hand. He wore soft leather, fingerless driving gloves which were sodden with the rain. Suddenly my fear of looking foolish and cowardly rose above my fear of falling and, gripping the roofer's hand with all the faith of a drowning man clutching at a straw, I clambered up the last few rungs of the ladder and launched myself stomach first onto the edge of the house roof. As I wriggled my way further into the lead lined gulley between the two peaks of the roof I slowly realised that at some stage I had to do all this in reverse in order to get back down again. Up here I could taste the salt on my lips. It was what I imagined it would be like to be on a ship in a storm. I suddenly had a terrible mental picture of the two workmen having to remove a section of the roof in order to lower me back inside. I could feel sweat mingling with the rain running down my spine.

'See?' said the shorter roofer, a small, lithe fellow whose visible skin was burned mahogany brown by the sun, and whose confidence and agility on the roof had already reminded me more of a monkey than a man. He stabbed a podgy finger at the edge of a slate which obediently moved out of position.

2

Two other nearby slates, disturbed by the movement, slipped downwards and revealed the aged wooden laths to which they had been fastened. The roof was not lined and I could see straight through into the loft. I instinctively reached to push the slates back into position to stop the rain getting in but all I succeeded in doing was dislodging another half a dozen slates.

'The whole roof is rotten,' said the taller roofer with all the cheerfulness of a man who is not going to have to pay for the repairs but who, indeed, realises that he has found himself a couple of month's profitable work. 'You need new battens, new slates and new nails. Your valleys need new lead too.'

'Copper,' said the mahogany brown roofer.

I looked at him quizzically.

'Copper nails,' he said. 'They're a bit more expensive but they last longer. Especially with the salt air.' He kicked at the roof in that idle sort of way that a motorist will kick at the tyres of a car he's thinking of buying and a dozen loose slates slid a little further out of position. 'Your coping tiles are loose too. The mortar has gone.' He steadied himself against a chimney stack as a strong gust of wind caught him unexpectedly. 'And you've got woodworm.'

'Thought it better that you saw for yourself,' said the taller roofer. He slid his fingers into one of the gaps that had appeared in the roof and, like a conjurer producing a rabbit from a hat, pulled out the top half of a nail and offered it to me. 'Rusted right through,' he said. 'Hand made.' he added. 'This roof hasn't had any work done on it since the house was built.'

I took the nail from him, examined it and for no very good reason slipped into my coat pocket. 'Thank you,' I said. 'I think I'll go down now.'

The taller roofer must have seen the look of apprehension on my face. 'Don't worry!' he said. 'If you fall you'll hit the ground before you have time to worry about it!' He laughed and his partner laughed with him. I did not laugh but edged backwards towards the ladder and somehow wriggled round into a position from which I could swing my legs over the edge of the roof. I then gingerly climbed down the swaying

3

ladder. As soon as I had my feet back on the ground I hurried round to the back door to see my wife, leaving the roofers to climb down and tidy up their ladders by themselves.

'The bad news is that we seem to need a new roof!' I told Patsy, who was standing in the kitchen of Bilbury Grange watching a saucepan full of cold water fail to boil on a small primus stove we had borrowed from Dr Brownlow. I pushed back my hood and wiped the rain from my eyes with the back of my hand. The only kitchen furniture we had was an old pine table and three unmatched dining chairs (two of which had, for some inexplicable reason got legs of uneven length). We had bought a second hand cooker from a dealer in Barnstaple but, despite several promises, it had not yet been delivered. 'The good news is that if you stand in the right spot on the edge of the roof we've got a sea view.'

Patsy half smiled at my feeble attempt to make fun of our problems. 'Mr Naughton is here,' she said. 'He's down in the cellar. He says he thinks we've got woodworm.' Mr Naughton was a builder we'd asked to come and give us a quote for some essential restoration work. Patsy looked at me and swallowed hard. 'Have we done the right thing?' she asked.

Still dripping with rain I instinctively reached out and pulled her to me. 'Of course we have!' I insisted. 'Things can't get much worse can they?' She threw her arms around my neck and clung to me as though she were drowning and I were a life-raft.

Just then the door from the cellar burst open and a bald, burly man in a brown boiler suit marched in. He was holding a piece of wood that seemed to have mushrooms growing out of it. 'Dry rot!' exclaimed Mr Naughton with ill disguised delight. He shook his head and sucked in air as though he was about to go pearl diving. 'You've got dry rot in your joists and your floorboards. Nasty. Very nasty. Do you want to come and have a look?'

'No, thanks,' I said, wearily. 'I'm happy to trust your judgement.'

I have noticed that builders always do everything they can to make house owners feel uncomfortable and anxious. I think it must be something they are taught when they are apprentices. I suspect the theory is that if you terrify the customer

4

he will expect a bank shattering bill and feel happy and relieved when it turns out to be merely outrageous. (As I was to discover later builders also have a habit of starting a job and then disappearing for hours, days or even weeks at a time. I am convinced that they do this so their customers don't ever dare complain about the things they do when they turn up. Customers are so grateful when the wretched builders arrive that they gladly put up with the mess and the chaos and they bite their tongues when the workmen settle down for their obligatory tea breaks at fifteen minute intervals.)

Patsy was so depressed by Mr Naughton's gloomy prognostications that she burst into tears. It was beginning to look as though the rest of 1972 wasn't going to be easy.

*   *   *

It may sound rather clichéd but things didn't seem quite so bad after we'd had a cup of tea. It wasn't so much that the tea worked miracles but simply that taking a few minutes to drink it gave us a chance to put things into perspective. When we had bought Bilbury Grange we had both known that it was going to need a lot of work. Although buying it had taken virtually every penny we'd been able to raise, we had bought it relatively cheaply and so we had a little money left over from the bank loan which we had set aside for repairs.

Right from the start we had known that we wouldn't be able to do everything at once. If we had wanted something small and neat and faultless we would have chosen one of the new semi-detached houses being built on the Barnstaple road.

It is true that we hadn't expected to have to replace the roof and the floorboards, and we hadn't known that the house had woodworm and dry rot, but when we thought about it we realised that by dealing with these fundamental problems right at the start we would at least be ensuring that we ended up with a solid building.

We wanted to turn Bilbury Grange, so long a derelict house, into a home and it would have been a lot more expensive if we had started to decorate and furnish the house and had then found out that it needed partly rebuilding.

5

These were the arguments we used to cheer one another up and to a very large extent they worked.

We sent Mr Naughton and the two roofers away with strict instructions to submit their estimates for the work they considered essential and I hung my still dripping coat up in the back lobby. Then Patsy had opened a can of beans, poured them into a pan and started to heat them on our small stove. I put two slices of bread into our only electrical appliance - an automatic toaster.

Bilbury Grange had been built in the last part of the 19th century for a rich businessman from the Midlands who had retired to Devon to spend his days hunting, shooting and fishing. We still hadn't found out the name of the architect who had designed the house but the businessman had clearly either had taste as well as money or else he had at least had the wit and intelligence to allow someone with good taste to make all the major building decisions.

The front entrance to the house was on the south side of the building with two short stone staircases, one from the right and one from the left, joining underneath a stone canopy which was held up by two massive stone pillars. Two large and fierce looking stone lions (one of which had, sadly, lost part of its tail) guarded the two halves of the front door which opened into a large reception hall. This was dominated by a massive stone fireplace which was so large that it had two stone seats built into its sides. On the western side of the house a second entrance door, this time guarded by two stone eagles, led into a corridor which passed a boot room, a gun room and a games room before entering into the reception hall area alongside the fireplace.

The main part of the house was square, with four large reception rooms on the ground floor and a beautiful swirling staircase leading up to the first floor. There were six main bedrooms, two small bedrooms, and a junk room in the attic. A smaller, far less impressive staircase twisted its way around the back of the house and led directly down into the kitchen. The door down into the cellars, which ran underneath the whole of the main part of the house, was also in the kitchen.

The back door of the house led out of the kitchen into a cobbled courtyard, the entrance to which was through the centre of a now almost derelict coach-house which, despite its dilapidated appearance, still had its own clock tower. The other two sides of the courtyard were made up of stables and other outbuildings.

To get from the lane to the house you had to drive between a pair of rather tumble down stone pillars and a pair of rusting iron gates. You couldn't see the house from the lane because it was hidden behind a small copse and a clump of massive rhododendron bushes. The driveway which led up to it and which twisted in between the trees was no more than a quarter of a mile long.

The gardens around the house, which had clearly once been landscaped, had been allowed to fall into disrepair. We had a small stream and a lake with an island in the middle of it, but although the stream was still running the lake had become choked with weeds. In the days when it had been built the house had been in the centre of a small estate but the agricultural land had long since been sold off and all that now remained were two medium sized fields which contained more than their fair share of nettles and thistles.

All this may sound rather splendid but as we sat at our badly stained pine table (we didn't have a table cloth) eating our baked beans on toast off paper plates we didn't feel very splendid. In fact we didn't yet *feel* as if it was our house. We both felt more like intruders who had broken in and we half expected someone in authority to storm into the kitchen and throw us out into the cold and windy rain of a Devon spring.

* * *

We had just finished eating our single course meal when the telephone rang.

The only telephone point we had was in the hall about half a mile away, and at first I didn't hear the bell. But Patsy did. She ran off as quickly as she could while I put our empty bean tin and dirty plates into the dustbin outside the back door and started to wash our knives and forks. Patsy reappeared a minute or two later.

'It's the editor of your paper,' she said, breathlessly.

'What does he want?'

7

'He didn't say. But he sounded a bit cross.'

I had forgotten about the local paper, 'The Barnstaple, Bideford and Bilbury Herald' but I shouldn't have done. For several months I had been writing a weekly medical column for them. The Editor was ringing to say that they didn't have any copy for the next edition.

'We need a column from you in an hour!' said the editor, crossly. 'Otherwise there will just be an empty space in the paper.'

I felt very bad about forgetting to send in a column and I apologised profusely. I didn't get paid very well for writing the column but I enjoyed doing it and I tried to be as professional about it as I could be. Besides, with Bilbury Grange to restore, we needed every penny we could lay our hands on.

'I tried to ring you at the surgery but they told me you were on holiday,' said the editor. 'Your receptionist, a Miss Jackson, said you'd ... '

' ... Johnson.'

'Pardon?'

'Her name is Johnson. Doreen Johnson.'

'Johnson. She said you'd got married, and gone off on your honeymoon but that she thought you'd probably be at home.'

'That's right. We're having our honeymoon here.'

'Why the hell didn't you tell us you were getting married?'

'I'm sorry. It was a very quiet do – just family and close friends.'

'But you should have told *us*,' insisted the Editor. 'We could have sent a photographer along and put something in the paper.'

'We didn't really want anything in the newspapers,' I said. 'We're both rather shy.'

'Baaaah!' snorted the editor, who clearly didn't believe me, even though it was the truth. 'You didn't have to be in any other papers but you should have told us. You write a column for us, for God's sake! Next time you get married you just make sure you ring us beforehand, right?'

'There won't be a next time!' I laughed.

'Hrrmph.' snorted the editor. 'That's what they all say.' He shouted at someone in the background. 'Who's looking after your patients?' he asked me.

'Dr Brownlow. He was my predecessor. He kindly offered to come out of retirement for a week.'

'Having a good time?'

'I beg your pardon?'

'Are you having a good time? You're on your honeymoon aren't you? People are supposed to enjoy themselves on their honeymoons.'

'Yes, thank you!'

'Ring in your copy within the hour, right?'

I promised I would, though I didn't have the faintest idea what I would write about, but my words were wasted on an empty telephone for the editor had severed the connection without saying 'goodbye'. He always put the telephone down when he'd finished saying what he wanted to say, or when he found a conversation beginning to bore him, and I still found it rather disconcerting. I hurried back to the kitchen, found Patsy and told her that I had to write a column. I then spent ten valuable minutes trying to find my typewriter and a piece of paper. In the end I gave up and wrote my column in pencil on two clean paper plates. By the time I had finished and had dictated the copy to a reporter at the paper there were just three minutes left of my allocated hour.

* * *

Patsy and I had been married for two and a half days.

When we had first met I had been living at the Duck and Puddle public house in Bilbury and she had been working there as a waitress. I had just qualified as a doctor and had taken a job as an assistant to a rather eccentric general practitioner called Dr Brownlow. After a few months Dr Brownlow had decided to retire when the chance discovery of an underground river on his land gave him the opportunity to set up a business selling bottled water. I had accepted eagerly when he had offered me his practice.

It hadn't taken Patsy and I long to fall in love and when Bilbury Grange had come onto the market within a few days of Dr Brownlow offering me his practice the omens had seemed irresistible. I had a reliable, steady job and we had somewhere to set up home together. Patsy and I had decided

9

to get married and had agreed to buy Bilbury Grange with money we didn't have but had been told we could borrow from the bank.

We had decided to spend our week long honeymoon getting settled into the house, trying to find some cheap, basic furniture and organising the builders who would help us repair and rebuild the house. Although the house wasn't really habitable we had decided to move into it straight away; partly to save money which would we would have wasted renting somewhere else, and partly because we didn't want to waste any time before getting started on the restoration, but mainly because we couldn't wait to move into our new home.

* * *

CHAPTER TWO

Twenty four hours later the two roofers stood silently in the kitchen while Patsy and I read their estimate for re-roofing Bilbury Grange. They looked rather out of place standing, and steaming slightly, on our level kitchen floor. They both still wore their green rubberised waterproofs but their coats were unfastened and I could see that around his waist each man wore a worn leather holster which carried a hammer and a pouch full of nails.

The two men brought with them a smell of wet rubber. Through habit they both stood with their legs wide apart and this made them look as though they'd just climbed down off a pair of horses. The look of them rather reminded me of cowboys and I couldn't help hoping that there was no sinister significance in this.

'I think you must have made a mistake,' I said, turning the single sheet of paper around and putting my finger on the figure at the bottom. Apart from the amount we had paid for the house it was the largest single sum of money I had ever been forced to contemplate.

The taller and stouter of the two roofers, the one with the moustache and beard, who seemed to be in charge of financial matters, pulled a pair of spectacles out from somewhere underneath his waterproofs and peered at the paper as though he was looking at it for the first time.

'No,' he said. 'No mistake. That's the estimate. You've got a big roof. It needs a lot of work.'

'And a lot of slates!' added his partner, clearly accustomed to taking on a supporting role. 'You must have a quarter of an acre of roof up there.'

11

'That's another thing.' I said 'I'm a bit worried about the slates. Are you sure that new slates will look right on an old house?'

'Best asbestos!' said the stouter roofer, defensively. 'You won't be able to tell the difference.'

'Can't you reuse our existing slates?' asked Patsy. 'Surely they haven't all gone rotten?'

'Most of them will get broken when we take them off,' said the stout roofer. 'If we have to try and re-use them it'll take us much longer to get them off. And we'll never be able to get any slates to match the ones we do break.'

I accepted that the roof needed re-slating but I wasn't happy about any of this. 'I'm not sure.' I said. 'We'll think about it and let you know.'

'You've got our number,' said the thinner roofer. 'It's on the estimate.'

'You won't find a cheaper price anywhere else,' his partner warned us.

They turned and left, leaving Patsy and I and the bill alone in the kitchen. I put the bill down on our stained old table and Patsy and I sat on two of our three mismatched dining chairs. I looked round at the chipped and fading cream paint-work on the walls and woodwork, at the huge floor to ceiling built in china cupboards, at the massive glazed white sink and the huge old taps which were fed by piping which shook every time they delivered water and thought of the floorboards underneath us which had provided bed and board for rather too many woodworm. I thought of the dry rot spores growing merrily in the cellar and the slates slipping off our roof and I wondered, just for a moment, whether or not we might possibly have taken on more than we could cope with.

'Are things going to be all right?' asked Patsy, quietly.

'Yes.' I said, with far more certainty than I felt.

'How can you be so sure?'

'Because the worst that can happen is that we get thrown out of here and have to live in a tent in a field and even then we'd have each other and I wouldn't care so what have we got to worry about?'

Patsy smiled. 'I do love you,' she said.

'And I love you,' I said. 'And that's the only thing that

really matters.' I stood up, moved around the table, lifted Patsy to her feet and kissed her.

'I think we're both mad,' she said. 'Stark raving, certifiably bonkers.'

'I think you're probably right.'

'Was that the front door bell?'

I said I thought it was.

With great reluctance I let Patsy go and then sprinted out of the kitchen, along the back corridor, through the doors into the huge reception hall at the front of the house and across the reception room. I was slightly out of breath when I pulled open the front door and couldn't help thinking that whatever else happened living in Bilbury Grange would help make me fit.

Thumper Robinson and his girlfriend Anne were standing there. Anne had their baby in her arms. Thumper was holding a bunch of freshly picked spring flowers. I noticed with delight that the rain had stopped, that the sky was blue and that the sun was shining for the first time in two days.

'Hello!' said Thumper. 'We thought we'd drop in and see how you were getting on. Tell us if it isn't convenient and we'll go away again.'

'Come in!' I said. I was truly delighted to see them both.

'Isn't this place amazing?' said Anne, looking around her, wide eyed with astonishment. 'Do you know I've never seen it before?'

'It's all a terrible mess,' I apologised. 'Patsy's in the kitchen. Follow me.' I led the way back through to the back of the house.

'Shouldn't you have put knife nicks in the door posts so that you could find your way back?' called Thumper with a laugh. 'This place is enormous!' Our footsteps echoed on the bare wooden boards.

Patsy was as pleased to see our visitors as I was. Although we didn't realise it at the time this was for both of us a moment we would always remember, for Thumper and Anne were the first visitors we had welcomed to our home.

'Would you like a cup of tea?' she asked when she'd made a fuss of the baby. I confess that I made a bit of a fuss of the baby too. He is, after all, named after me in memory

13

of the fact that I helped to deliver him in a field.

'I'll have a cup in a minute or two,' said Anne. 'When you've shown us round.'

'I'd better put the water on to boil now,' said Patsy. 'It takes rather a long time,' she warned. She filled our only saucepan, lit our tiny camping stove and then balanced the former on the latter. Despite half a dozen telephone calls our new second hand cooker still hadn't arrived from the shop in Barnstaple.

'Why are you using bottled water?' asked Thumper.

'It's out of the tap,' explained Patsy, 'but it comes out a bit brownish so we filter it through some coffee filter papers we found in a cupboard.'

We ignored Thumper's look of distaste and took our first visitors on our tour of Bilbury Grange.

'You do like a challenge, don't you?' said Thumper, with a grin when we got back to the kitchen. The water in the saucepan was boiling and Patsy put tea bags into our only two mugs. 'I'm afraid we don't have any milk,' she apologised.

'Or sugar.' I added.

'I'm not surprised!' said Thumper. 'I'm amazed you can afford the tea bags!'

'Thumper!' said Anne, sharply but Patsy and I were both laughing. 'Aren't you having a cup?' Anne asked us both.

'Not thirsty,' said Patsy.

'Just had one,' I said.

'You've only got two mugs haven't you?' said Thumper, perceptively.

Patsy and I looked at one another and exchanged thoughtful glances.

'I've never been in a house where they had more bedrooms than cups,' said Thumper, with a grin.

'How long has it been empty?' asked Anne, who seemed rather embarrassed by Thumper. 'Didn't it used to be owned by someone who was in advertising?'

I nodded. 'An American called Pironi owned it for a while but I don't think he came here more than half a dozen times in as many years. Hardly anyone ever saw him. Then Mike Trickle, the TV personality, bought it but I don't think he ever stayed here.'

'So it must be several years since anyone has actually lived here?'

I nodded.

'Where are you staying?' asked Anne. 'The Duck and Puddle?'

'No,' replied Patsy. 'We're going to live here.'

Anne blushed strongly. 'I'm sorry!' she said. 'I just thought ... ' She looked around the kitchen.

'I know,' said Patsy. 'It's all a bit of a mess. But we can't really afford to pay money out for a room because we need every penny we can raise to repair the house. And anyway we want to be here so that we can keep an eye on things.'

'It's no worse than our place was for ages,' Thumper reminded Anne. 'Just bigger.' He looked around the room and whistled. 'Difficult to know where to start, isn't it?' He paused. 'Still,' he said, 'at least the fabric of the building is sound. Roof and stuff. That's what really costs the money.'

'We need a new roof,' said Patsy.

This time it was Thumper's turn to look embarrassed. 'I thought you must have had it surveyed ... ' he said. 'And the roof *looks* O.K.'

'The bank had a survey done, but it didn't show up anything too bad,' I told him. 'We knew we wanted the house and it was an auction so we didn't really have time to have our own done.'

'When you say you need a new roof,' said Thumper, 'do you mean that you need a new roof? Or just that it needs an overhaul?'

'According to the roofers the roofing nails that hold the slates in position have all corroded and our battens have all got woodworm.' I said. 'They say we need a new roof.'

Thumper scratched his head. 'I hate to think what that'll cost you.'

I picked the estimate up off the table and handed it to him. He looked at it and his mouth actually fell open. He stared at it for a few moments, showed it to Anne and then handed the piece of paper back to me. 'You haven't agreed to this, have you?' he asked me, quietly. I'd never seen him look quite so serious.

'No. We said we wanted time to think about.'

15

'Where did you find them?'

'We just picked them out of the telephone directory.'

'Can you afford that sort of bill?'

'No. But do we have any choice?'

'Do you really want this place roofed with horrible, shiny blue artificial slates?'

'No. But they said they were a lot cheaper and the cost is important.' I was surprised to hear myself defending the two roofers.

'And they said we wouldn't be able to tell the difference between asbestos and the real thing,' added Patsy.

'Asbestos slates are a lot easier to work with and they'll be able to make a bigger profit if you let them use asbestos,' said Thumper. 'But they'll look vile.' He waved a hand around. 'This is a beautiful house,' he said. 'It needs restoring with love.' He paused. 'Love doesn't always come cheap,' he reminded us.

I trusted Thumper and I knew that he was right, but he wasn't telling me anything that in my heart I didn't already know. Our problem was that although we loved the house we neither of us knew very much about builders. And we were both frightened by the fact that restoring Bilbury Grange was going to cost us far more money than we had expected – or that we had available.

'What do you think we should do?' Patsy asked him.

'Well, for a start, you should re-use the slates that are on the roof,' he told us. 'Slates don't really rot, though some of them will have weathered. And with a little care it should be possible to save at least two thirds of them, especially if the nails holding them in have corroded.' He picked up his mug of tea and drained half of it in one gulp. 'That was horrible,' he said, making a face and shaking his head.

I was puzzled. 'But the guys who left us this estimate said the slates would be broken when they took them off. Why would they lie?'

'What would you do with the old slates if you knew you were having new asbestos ones put on?'

I shrugged. 'Nothing.'

'Exactly. You'd be grateful to let them take the old ones away, wouldn't you?'

'Yes.' I agreed.'I suppose so.'

'The crooks who gave you this estimate will sell your slates to someone else,' Thumper said. 'They've probably already got a buyer.'

'I'm glad you came round,' said Patsy, meaning it.

'So am I!' said Thumper. 'It makes me go cold inside to think that you might have let these crooks rip you off.' He grinned at us. 'I do the ripping off in Bilbury!' he said, only half joking. 'I don't like con artists coming into my village and I take a really dim view of it when I find that they're trying to rip off my friends.'

'You shouldn't say that,' said Anne.

'What?' asked Thumper.

'That about you doing the ripping off. I know it's all right with the Doctor and Patsy because they know you're only joking. But you shouldn't say that you rip people off.'

I couldn't help wondering just how much Anne knew of the things that Thumper did to earn his living.

Thumper laughed. 'Of course I do!' he said. 'It's just that most of the time I rip off insurance companies and people like that who don't count.'

'So you don't think it will cost us that much to have the roof done?' Patsy asked him.

'Not unless you want it covering in gold leaf!' replied Thumper. He looked across at me. 'Why didn't you give me a ring before you got these cowboys to give you a quote?'

'I didn't like to bother you,' I said, telling him the truth. 'I knew you'd help us but ... '

'Have you had anyone else here giving you quotes?' Thumper asked us.

'A builder named Naughton came,' said Patsy. 'He says we've got dry rot in the cellars. We've got to have new floorboards.' Thumper held his head in his hands. 'Not 'Naughty' Naughton?'

'Do you know him?'

'Big, fat chap? Usually wears a brown boiler suit? Carries a briefcase with him?'

'Yes.'

'I know him.' said Thumper. 'Telephone directory again?'

Patsy nodded.

17

'You have been doing well,' he said. 'I'm surprised at you Patsy. Don't you remember that case that was in the papers five or six years ago about the builder who was accused of laying a tarmacadam drive so thinly that it cracked the first time the bloke drove his car onto it?'

'Vaguely,' agreed Patsy, after a moment's thought.

'That was your man Naughton,' said Thumper. 'Did he give you a piece of wood with your dry rot on it?'

'Yes.' I said. 'It's outside the back door.'

'Show me?'

I opened the back door, fetched the piece of wood with the dry rot growing in it and showed it to Thumper who examined it carefully. For the first time I looked at it closely too. There were small white clumps that looked like mushrooms, long strands that looked like thick strands of a giant spider's webs and small orange pellets that looked like small orange pellets. The whole thing smelt strongly of mushrooms.

'He said he got this out of your cellar?'

'Yes.'

'How do we get down there?'

Patsy and I both jumped up and went over to the door that led down into the cellars.

'Bloody hell!' said Thumper a few moments later, walking around underneath our house and clearly amazed by the vastness of the cellars. 'How many rooms are there down here?'

'Nine,' I told him. 'Four wine cellars, one coal cellar and four storage rooms.' I was especially proud of the wine cellars which had brick wine storage bins built into them. They were so large that I still hadn't explored them properly. As I wandered about I saw the dusty neck of a wine bottle poking through a clump of cobwebs. I moved closer, brushed aside the cobwebs and realised that there were several other bottles lying alongside and below it. They had clearly been forgotten by some former owner. Most old houses that haven't been occupied for a while contain derelict beds, old sofas and vermin. Ours also had a few bottles of wine.

'Amazing!' Thumper walked about poking at the walls and sniffing at the floorboards above him.

'Is that dry rot?' I asked him, pointing to a huge white matted clump that looked like a bunch of old spiders' webs.

18

'No.' said Thumper, glancing at it. `That's old spiders webs.'

'What about that thing that looks like a mushroom?'

'It's a mushroom,' replied Thumper. 'Let's go back up into the kitchen.'

The three of us followed him back up the stairs into the kitchen. 'There's no dry rot down there.' said Thumper firmly.

'Are you sure?' asked Patsy, frowning. 'But what about that piece of wood Mr Naughton brought up? Hasn't that got dry rot?'

'That's got dry rot,' confirmed Thumper. 'But it's not out of your cellar.' He grinned. 'Get me some old newspapers and some matches.'

'What on earth for?' asked Patsy, puzzled.

'We're going to burn this,' said Thumper, picking up our piece of wood with dry rot growing in it. 'It's probably the only bit of dry rot around here. I don't want any of these spores infecting your house.' Patsy rummaged around in a cupboard and found some old newspapers. I handed Thumper the box of matches that Patsy used to light our camping stove and we followed him out into the courtyard where he built a small bonfire and burnt the piece of wood.

'But if that wasn't out of our cellar where was it from?' I asked Thumper when we were back in the kitchen again.

'Out of his briefcase,' replied Thumper. 'Naughty always carries a bit of dry rot around with him. He keeps a clump of it growing in an old barn he's got. Has he given you the estimate yet for putting new floors in?'

'No,' said Patsy. 'He said he'd post it to us.'

'Promise me you'll let me see it when it comes?'

'O.K. But why?'

'Because it'll be a wonderful work of fiction,' said Thumper with a grin. 'And it'll make your roofing estimate look like petty cash.'

'So we don't need new floorboards?' Patsy came across to me and hugged me.

'No. The ones you've got are absolutely fine. There's a bit of woodworm here and there but no more than you'd expect in a house this old.' Thumper shook his head with disbelief.

'What a prize pair,' he said. 'I can't wait to tell Frank about you two.' (Frank is the landlord of the Duck and Puddle, the Bilbury pub, and I knew I was going to have to put up with some teasing from him and the regulars.)

Patsy, her arms around my neck, whispered something in my ear. I didn't quite catch what she said and asked her to repeat it. She blushed, looked embarrassed and buried her head in my shoulders. She wouldn't tell me what she'd said but pushed me across to the far side of the kitchen so that we were out of earshot of Anne and Thumper. 'Excuse us, for a moment!' I called across to them, laughing.

'Why don't we ask Thumper if he can help us,' Patsy whispered. 'Maybe he'd help make sure we don't get cheated by builders and roofers.'

'I don't like to ask,' I whispered back. 'It's taking advantage of a friend.'

'We could pay him!' whispered Patsy. 'Hire him as a consultant or something. A sort of building supervisor?'

It was a marvellous idea. I told her so and turned back to Thumper and Anne.

'We've got a proposition for you!' I told Thumper. I explained what it was. 'But only if you've got the time and only if you'll let us pay you.'

Thumper seemed surprised. 'I don't want any money from you!' he insisted. 'I'll be very happy to help. But I don't want you to pay me.'

'But don't you see, we won't ask you to do anything if we can't pay you,' I told him. 'That's why we nearly got into that terrible mess with the roofers.'

'Not to mention Mr Naughton,' added Patsy.

'Have you got time to help?' I asked.

'Of course he has,' said Anne, without hesitating. She turned to look at Thumper. 'He's been complaining that things have been quiet recently. And to be honest we could do with the money.'

'Have you?' I asked him. 'Have you got the time?'

'Yes,' agreed Thumper. 'Of course I have. And I'd love to help. It's a wonderful house and I'd really love to help put it back together again. But I don't want to take money off you.'

'You must see it from our point of view,' said Patsy. 'We

20

desperately need someone we can trust. Restoring this house is going to be a big job. But we can't keep asking you for help if we aren't paying you. You've got bills to pay ... '

'And Frank doesn't give his beer away!' I pointed out.

Thumper scratched his head.

'If you won't help us we'll hire those roofers and get Mr Naughton to do all our building work,' threatened Patsy.

'O.K!' agreed Thumper, holding up his hands in mock surrender. 'O.K. I give in.

'Wonderful!' I said. I held out a hand. 'It makes great sense for all of us.'

'You haven't heard what I'm going to charge you yet,' said Thumper. 'And there are two working conditions I want sorting out before I start.'

'O.K.' I said. 'What are they?'

'I want milk and sugar in my tea,' said Thumper firmly. 'Not milk or sugar. Milk *and* sugar.'

'You're a hard negotiator,' sighed Patsy. 'But I suppose we can manage that.'

Thumper agreed to start work the following day after he had delivered a pile of logs to a hotel in Lynton.

*   *   *

After Thumper and Anne had gone Patsy and I spent the rest of the day cleaning and tidying up. It's amazing how much rubbish accumulates in any house that is theoretically 'empty'. There was a huge pile of unsolicited mail in the reception hall and there were half a dozen broken beds and old sofas lying around in the other rooms.

We carried and dragged everything we could find out into the courtyard at the back of the house. Getting rid of the stuff that we could burn was easy but getting rid of bedsprings and other bits and pieces of assorted metal promised to be more of a problem. There was a lot of it: an old water heater, a broken refrigerator, part of a cooker and, inexplicably, a broken car exhaust system that we found in a bedroom.

I put all the burnable items, the moth-eaten curtains, the threadbare carpets and the seemingly endless piles of old newspapers and magazines into several heaps and used some of the unsolicited mail to start a bonfire. I like lighting bonfires and this one seemed especially cathartic. Removing the debris left behind by former owners seemed to be an essential part of making Bilbury Grange *ours*. I was so preoccupied with what I was doing that I completely lost track of the hours, and the light evening meant that there was no darkening of the skies to remind me of the time.

'Are you hungry?' called Patsy, suddenly appearing from one of the downstairs rooms as I dragged a pile of old curtains down the main staircase and into the reception hall. At the sight of her I couldn't help bursting out laughing. Her blue jeans, her once white tee shirt, her face, her hands and her hair were all covered in a mixture of dust from the house and soot from the bonfire. She had tied her hair back with a red ribbon and her forehead was smeared with black marks where she'd wiped away the sweat. 'What are you laughing at?' she demanded, rather indignantly.

'Look in the mirror!' I told her, nodding towards a massive gilt framed mirror that was still screwed to the wall opposite the fireplace. The frame was chipped in several places and the mirror needed new glass. Whoever had left it had clearly decided that it was worthless. They had, I thought, very probably been right.

Patsy dropped the piece of carpet she was carrying and walked across to the mirror. She looked at herself without any apparent surprise and beckoned to me to join her. I dropped my pile of curtains and walked across to the mirror.

'Now you look!' she said, grinning at me.

I looked even more bizarre than she did. I had a huge spider's web draped over one side of my head and my face was, if anything, even grubbier than hers. 'We look a bit of a mess, don't we?' I laughed. Patsy reached up and removed the spider's web from my hair with her hand. Then she wiped her hand on the back of her jeans. I put my arm around her and pulled her towards me. 'You don't have any regrets about buying this crazy house, do you?'

'None whatsoever.'

We kissed. Somehow she still smelt sweet and her lips were warm and soft. Her kiss made me feel twelve feet tall. After what seemed like a lifetime we reluctantly parted.

'Are you hungry?' whispered Patsy, gently lifting her lips

from mine, lifting her head backwards and pushing me away with her hands. 'Because I'm absolutely starving.'

'Me too!'

We washed in brown, cold water in one of the bathrooms upstairs. The bathroom was huge and had two massive cast iron white baths standing side by side in the middle of it. The baths were so large that Patsy claimed that she'd swum a full stroke underwater in hers. We left our dirty clothes soaking in the water and dried ourselves on two huge, white, fluffy bath towels that Frank and Gilly had given us as a wedding present. Then Patsy drove to the fish and chip shop in Combe Martin with strict instructions to make sure that my meal was well doused with vinegar and liberally sprinkled with salt, while I stayed behind to feed the bonfire and to make sure it didn't get out of control – at the same time trying hard not to get so close to it that I covered myself in smoke and soot again.

By the time she returned twenty minutes later I had cleared away the last of the curtains and the carpets and the bonfire was belching forth clouds of black smoke. I sat down at the kitchen table with the back door safely closed and through the window watched the flames rising around an old wardrobe with missing doors which I had found in the attic.

'Oh, darn it!' said Patsy, unwrapping the two parcels she had brought back with her. The smell was wonderful. 'I've forgotten to bring anything to drink.'

'I think I saw a couple of bottles of wine abandoned in the cellar,' I remembered. 'I'll go and fetch one. Do you have any preferences?'

'Chateau Lafitte 1897!' laughed Patsy.

'No. I mean what colour? Red or white?'

'I don't mind. Anything you can find.'

I got up from the table and went down into the cellar. There were more bottles than I had at first thought – probably two dozen in all. Knowing nothing at all about wine I pulled out a few of the bottles and examined the labels. They all came from the same bottler. I plucked a bottle at random and took it back upstairs. Sadly, it seemed that whoever had left the wine had known what he was doing for it tasted rather bitter and we ended up pouring most of the bottle down the sink and drinking plain water with our chips. But fish and chips had never tasted so good, and whatever its original colour our filtered water tasted sparkling and fresh. I made a mental note to throw out the rest of the wine sometime.

By the time we had finished our meal the sun had set and it was dark outside. The bonfire had died right down to a few smouldering embers but when we took our dirty paper plates and the paper in which our fish and chips had been wrapped and threw them all onto the fire the flames flickered brightly for a few moments and lit up the courtyard in the darkness of the evening.

I don't know whether it was the heat of the fire, trapped in the courtyard by the thick stone walls of the house, stables and coach-house, but the evening seemed warmer than the day had been. Leaving the debris of our meal to burn away Patsy and I walked out of the courtyard, past the walled vegetable garden and down to the lake, lit now only by moonlight filtered romantically through the towering trees around it. We found an old cast iron garden seat underneath what had been a rose bower and I kicked and pulled the brambles from it so that we could sit down. Above the lake we could see a thousand insects hovering and flitting and the occasional splash proved that there were still some fish in the water. I put my arm around Patsy and we sat there wrapped together in the half dark, sharing our love and our dreams alone and silent. Despite all our problems I had never before felt such freedom, such contentment, such happiness and such hope for the future. I felt excited and apprehensive and incongruously suddenly remembered the first night I had slept under canvas when I was a boy. My father had erected a small tent on the back lawn and I'd slept there with the tent doors securely knotted against the night with double bows and with the moonlight shining so brightly through the canvas that I could see to read by it.

We sat and I thought how lucky I was to have found Patsy and how very, very lucky I was that she loved me as I loved her.

Suddenly, I felt her shiver as the cold of the night descended and I took her back into the house, tiptoeing through the lace-work of tripwire brambles laid across the paths, and giggling with fake alarm as bats swooped and pirouetted low overhead.

*　　*　　*

I was woken the next morning by bright rays of sunshine streaming through the uncurtained bedroom windows; the natural shafts of sunlight that had woken me clearly visible as they lit up a million specks of dust floating around the room. It seemed a far nicer way to be woken than to be yanked into awareness by the shrill, insistent, unforgiving ring of an alarm clock and I wondered why no one had ever invented an alarm clock which produced artificial shafts of sunlight instead of noise.

We had chosen a bedroom on the south east corner of the house, mainly so that we would wake every morning with a view of the rising sun, and we had slept on the one bed we had chosen to keep, an old iron bedstead with a soggy mattress.

I groaned as I struggled to sit up and rubbed my aching back. I wasn't sure whether it ached because of all the old furniture and debris I'd dragged out of the house the day before or because of the soggy mattress. I looked at Patsy, still sleeping, and couldn't help thinking that I had never before seen anyone so beautiful nor so innocent. Ben, the black and white collie I had inherited from an old tramp, had spent the night sleeping at the bottom of the bed. (Despite repeated questioning the tramp had never been able to tell me why he had called his dog Ben, despite knowing that she was a female). She stood up, stretched, yawned and went straight to the door when she saw me clambering carefully out of bed.

I stretched and then put my finger to my lips to tell her to keep quiet so that we didn't wake Patsy. She stood by the open door and waited; her ears pricked, her tongue hanging out and her tail wagging. Ben was clearly looking forward to the new day too.

Downstairs I opened the back door, which we hadn't even bothered to lock (we didn't have anything to steal and what, in any case, is the point of locking up a deserted house which has two dozen ill fitting windows?) and watched as Ben scam-

25

pered off into the courtyard. She stopped for a moment to sniff at the burnt out embers of the bonfire and then disappeared at top speed through the archway underneath the coach-house clock tower. Moments later I heard her crashing about in the undergrowth. I filtered some water through the last of our coffee filter papers (making a mental note to see if Peter Marshall at the village shop had any more for sale), filled the saucepan and lit our camping stove (making another mental note to telephone the cooker supplier in Barnstaple to see if there was any chance of us receiving our cooker) hunted around for something to eat and realised that we had nothing (making a mental note to buy some bread and other supplies from the village shop) and put our one remaining tea bag into one of our two mugs (making a mental note to buy some cheap crockery).

Realising I already had so many things to remember that I was quite certain to forget most of them I fished a stub of pencil from one of the kitchen drawers and, in the absence of a notebook, started to write out a list of things to do on the yellowing paint on the wall above the sink. To the list of things we needed to buy I added 'notebook' since carrying the kitchen wall with us when we went to the shop seemed a little impractical. As I did this Ben reappeared, bursting through the back door, which I had left open, and depositing a live and apparently perfectly healthy baby rabbit at my feet.

The rabbit and I stared at one another and I'm not sure which of us was most startled. Ben sat and watched us both as though conducting some personal experiment. The rabbit recovered first. He sat bolt upright, his ears standing up and his nose twitching, and then scampered off around and around the kitchen. I opened the back door even wider to encourage him to escape that way, but either the rabbit wasn't about to fall for what he thought was a trap or else, like the rest of us, he had fallen in love with Bilbury Grange. He turned around through one hundred and eighty degrees, ran off in the opposite direction and disappeared into the corridor. I hurried after him but by the time I had got to the doorway he was nowhere to be seen. Ben, who hadn't moved a muscle, put her head to one side and raised an eyebrow quizzically.

I made Patsy a cup of black tea and carried it upstairs.

I had hoped to wake her with a kiss but Ben clearly thought that was a sloppy idea. She leapt onto the bed, got a corner of the blanket in her teeth and pulled and pulled until Patsy woke up.

Just then I heard the sound of a vehicle in the driveway. I looked out of the window and saw that Thumper, who had already delivered his pile of logs, was arriving to start work.

* * *

CHAPTER THREE

Thumper had packed the back of his truck with tools and had brought his ladder too. We decided that while Patsy drove down to the village shop to buy some milk, sugar, bread and other essentials Thumper and I would take a look at the roof. 'There's no point in doing anything inside the house until we've got the roof sorted out,' he pointed out sensibly.

'You do need new battens,' he said, ten minutes later, as he peered through the gap the two roofers had left. I stood in comparative safety at the top of the ladder. He bent over and showed me a small piece of wood that crumbled in his fingers. 'But the beams all look sound enough. There are a few worm holes but they built this house with old ships' timbers and they're mostly too hard for woodworm to get into.'

'Ships' timbers?'

'Wood goes rock hard when it's in salt water for a long time,' explained Thumper. 'Woodworm prefer soft wood because it's easier to eat.'

'What about the slates?'

'We can reuse most of them. But we'll have to try and find a few thousand old ones to replace the ones that are already broken and the ones that break when we prise them off.'

We clambered down from the roof and Thumper said he knew of a place near Tiverton, about forty miles away, which would probably have the slates we needed in stock. 'Are you thinking of restoring the coach-house and the stables?'

'Yes. I suppose so. Eventually.'

'Then if you can afford it the sensible thing will be to buy more slates than you think you'll need. If you end up short you'll probably never be able to match the size and colour. If you buy too many we can always just store them and use them later.'

We climbed down from the roof just as Patsy got back from the shop and decided to go to Tiverton straight away. Thumper had brought down one of the loose slates so that he could make sure the ones we bought were the right size.

As we walked towards the front door Patsy climbed out of the Morris her arms laden with the old fashioned, stout, brown paper bags that the village shop still used. 'Peter said we could put it all on your account,' she said. 'So it didn't cost me anything!'

I'd been living in Bilbury for over six months and I still hadn't had a bill from Peter Marshall, the local shop keeper, taxi driver, postman and undertaker. Occasionally, I worried about this unseen liability, but since we needed all the credit we could get I wasn't about to rush down to the shop and force Peter to let me pay cash.

I reached into the car and picked up the remaining bags. 'I've got some salad stuff,' said Patsy. 'Lettuce, tomatoes, spring onions and cheese. Plus two fresh loaves, a box of cornflakes and a couple of packets of biscuits.'

'Milk? Sugar?' asked Thumper, following us into the kitchen. 'Did you remember the milk and the sugar?'.

'Yes!' laughed Patsy. 'I've got your milk and sugar. And I bought a couple of bottles of this in case it gets hot.' She pulled a large brown glass bottle of dandelion and burdock out of one of the bags.

'I haven't seen that stuff since I was a kid!' I exclaimed, as I helped Patsy stack the food she'd bought neatly on the kitchen table. I carefully wrote 'fridge' on the first page of the notebook she'd brought back. 'I didn't know they were still making it.'

'They probably aren't,' said Thumper drily. 'Just because Peter is selling it that doesn't mean that anyone is still making it.'

'That reminds me,' said Patsy. 'I managed to get these coffee filter papers very cheap. Peter says that no one in the village has got a machine that fits them.'

'How cheap is very cheap?'

'I don't know. He didn't say.'

'We'd better have a look at your water supply when we get back,' said Thumper. 'Though it's probably just some rust in the holding tank that's turning your water brown.'

The three of us squeezed into the cab of Thumper's truck, Ben made herself comfortable on my knees and we headed off for Tiverton in search of slates.

*   *   *

Just over an hour later we were driving gloomily back out of Tiverton. But instead of driving towards Bilbury we were heading north, out of Tiverton on the Bristol road. The sun had disappeared and the skies were grey and overcast.

'Sorry!' the man at the builder's yard had said. 'We don't have anything that size.' Ironically, there were tens of thousands of slates in dozens of different sizes stacked neatly all around the outside of the old caravan that he used as an office. 'They haven't made anything that size since I've been in the business.' Since he was in his late sixties and had already told us that he'd been in the building reclamation business all his life I found this distinctly depressing. He suggested that we try a builder's yard on the outskirts of Bristol.

'Do the slates we buy have to be the same size as our existing slates?' I asked Thumper as we started the drive back to Bilbury.

'They do really,' Thumper confirmed unhappily. 'Otherwise fitting them onto the roof will be like doing a jigsaw puzzle. And they'll look pretty odd too.'

We were driving through Taunton when Patsy suddenly shouted at Thumper to stop. He put his foot on the brake so suddenly and so sharply that Patsy and I nearly went through the windscreen while poor Ben fell off my lap and landed on the floor at my feet. Fortunately, only her pride seemed to be hurt.

'What's the matter?' demanded Thumper.

'Back up a bit,' said Patsy, excitedly, reaching across me and winding down the window.

Thumper put the truck into reverse and backed up, narrowly missing a group of holiday-makers in a Ford Cortina. 'Say when!' he told her.

'When!' said Patsy. 'Here! Look!' She pointed out of the now open truck window at a large, derelict building that was being knocked down. There was a crane parked in front of it with a huge iron ball hanging from it on a long chain. The crane driver was swinging the ball backwards and forwards so that he could use it to knock holes in the structure of the building.

'What is it?' I asked her. I couldn't see why we'd stopped.

'Slates!' shouted Patsy, gleefully. She pointed in the direction of the disabled building. 'Look!'

Thumper and I followed her outstretched hand and stared at the building. It had a slate roof, and two men in shorts and vests were standing on it. They were systematically smashing the slates with a couple of sledgehammers.

'That building looks quite old,' said Patsy. 'Maybe their slates would fit our house?'

'It's a long shot,' said Thumper pessimistically.

'Quick, quick!' said Patsy. 'Before they smash them all up.'

We all climbed out of the truck and hurried onto the demolition site. Thumper was carrying the sample slate we'd brought with us.

'Hey!' yelled a large man. He had a huge stomach which hung over the leather belt around his filthy jeans. 'You can't come on here. This is private. And it's dangerous.' he added. Ben growled at him but kept her distance.

'We're looking for some slates like this,' said Thumper, holding up the slate from Bilbury Grange. 'We're prepared to pay you cash.'

'These slates won't fit anything,' said the man with the huge belly. 'We checked 'em out. They're an odd size.'

'Could we just compare one with ours?' asked Thumper. He took a grubby and crumpled five pound note out of his back pocket and handed it over.

'Don't suppose it will hurt,' agreed the man, pocketing the note and walking a little closer to the building. He yelled up to one of the men on the roof, asking him to throw down one of the slates. The man prised off a slate and threw it down. For a moment I thought that the man with the overhanging stomach was going to attempt to catch it in his hands

31

but he wasn't quite that stupid. Luckily the slate didn't break when it landed on the ground. Up on the roof the two men who had been smashing the slates went back to work. The fat man picked the fallen slate up and brought it over to us. He handed it to Thumper. Thumper held it up against the slate we'd brought with us. Both were exactly the same size.

'Brilliant!' said Patsy, almost jumping off the ground with excitement. She pointed towards the roof of the building they were demolishing. 'Tell them to stop!'

'The colour's not right,' said Thumper casually and critically. 'But we can probably use them. How much?'

'How many do you want?'

Thumper looked up. 'All that you've got left.' The two men on the roof were still smashing slates. Patsy looked across at me with agony on her face. I knew she wanted me to tell the fat man to ask the two men on the roof to stop smashing slates. But I knew Thumper didn't want the fat man to realise how much we wanted the slates. I reached for her hand and pulled her away.

'Cash?' I heard the man say.

'Cash.' agreed Thumper. 'On delivery.'

The man scratched his head.

I heard Thumper offering a price for every whole slate. Then the fat man made a counter offer. He wanted a fixed sum for all the slates they'd got.

I heard Thumper raise his offer, still insisting that he would only pay a sum for each individual, complete slate.

I thought Thumper was being very sensible in wanting to pay for individual slates.

To my surprise and delight the fat man agreed to Thumper's offer, turned round, walked towards the building and shouted to the two men on the roof to stop smashing up the slates that were now worth money.

'Great!' said Thumper, turning to us with a broad grin on his face.

'Are they really the wrong colour?' asked Patsy, anxious now.

'No.' said Thumper. 'They're perfect.' He winked at us. 'I'll go and tell them where to bring the slates.' He turned

32

as he started to walk away. 'All you've got to do is find the cash.'

'Oh good,' I said. 'As long as that's all.'

*   *   *

We drove back to Bilbury feeling very pleased with our-selves, and as we arrived home the sun, which had been hiding for most of the morning, shone brightly again.

'I'll make us a nice salad for lunch,' promised Patsy. 'We can eat outside in the garden.'

While she headed for the kitchen Thumper and I started to walk around the house. We needed to prepare a list of other essential work.

'I'm glad to see that you're keeping all your scrap metal,' said Thumper, as we passed the pile of old boilers, bits of exhaust pipe, springs and other assorted pieces of unburnable rubbish.

'I don't really know what to do with it,' I confessed.

'I'll take it into Barnstaple,' said Thumper. 'I know a scrap metal dealer who'll buy all that from you.'

I stared at him in amazement.

'Never throw anything away,' he said, very seriously. 'Even the old battens off the roof are useful. They'll make terrific firelighters.'

Suddenly Patsy came running towards us, holding two rather limp looking lettuce leaves.

'Someone's stolen the lettuce!' she shouted. Thumper and I followed her back to the kitchen.

'Are you sure there's nothing else missing?'

'Just the lettuce,' said Patsy. 'All except these two leaves.'

It was then that I remembered the rabbit that Ben had brought into the house that morning.

*   *   *

CHAPTER FOUR

Suddenly it was time for me to start proper work again; to put down my broom and pick up my stethoscope. I had almost forgotten that I still had to earn a living. Some people would have probably thought of it as a strange honeymoon but I couldn't have wished for anything better.

In some ways Bilbury Grange now looked more of a mess than ever. There were piles of rubbish all around the outside of the house, and the scaffolding company that Thumper had hired had almost finished surrounding the house with rusty poles and brackets. Patsy said it made the house look as if it was in the intensive care unit, and she was right.

Exactly a week after Patsy and I had moved into Bilbury Grange I got up at my usual time but, instead of clambering into my tattered and now rather stained shorts and going outside to help Thumper, I dug out my faithful old sports jacket, the one with the leather patches on the elbows and the large ink stain on the lining, and my only decent pair of grey flannels and tried to make myself look more like a general practitioner than a labourer. It wasn't easy. The sun had shone for most of the week and had bleached my hair and tanned my skin, and the exercise had toned up my muscles and I definitely *felt* more like a labourer than a doctor.

At eight thirty I kissed Patsy goodbye, promised her that I would be home in three hours for my lunch if there weren't any emergencies, and climbed into the Morris to drive to the surgery. One of our reasons for buying such a large house was that we wanted to use part of the building as a surgery, but for the time being it was obviously quite impossible to see patients at what was, to all practical extents, little more than a building site. Fortunately, Dr Brownlow had agreed to let me continue to see patients in the surgery at his home. At eight thirty-five Patsy and I finally managed to drag ourselves apart and I started up the car.

I was driving slowly down the driveway away from the house when I heard Patsy shouting. I looked in the driving mirror and saw Ben bounding down the drive behind the car. I skidded to a stop, reached over and opened the front passenger door. Without breaking her stride Ben leapt straight into the car, settled herself down on the front seat and stared at me reproachfully, as though cross with me for forgetting her. I stuck my head out through the open window and looked behind.

'Ben seems to be coming with me,' I shouted back to Patsy.

'If I run after the car can I come with you too?' shouted Patsy, laughing.

I pipped my horn in a final goodbye and shot off down the drive, narrowly missed Thumper who was just arriving to carry on working on the roof, and headed for Dr Brownlow's house and my first surgery as a full time, self employed totally-in-charge general practitioner.

Although I had only been away for a week so much had happened that it felt strange to be back sitting behind Dr Brownlow's massive old oak desk, with Miss Johnson fussing around giving me messages and trying to get me up to date with what had been happening in my absence. She was wearing her pink flecked two piece suit and her two rows of pearls, which I knew she only wore on special occasions, and I felt touched. I was pleased to see that absolutely nothing had changed. Even though it was early summer and clearly going to be another warm day the waiting room still smelt of rain soaked mackintoshes and galoshes and the consulting room, unlit by natural light, still had a rather damp feel to it.

The first patient that morning was an elderly lady called Miss Phillips who had come to live in the village just a few days earlier and who had never been to the practice before. Neither of us had any idea just how much she was going to change my life.

Miss Phillips told me that she had moved to Bilbury because

she found life in the city just too tiring. She said she had a long standing nervous condition and had suffered with a weak heart for most of her life. We had no medical records for her since she was not yet officially a patient of ours, but I guessed that she was probably in her mid sixties. She was slim and rather frail looking and wore a flowered dress and a pale pink cardigan. Her hair, which was white, was mostly hidden by a straw bonnet decorated with a small bunch of real daisies. She carried a rather large raffia work shopping basket, a folded parasol and wore white lace gloves. She looked like a refugee from another century.

'How do you like Bilbury, so far?' I asked her. Although I was still a newcomer to the village I thought of myself as a native and I wanted everyone to like it as much as I did.

'It's wonderful!' murmured Miss Phillips. 'So quiet and peaceful.' She told me that she had lived in a flat in London where she had been a virtual prisoner; afraid to go to the shops, afraid to visit friends and afraid to go for a walk in the park. I thought she looked tired.

When I asked her what I could do to help her she reached into her basket and pulled out a small white cardboard box which contained half a dozen capsules. 'My doctor in London insisted that I take three of these every day,' she told me. 'They are for my nerves.' With some slight reluctance she handed the box over to me. Her movements were slow and she had a slight tremor when she moved.

I examined the box carefully. It bore nothing except the name of the company and a scribbled note saying 'Take as directed'. I had never seen the capsules before though I knew the name of the manufacturer very well. I handed the box back. 'Do you know what they're called?'

'I wrote down the name,' said Miss Phillips. She smiled rather nervously. 'My memory isn't as good as it was.' She reached into her bag again and took out a piece of paper. She handed it to me. It had the word 'Angipax' written on it.

'How long have you been taking them?' I asked. I had never heard of the pills.

She thought for a moment. 'Six months or so. I think.'

'Do they help? Do they make you feel better?'

'I don't know,' said Miss Phillips, rather surprisingly. 'But I'd like to stop them now that I'm living in the country.'

I said I thought that sounded a good idea.

'I thought I should ask your permission first,' said Miss Phillips. 'My doctor in London never liked me doing anything with asking him first.'

'Very sensible,' I agreed. I reached behind me and took a large book off a shelf. 'I'll just check up to see what the manufacturers say about those pills of yours.' I flicked through the index of the reference book but couldn't find 'Angipax' listed anywhere.

'I don't expect they'll be in there,' said Miss Phillips. 'They're very new. My doctor used to get them for me specially.'

I plucked another book off the shelf, found the telephone number for the drug company concerned and rang the Medical Director.

'Do you make a drug called 'Angipax'?' I asked him, when I got through.

He sounded a little surprised but said that they did.

I described one of the capsules.

'That's right. Are you one of the trial doctors?'

That explained why the doctor in London had given Miss Phillips the capsules instead of sending her to the chemist with a prescription. The doctor was being paid by the drug company to test the new drug on his patients.

I explained the situation. 'Miss Phillips wants to stop them. Is it safe for her just to stop them overnight?'

'Oh, yes!' said the Medical Director immediately. 'No problem.' He paused. 'Are there any capsules left?'

'A few.'

'I'll send someone round to pick them up.'

I said he needn't bother going to so much trouble and that if he wanted the capsules back I'd put them in the post, but he said he would rather send someone round. I put the telephone down and told Miss Phillips that the company making 'Angipax' had confirmed that it was safe for her to stop them.

'That's wonderful,' said Miss Phillips. 'Thank you, doctor.' she smiled at me and stood up. 'Do I pay you or your receptionist?' She took out a rather plump looking purse.

I must have looked as puzzled as I was.

'My doctor in London always liked me to pay him directly,' said Miss Phillips.'He said it made the accounting easier.' She smiled again. 'And I prefer to pay each time rather than allow a bill to build up.'

'If you're going to live in Bilbury and you would like me to look after you Miss Johnson will give you a form to sign,' I told her. 'There isn't anything to pay.'

'Oh!' said Miss Phillips, clearly surprised.

'This is a National Health Service practice.' I explained. 'We don't have any private patients. The Government will pay me to look after you.' I couldn't help thinking that the doctor must be making a fortune. His patients were paying him for treatments which the drug companies were undoubtedly also paying him to try out. I asked Miss Phillips to leave her capsules with Miss Johnson and to tell her that someone from the drug company would be round to pick them up.

Miss Phillips thanked me profusely and walked slowly towards the door. I waited until I'd heard her footsteps disappear down the corridor before I pressed the buzzer underneath my desk to tell the next patient to come in. I didn't know why, but Miss Phillips had worried me.

*   *   *

When I'd finished the morning surgery Miss Johnson said that Dr Brownlow had asked me to call in and see him. She told me that he would be in the converted barn where he was supervising the water bottling plant he had set into operation. Dr Brownlow had retired from general practice to run a business selling bottled water to restaurants and supermarkets.

'Thank you for standing in for me last week!' I said. 'How's the water business?'

'It's looking good!' said Dr Brownlow. He looked ten years younger than he had when I'd last seen him.

'So are you!' I told him. 'Running a business clearly agrees with you.'

'I like it,' admitted Dr Brownlow. 'I like the challenge.' He put down the sheaf of papers he was holding. 'I just wanted to ask you how you were getting on with Bilbury Grange. How are you enjoying married life? And how is Patsy?'

'I'm enjoying married life very much,' I said. 'And Patsy is very well. But the house is coming on slowly.' I told him about the problems with the roof and about the dry rot in the cellar and about how Thumper had agreed to help us.

'I heard that Thumper was helping you,' said Dr Brownlow. 'I'm pleased. Not that you need a new roof but that you've got Thumper working with you. You can trust him.'

'I know,'I said.

'A lot of people think he's irresponsible and unreliable,' said Dr Brownlow. 'A bit of what we used to call a wide boy. But I've always found him to be honest.' He smiled at me. 'But then I don't run an insurance company.'

I smiled back. 'I don't think he's the only person in Bilbury to regard insurance companies as fair game. I can't really understand why they still sell policies in Bilbury.'

'Simple,' said Dr Brownlow. 'The Bilbury claims all go into the computer as Devon claims. And fortunately for us the rest of Devon has got some pretty honest citizens.' Unexpectedly Dr Brownlow reached out and put a hand on my shoulder. 'You'll probably find it difficult for a while,' he told me.

I must have looked puzzled.

'Buying and trying to restore a large house.' he explained. 'But you're doing the right thing. When I bought this place people said I was mad. But I've never regretted it. A small new house may be easy to run but it won't have much soul. A big old house with character will give you a challenge, cement your marriage and repay your love. And you've bought it at the right time. As you get older and try to make decisions you'll find it gets more and more difficult. Whenever you want to do anything challenging you'll think of too many problems; you'll know too much, you'll know of so many things that can go wrong that you'll freeze. You'll find yourself more and more incapable of making decisions, more and more incapable of taking risks and increasingly content to sit back and accept things as they are.'

'That's hardly true of you!' I pointed out. He had, after all, given up his medical practice to concentrate on building up a business selling bottled water.

'Ah, that's different!' said Dr Brownlow. 'When you get to my age you realise that time is running out and that if you don't do something today then tomorrow may be too late. You learn to do things by instinct or not to do them at all.' He stretched his neck first to one side and then to the other. He had bad arthritis in his neck, and although I knew it must have been painful he never complained about it. 'Besides, when you get to my age you learn to let the future worry about itself.'

'Would you like to come over and have a look at the house sometime?' I asked him.

'I'd love to!' said Dr Brownlow instantly. 'When would be convenient?'

'We can't invite you for a meal just yet,' I apologised. 'We don't have a cooker. Or any crockery.'

'That's all right! I'd just like to see Patsy and the house.'

'This evening then? About eight?'

*   *   *

Patsy had prepared a large pile of salad sandwiches for our lunch and we ate them outside, sitting in the garden. Ben sat down beside us chewing on a bone. Thumper had gone back home to have his lunch with Anne.

'Thumper says we ought to get a proper roofing firm in to do the roof,' said Patsy. 'He says there's plenty of other stuff for him to be getting on with but that if he tries to do the roof by himself we'll never get all the essential jobs done before the winds start at the end of the summer.' Bilbury gets a lot of strong south westerly gales, and properties which are not well prepared can suffer badly. 'Oh, and he says there are half a dozen dead trees that need to come down too.'

'Does he know anybody we can trust to do the roof?'

'He's suggested that we get three firms to come out and give us estimates,' said Patsy. 'He'll talk to them and tell them exactly what we want. And he says could you have some cash ready for when the slates are delivered on Wednesday.'

'Does Thumper have any idea how much it will cost us to have the roof done?'

Patsy told me. Thumper's guess was much lower than the

estimate we'd received, but it was still an awful lot and would use up most of the money we had set aside from the bank loan for doing other repairs.

'It's going to take us longer to get the rest of the house put straight,' I told Patsy, as I took a large bite out of a tomato sandwich.

'Because of the money?'

I nodded.

'Are things going to be all right?'

'Of course they are!' I assured her, with far more confidence than I felt. Getting the roof done really had been an unexpected problem.

'Honestly?' said Patsy, who clearly didn't believe me.

I paused. 'I don't know.' I admitted.

'That's better. I want the truth, you know!'

At five minutes to two I kissed Patsy and stood up. Ben stood with me and started to wag her tail. 'I'd better get started with the afternoon visits,' I told her. 'Otherwise I'll never finish this evening's surgery.'

'Are you sure Dr Brownlow isn't expecting a meal tonight?' asked Patsy, for the tenth time. She had looked very worried when I had told her that Dr Brownlow was coming.

'Absolutely! He just wants to come and see you and look at the house. Talking of meals did you manage to speak to the cooker people?'

'They promised to deliver it this afternoon,' said Patsy, without much confidence.

*   *   *

I had five visits to do on my first afternoon back at work and I arrived at Dr Brownlow's house with only a couple of minutes to spare before the evening surgery.

'A man came to pick up those capsules Miss Phillips left,' said Miss Johnson. 'He'd driven all the way from Bristol!'

It seemed very odd that anyone should drive over a hundred miles each way to pick up a few capsules, but there was a full waiting room and I didn't have time to think any more about it. Anyway, I'd always suspected that drug companies had more money than sense. Ben and I went straight into the consulting room. I pressed the buzzer to start the surgery and she curled up beside my feet and went to sleep.

It was an uneventful though rather long evening surgery. The first nine patients I saw were all early holiday-makers. There were four cases of mild sunburn, two children with insect bites and three patients with colds in the first thirty minutes. Most of the villagers would not dream of visiting the surgery with such trivial ailments and I was beginning to despair of seeing anyone I knew when in walked Nigel Woodloe.

Nigel and his wife Karen used to work in London and come down to their cottage in Bilbury at the weekends. He had a job as a currency dealer for an American bank in London and she had an equally important job with an old fashioned England merchant bank. I knew that they had recently given up their jobs and had decided to live in Bilbury full time, though I didn't know what they had decided to do to earn a living or whether they had earned so much money that they could retire.

'I've got a terrible back,' said Nigel, lowering himself into the chair on the other side of the desk with great caution and holding the right side of his back. 'I wonder if you'd be kind enough to sign me off work so that I can collect some sick pay.' He was still wearing the dark suit, white shirt and red tie of a banker's uniform, though whether or not this was in my honour I didn't know.

'Are you working, then?' I asked him.

Nigel looked embarrassed. 'Not exactly,' he confessed. He lowered his eyes. 'But I still have a valid sickness insurance policy which pays out if I can't work for any reason.'

'And you want to make a claim?'

'Things are a lot harder than we anticipated,' admitted Nigel.

'I'd better examine you!' I told him. 'Could you pop onto the examination couch?'

Nigel levered himself up out of the chair, took off his jacket, staggered across the room and collapsed onto the couch. Although he looked bad I couldn't find anything wrong with him. I told him so. He climbed off the couch, walked back around my desk, put his jacket on and sat himself down again. This time he clutched the left side of his back.

'We thought we'd be able to survive on what we could grow and what we could earn doing odd jobs,' he confessed. He looked very guilty and was clearly not very good at taking advantage of the system. 'But the slugs have eaten most of our seedlings, and apart from two days selling ice cream I haven't been able to get any work at all.' He bit his lower lip.'Things are a bit desperate.'

I wrote out a sick note. 'It's almost impossible to disprove backache,' I told him. 'But if by any chance you get examined by any other doctor try to remember which side of your back hurts.'

Nigel went very red.

'When you came in it was the right side which hurt,' I explained. 'Now it's the left.'

'Oh.' said Nigel, simply. 'I'm sorry. Thank you.'

'Do you regret coming down here to live?' I asked him, handing him the sick note he needed.

'No!' Nigel replied without hesitation. 'Absolutely not!' He took the sick note I held out and nodded his thanks. He stood up.

I waved a hand.

'Really,' he said. 'I appreciate it.' He folded the sick note up into four and put it into the inside pocket of his jacket.

After Nigel there were another twelve patients: three visitors and nine locals. The visitors included a child with a sore throat, a diabetic needing a supply of insulin and a girl who had come on holiday with her boyfriend and who rather belatedly wanted contraceptive advice and threatened to get herself pregnant if I didn't help her immediately. The locals included three arthritics wanting prescriptions, a patient with high blood pressure needing a check up, a woman with early menopausal symptoms, two children needing injections, a woman who thought she might be pregnant but rather hoped she wasn't and a man with a genuine bad back.

I finished the surgery at 7.40 pm and Ben and I got back home just before 8.00 pm to find that Dr Brownlow's elderly Rolls Royce was parked in the driveway and he was having a guided tour of the house with Patsy on his arm. Thumper had long since gone home for his tea, leaving behind a lengthy list of requests, queries and instructions. Two of the three roofing firms Thumper had recommended were sending men along to give estimates (the third firm said they were too busy) and it was no surprise at all to hear that the cooker still hadn't arrived.

'It's marvellous!' said Dr Brownlow, enthusiastically, when we'd shown him everything. It was now dusk and we were sitting by our rather stagnant ornamental lake being bitten by a variety of insects. 'There's no disputing that it's a challenge and a lot of people would say that you're mad, but it'll be worth it in the long run.'

Patsy reached out, took my hand and squeezed it. We both valued every scrap of encouragement.

'We'd better go in!' I said, unromantically. 'I don't know about anyone else but I'm being eaten alive.'

'Oh no!' said Patsy, putting a hand to her mouth as she suddenly remembered something. 'I'm sorry! You haven't eaten yet have you?'

'Not since lunchtime!'

'You can have a sandwich or I'll go and fetch fish and chips.'

'Let me treat you!' said Dr Brownlow, standing up. 'I haven't had fish and chips for ages. Is that good chip shop in Combe Martin still open? The one down near to the beach?'

We both nodded. 'I'll be back as soon as I can,' promised Dr Brownlow.

True to his word he was back before the saucepan had boiled on the camping stove.

'Come on!' said Dr Brownlow, excitedly. 'Make the tea afterwards. Eat these while they're still hot. They smell marvellous.' He handed us each a hot parcel of fish and chips and we ate them with our fingers out of the paper.

'That was the best meal I've had for years!' said Dr Brownlow sighing and sitting back with a broad smile on his face. 'I'd forgotten how good fish and chips taste.' He looked thoughtful for a moment. 'Do you know,' he said, slowly and deliberately, 'I think I get more real pleasure from eating fish and chips wrapped in paper than I do out of eating the most expensively cooked cordon bleu meal in the most elaborate surroundings.'

'I agree with you,' I said.

44

'And no washing up!' said Patsy, standing up and starting to make the tea. We had acquired two extra mugs that Thumper had brought with him and Patsy had declared her intention of going into Barnstaple and buying some crockery from a cheap store she knew.

'What do I do with this?' asked Dr Brownlow, holding up his empty fish and chip wrappings and looking around for a waste bin.

'There's a rubbish pile outside,' I told him. I got to my feet and headed for the back door. As I passed him I went to take his wrappers from out of his hands. 'No, it's O.K!' he said. 'I can manage my own rubbish. It'll make me feel virtuous.' He followed me to the back door and out into the courtyard. Ben, who thought we were all going for a walk, got quite excited.

'I thought you were poor!' said Dr Brownlow, tossing his chip wrapping paper into a half full cardboard box that I had earmarked for burning and picking a bottle from another box. It was the bottle that had contained the wine we'd abandoned the previous evening. Ben, who had run away towards the vegetable garden now turned and waited for me.

'Oh, it was just some stuff I found in the cellar,' I explained. 'It was undrinkable.'

But Dr Brownlow wasn't listening. He was carefully examining the label. 'You didn't buy this, did you?'

I shook my head. 'No I found it in the cellar.' Ben, who had decided I wasn't going for a walk after all, started to run back towards the house.

'Is there any more like it down there?'

'Yes. I'm not sure how many bottles, but they're all the same. But it's gone off otherwise I would have opened a bottle to go with our chips.'

'Show me,' said Dr Brownlow, suddenly very serious. He waved me into the house. With Ben following us I led the way down into the cellar and pointed out the bottles of wine that I had found. Dr Brownlow pulled each one out of its hole and carefully examined the label.

'Are these all yours?' he asked me.

'Yes. We bought the house and contents. But we've burnt most of the contents.'

'You're absolutely sure?'

'Yes!' I said, rather impatiently. 'Why?'

'You don't know what these are, do you?'

'No.' I had by now realised that something serious was going on.

'This is Chateau Lafite Rothschild,' said Dr Brownlow. 'Bottled in 1925.'

'Is it valuable?'

'A few years ago half a dozen bottles of this went for over £500!' said Dr Brownlow, carefully replacing the bottle that he had been holding.

I was so shocked that I nearly fell over. When I had recovered I raced back up the stairs towards the kitchen. On the way up I met Patsy who was coming down to see what we were doing.

'Do you want the bad news or the good news?'

Patsy looked startled. 'What bad news? What do you mean?'

'That horrid bottle of wine we threw away last night was worth around £100!' I told her.

'Oh no!'

'But the good news is that we've got another eleven bottles of exactly the same wine down in the cellar!'

Patsy threw her arms around my neck, I lost my footing and we both stumbled down the stairs. We scrambled to our feet to discover that my best grey flannels had a tear along one leg, but I didn't care.

'That will help pay for our new roof!' said Patsy.

Ben, attracted by all the excitement, came racing over towards us and started to lick my face excitedly.

'I take it the news isn't unacceptable, then?' said Dr Brownlow.

'It's marvellous!' I said, shaking him by the hand. 'I'm really glad you came round this evening. I was going to dump that wine.' Patsy, who had cobwebs caught in her hair, reached across and kissed him on the cheek.

Dr Brownlow grinned at us both. 'Shall we have a cup of tea to celebrate?'

*   *   *

CHAPTER FIVE

The Sunday after we had moved into Bilbury Grange Patsy and I went round to have tea with her parents at their farm. Patsy's sister, Adrienne, who was eager to start her own complementary medicine practice, had gone to London for a three day course in iridology and so, since it was the lambing season, Mr Kennett was extremely busy.

'Come and give us a hand Patsy,' he said, when we'd finished our salmon and cucumber sandwiches and our tinned fruit salad with fresh cream. 'I've got twelve lambs that need feeding.' He took his old blue coat down from behind the living room door, and put it on. It had long since lost both its buttons and its belt so he tied it tightly around the waist with orange baler twine. He then slipped his wellington boots on.

Patsy and I trooped outside in Mr Kennett's wake, calling in at the kitchen to pick up a pan of reconstituted powdered ewes milk which had been warming. We left Mrs Kennett, who was, as always, as quiet as a mouse and who never seemed to have anything to do with the farm, to clear away the table. I left Ben sitting in the living room alongside Mr Kennett's two dogs and gave her strict instructions to stay where she was. Fortunately, the three dogs seemed to get on well together.

The lambs which needed feeding were huddled together on a thick bed of straw in one corner of an old barn. The corner of the barn had been fenced off with old wooden boards. As soon as they saw Mr Kennett the lambs leapt to their feet and started to make a tremendous noise. The strongest pushed to the front and tried to jump over the wooden wall of their temporary pen.

'Why do these need feeding?' I asked Patsy quietly. I knew nothing at all about farming.

'Some of them are orphans,' explained Patsy. 'We always lose a few mothers in childbirth. And if a ewe has more than two lambs she won't be able to feed them all so we have to take over.'

I watched as Mr Kennett decanted warm milk into four pint sized feeding bottles fitted with red rubber teats. He gave two of the bottles to Patsy and kept two for himself. Then he climbed over the fence and started feeding the noisiest and pushiest of the lambs. As he did so several others tried to suckle on his coat. 'That's where all my coat buttons went,' he explained to me with a gummy grin. Patsy stayed on the outside of the pen and fed two of the lambs through a gap in the wooden boarding. When the first four lambs had emptied their bottles Mr Kennett and Patsy rinsed the bottles and the teats, refilled them with milk and started to feed another pair each.

'Them last four aren't going to make it,' said Mr Kennett, without emotion, nodding towards the four lambs which had not yet been fed. 'They're always last.' Two of the lambs were clearly suffering from diarrhoea and all four were noticeably smaller and weaker than the others. Like their brothers and sisters they all had numbers painted on their sides. One, a pretty little thing which was completely black, could hardly stand and seemed to be shaking and shivering though whether with cold, fear or general debility I did not know. 'They need two hourly feeds,' said Mr Kennett. 'And they need electrolytes. But they aren't worth the trouble.'

'Do you want to try?' Patsy asked me when it was the turn of the last four to be fed.

I hesitated for a moment before answering that I would. Without a word Mr Kennett rinsed and then refilled the four feeding bottles and then gave two to me and two to Patsy. 'I'll leave you to it,' he said.

'Just make sure that you keep the end of your bottle up in the air,' said Patsy. 'Otherwise they'll suck in air.'

I poked my two feeding bottles through the wooden boarding of the pen but the two lambs I was trying to feed were repeatedly pushed out of the way by stronger lambs which had already been fed. However much I tried to push the bigger lambs away they kept on coming back and the two weak lambs I was trying to feed seemed to get hardly anything to drink. Even when they did manage to get the teats into their mouths they were quickly nudged out of the way. I glanced to my right and saw that Patsy had managed to wedge her two runts into a corner so that she could make sure they were fed. The barn was filled with the sound of sucking and slurping and Patsy's best dress was covered with splashes of milk.

I climbed over the boarding, holding my two bottles high above my head, and found myself being nudged and buffeted from all sides. Even the lambs who had just been fed were desperate for more. Two of the fittest jumped up and left unpleasant looking streaks down the front of my only half decent pair of trousers. (The pair that Patsy had already had to repair after my fall down the cellar steps). Deciding that I now had absolutely nothing to lose, I crouched down with the two lambs I was trying to feed in a corner and protected them with my body while I fed them. Their tiny, bony bodies heaved as they desperately sucked at their bottles. When they'd finished I stood up feeling pleased with myself. Patsy, who had finished and had been watching me, started giggling when she saw the mess I was in. When I looked at her in surprise she pointed at the front of my jacket and trousers. I looked down and saw that both were covered with milk splashes. Two of the fitter lambs were butting one another and three others seemed to be playing a game of hide and seek under and around a rusty old piece of farm machinery.

'You haven't got another jacket!'

'I know.'

'And those are your only decent trousers!'

I nodded.

'So you're going to work in those tomorrow?'

'I don't care!' I told her. 'Those two poor little chaps weren't getting anything to drink.'

'They're girls not chaps,' said Patsy.

'Whatever. They weren't getting anything to drink.' I frowned and paused. 'When your father said that these four weren't worth the trouble, what did he mean?'

49

Patsy's smile disappeared and she looked embarrassed. She shrugged. 'You know . . . '

'No . . . I don't . . . Do you mean . . . '.

'He doesn't think they'll survive.'

'They'll die?'

'Yes.' said Patsy bluntly.

'They would survive if they were fed properly and looked after?'

'Probably.'

I turned round and looked down at the two lambs I'd just fed. They looked up at me and their eyes were full of trust and faith. I reached out a hand and they both lunged forward and took a finger each into their mouths. Their tails wagged furiously as they sucked hard, desperately trying to draw milk out of what they mistakenly thought were nipples. Strangely, they didn't stop when no milk came but seemed to get some comfort out of what they were doing.

'We can't just let them die.' I said. I could feel tears welling up in my eyes.

'They'd die anyway,' Patsy reminded me quietly. 'That's why they are here.'

To my shame it was something I hadn't even thought of. I hadn't related the tiny, woolly, loveable mischievous creatures in the barn with lamb chops on a plate. Suddenly, in that brief moment, deliberately breeding animals to kill and then eat seemed obscene beyond belief.

'We've got to save these four,' I told her.

She looked at me, puzzled.

'Take them home and feed them.'

I could see the uncertainty and confusion in her eyes.

'Your father won't mind, will he? He thinks they're going to die anyway.'

'But why?'

'I don't know why.'

But I did know. Because they had touched me. Because I felt guilty about the fact that I had eaten lamb and calf and pig and God knows what else. Because they seemed loving and loveable and they had looked at me with trust in their eyes. I did know why but I couldn't explain it. I felt embarrassed and uneasy and uncertain and I didn't want to upset

50

Patsy.

'They have to be fed every few hours.'

'That's O.K.'

'It'll mean getting up in the night.'

'I don't mind.' I could feel tears on my cheeks. I hurriedly wiped them away and blinked my eyes.

Patsy saw and came to me in a rush and flung her arms around my neck. 'You are a big softy,' she said. 'But I do love you. I'll help you look after them.'

'Do you think your Dad will let us take them?'

'There's only one way to find out.'

Hand in hand we walked slowly back to the farmhouse.

Mr Kennett, who had taken off his wellington boots and unfastened the orange bailer twine wrapped around his coat and was now settled back in comfort on the sofa thought about my request for a moment and then nodded. 'Good idea.' he said. 'If you're lucky you might make a few bob'. He paused, mulling something over in his mind. 'I'll let you have them at half price,' he said. 'Because you're family.' He reached out and shook my hand to confirm the deal then told me the price.

I reached into my pocket and handed over the coins.

'Take four of the stronger ones,' he said, with a sudden and unexpected burst of generosity.

'It's O.K., thanks,' I said. 'We'd like to take the four that were fed last.'

Mr Kennett looked at me as though worried that his daughter had married a man not suited to be let loose in the world of commerce and then shrugged, his anxiety for his daughter's welfare overwhelmed by simple self interest. He offered to deliver the lambs the next morning but when I said we wanted to take them home with us now he helped us load the four of them into the back of the Morris Minor and then put a small sack of lambs' milk, two spare teats and half a bale of straw into the boot. He wouldn't take any money for these items but said we could replace them whenever was convenient. Ben lay on the floor at the front of the car beside Patsy's feet and growled persistently all the way home. In the back the lambs 'baaaaaed' and 'maaaaaed' a lot and then fell asleep bundled up together on an old blanket

51

in an incomprehensible mixture of legs and tiny tails.

*   *   *

The slates had been safely delivered and stored in a massive pile which almost blocked the front drive. The roofers recommended by Thumper had begun removing slates and rotten battens from huge sections of our roof. Thumper himself had recruited a young man called Ernie to help him dig out bits of rotten wood from our window frames, soffits and door posts. Our four lambs, now christened Lizzie, Petula, Cynthia and Sarah-Louise, were happily ensconced in one of our stables, and although Patsy and I were both exhausted from giving them feeds every few hours (including throughout the night), we were getting great pleasure from their company. And a very excited wine dealer from a London auction house had rung to made an appointment to come to Bilbury to collect the wine ready to put it into a forthcoming auction. When Patsy had described the label to him he had, she said, positively drooled into the telephone. She said she didn't think she had ever heard anyone get quite so excited by anything. If his recommended reserve price did not prove to be unduly optimistic the money the wine would raise would pay for the roof repairs. There seemed some justice in the fact that although Bilbury Grange had given us a nasty financial surprise it had matched that with a pleasant financial surprise. We took it as a good omen.

At the surgery things seemed to be going quite well. I hardly ever saw Dr Brownlow, partly because he was busy helping to organise his new water bottling plant which seemed to have developed more glitches than even he had anticipated, but mainly, I suspect, because he was conscious of the fact that it was now my practice and he didn't want to get in the way. Many of the patients still missed him, and his daily presence in or around the surgery would have probably caused more than a little confusion. Miss Johnson was a tower of strength and inexhaustible fund of knowledge and information about the workings of the National Health Service bureaucracy and the idiosyncrasies of our patients. Just as important she also knew where everyone lived.

In a town or a city general practitioners can usually rely

on street names and house numbers to help them find their patients. But in Bilbury none of the lanes have names and none of the houses or cottages have numbers. Most of the buildings have names, but the signs are invariably covered up with ivy, rambling roses or weeds. Without Miss Johnson's instructions I would have wasted most of my days driving backwards and forwards and getting nowhere.

There was only one faintly grey spot on the horizon to darken our joy in living.

While having a drink in the Duck and Puddle with Thumper one evening I had heard a rumour that a London based property company was negotiating to buy several hundred acres of woodland and farmland to the west of the village and had applied for permission to build a large housing estate, a golf course, a holiday village, a hotel and a supermarket on the site. The rumour came from Frank Parsons, the landlord at the Duck and Puddle who said he'd heard it at one of his Licensed Victuallers Association meetings in Exeter. He said he had heard that the new hotel would have three bars.

However, none of us took this rumour very seriously. As much as we like Frank and enjoy his company, we know that sobriety and reliability are not his strengths and his trips to Exeter for the L.V.A. meetings cannot, in all honesty, be regarded as objective fact finding missions.

*   *   *

CHAPTER SIX

The following Tuesday was Patsy's birthday and I'd hoped for a quiet and uneventful day so that I could get all my work done a little early. I wanted to take her out to dinner at a new vegetarian restaurant in Ilfracombe which already seemed to have acquired an excellent reputation. I had taken my private and very personal vow to turn vegetarian seriously but rather to my surprise Patsy said that she too wanted to stop eating meat.

'You don't have to,' I told her when she announced that she too had decided not to eat meat again. 'It's just something that feels right for me.'

But Patsy was just as determined as I was. 'I used to cry myself to sleep at night when we had to send the lambs off to slaughter,' she told me while we were feeding our four lambs. 'I tried to harden myself to it by never getting to think of them as individuals.' She paused and for a long while neither of us said anything. 'That was one of the reasons why I went to work at the Duck and Puddle,' she told me. 'I just wanted to get away from the farm.'

Much to the annoyance of Sarah-Louise and Petula, who were both vigorously enjoying their early morning feed at the time, I put down my two feeding bottles and gave Patsy a tremendous hug. It occurred to me that if Patsy hadn't gone to work at the Duck and Puddle I might never have met her.

But the day was anything but quiet and uneventful.

The first thing that happened was that just as I got home for my lunch Miss Johnson telephoned from the surgery with an urgent message for me to visit Miss Phillips, the lady who had recently moved to Bilbury from London and who had visited me a couple of days earlier wanting to know if she could stop her tablets. Miss Johnson didn't know exactly what had happened but said that she had received an urgent call from a neighbour, a retired army Major called Arnold Kineton, who was regarded locally as a bit of an old fuss pot (Frank Parsons claimed that all old soldiers were wimpy and effeminate and that retired officers in particular were invariably more like old women than old women), but whose concern for the health and welfare of his neighbours was undoubtedly genuine. I sometimes got the impression that he looked after the other villagers in much the same sort of way that he once looked after his men. I asked Patsy to put my salad somewhere safe (our visiting rabbit was back again and lettuces, in particular, were only safe in cupboards) and drove off as speedily as the Morris Minor would take me to the cottage on the outskirts of Softly's Bottom where Miss Phillips lived.

Major Kineton was waiting for me on Miss Phillips' front porch. Even though it was a warm, humid day he wore a smart Harris Tweed jacket with beige cavalry twill trousers which had a razor sharp creases down the front, a yellow waistcoat and a paisley cravat. He had a neat little moustache and his grey hair (cut twice a week in Barnstaple) was parted immaculately on the left. Major Kineton always carried a walking stick made of a straight piece of young ash, though he never used it as a walking aid and usually carried it tucked under his arm like a swagger stick.

'I'm glad you've come, doctor,' said the Major, rather formally. 'I'm terribly worried about Miss Phillips.' He turned and led the way into the cottage as though it was his own and paused in the narrow hallway to show me into the living room. He stood to attention as I went through and then followed and stood behind me. There would have been some dispute about whether he or the doorpost was standing straighter.

The living room was neatly furnished with an expensive white leather three piece suite dominating the room. The suite was far too large for the cottage and was rather unexpected. After our first meeting I would have imagined that Miss Phillips would have chosen something floral. The walls were decorated with half a dozen hunting prints and a modern, imitation copper warming pan hung on a large nail over the slate topped fireplace. Every available surface in the room was covered with cats of all colours and all sizes. The only thing they had in common was that they were all made of porcelain or china. An elderly, exceedingly frail looking woman I had never seen before was slumped in one of the leather armchairs. She wore a red woollen dressing gown and underneath it I could just see an inch or two of an ankle length nightdress trimmed with lace. Her grey hair was uncombed and she was crying quietly. She was rocking backwards and forwards to comfort herself. As I entered the room another woman I didn't recognise came out of the kitchen. She wore a pair of smart charcoal grey trousers and a man's white shirt with what looked like a club tie. 'I'm Rachael Tweedsmuir,' she said, introducing herself. 'Miss Phillips and I live together.' She said this rather defiantly, as though half expecting me to make some comment of disapproval. I nodded and said I was pleased to meet her but this social nicety was ignored.

'She has been in a terrible state since she stopped her tablets,' said Miss Tweedsmuir, rather aggressively. She moved across the room, crouched down beside the older woman and took her hand in hers. 'She hasn't slept a wink and she hasn't stopped crying.' For a moment I was puzzled and then I suddenly realised that the woman in the chair must be Miss Phillips. I really hadn't recognised her.

'I spoke to the drug company,' I said, rather defensively. 'They said it would be perfectly all right for her to stop the tablets.'

'Well, look at her!' said Miss Tweedsmuir. 'Does she look all right to you?'

I had to admit that she didn't.

'She's certainly not herself,' said the Major, stepping forward. 'I can vouch for that.'

'Thank you, Major,' said Miss Tweedsmuir. 'I think we can manage now.' Dismissed, the Major backed out of the room and disappeared. He clearly knew his place. 'He came to bring us some mushrooms he'd picked,' she told me. It occurred to me that she wasn't a woman whose path I would have liked to cross.

56

I examined Miss Phillips carefully but could find no physical evidence of any abnormality. Her heart was beating strongly, her lungs were working well and her central nervous system seemed to be functioning reasonably well if rather sluggishly. But when I talked to her I could not get her to reply.

'She missed them once before and went like this,' said Miss Tweedsmuir. 'We were away with friends in Cheltenham and she'd forgotten her pills. She couldn't get any from the local chemist because her quack in London got them for her specially.'

'And she went like this?'

'Absolutely. Just the same. Crying. Depressed. Sleeping all the time. Wouldn't eat. Terrible.'

'What happened?'

'We went back to London early. She started taking the tablets again and she got better.'

'She didn't tell me about that,' I explained.

'She doesn't remember anything about it,' said Miss Tweedsmuir, very matter of fact.

'It sounds like a withdrawal syndrome,' I said. 'She'd better start on the tablets again.'

'I would have done that, doctor,' said Miss Tweedsmuir rather coldly. 'But Miss Phillips left the remainder of her tablets with you.' She was right, of course. I remembered that the drug company had sent someone down from Bristol to pick them up.

'I'll ring them back and ask them to let me have a supply,' I said. 'Then if Miss Phillips still wants to come off them we'll have to do it slowly.'

'That would probably be best,' agreed Miss Tweedsinuir. There was a hard edge in her voice that came quite close to sarcasm.

'Would you like me to arrange for Miss Phillips to go into hospital?' I asked.

'No! Certainly not.' said Miss Tweedsmuir very firmly. 'She's not well enough to go into hospital. That's the last place I'd send anyone in her condition.'

I didn't know what else to do and so 1 turned and headed for the door.

'Oh, one other thing, doctor...

'Yes?'

'Do you like animals?'

'Yes. Very much.'

'That's what I had heard. Our cat Ophelia has just had kittens. Could you give one a good home?'

I was, to say the least, rather taken aback. 'Yes.' I said. 'I suppose so.'

'Where do you live?'

I told her.

'Miss Phillips and I will come round and have a look when she's feeling better. If your home is suitable you can have one.'

'Oh.' I said. 'Thank you.'

I drove home via the surgery so that I could telephone the Medical Director of the drug company and ask him to let me have some tablets for Miss Phillips. He was unwilling, at first, to let me have any, but when I told him that if anything happened to Miss Phillips I would make sure that his company was blamed he agreed to send me the tablets I needed. This was a trick I'd learned from Dr Brownlow and it always seemed to work. Then I drove back home and finished my lunch.

*　　*　　*

I had still not quite finished lunch when the telephone went again.

'I've got Mr Lister for you,' said a secretary who sounded as if she had a small rock in her mouth. I waited for a few moments and then a man's voice came onto the line. Mr Lister was the editor of the 'Barnstaple, Bideford and Bilbury Herald' for which I wrote my weekly medical column.

'Got a bit of a problem with your column, doc!' said Mr Lister. 'Bit embarrassing really.'

'What's the trouble?'

'You seem to be causing a bit too much controversy. We've had a few letters from other members of your profession who object to some of your views.'

'Anything in particular?'

'Well you did a column for us warning about some of the problems caused by the whooping cough vaccine. That hasn't

58

gone down too well.'

'But the whooping cough vaccine does cause problems! Everything I wrote in that article was absolutely accurate.'

'Maybe. But some members of your profession think you're making things worse by worrying the public. They think these are problems that should be sorted out within the profession.'

I didn't know whether to laugh or to cry. 'But that's crazy!' I said. 'The profession isn't doing anything to sort these problems out. That was why I wrote about it in my column. Is that the only thing that's worrying you?'

'No.' said Mr Lister, drawing the word out. 'It isn't. You see, with a column like this you have to be very careful. Especially in a paper like ours.'

'I thought you told me that the readers liked the column?'

'They do,' agreed Mr Lister. 'Indeed, they do. At least the non medical readers do.'

'But the doctors don't?'

'Exactly. We had a lot of complaints about that article of yours telling readers how to change doctors and how to complain when doctors do things wrong.'

'I thought those were important issues!'

'In a way I agree with you,' said Mr Lister. 'But we want something a bit less, well, aggressive. We're not trying to change the world here, you know!'

I didn't say anything. Patsy who had heard my half of the conversation had come closer and was now sitting next to me. She looked worried.

'The thing is,' continued the editor, 'that you have to decide whether you want to write about what happens or you want to try to change things yourself. Those really are two quite different things.'

'But surely a writer should try to change things that he thinks are wrong!' I said.

'Not at all,' said Mr Lister. 'A journalist is a witness. His job is to report what happens. You're making the mistake of trying to make the news. Your problem is that you make people think. That's not really what we want in a newspaper.'

'But this is a column. Surely that's different?'

'Not really,' said Mr Lister, wearily. 'You can be controversial occasionally. That's fair enough. But only if you tell people what they already think, and certainly not if you start upsetting the establishment. People like to have their prejudices sustained. But we can't afford to upset important people in the town. If you carry on being too honest you'll struggle to make yourself any sort of career as a journalist. And you certainly won't do your career in medicine any good. You need to learn to compromise a little. Try not to rock the boat quite so much.'

'Can I ask who I've upset?' I asked him, though I wasn't sure any more that I cared. I wanted to rock the boat. I wanted to make a difference. I wanted to change things. I didn't see any point in doing otherwise.

'Well I don't mind telling you that we've had three letters from one doctor alone.'

'That wouldn't be the young Dr Brownlow, would it?' I had had a disagreement with Dr Brownlow's son a few months earlier when he had tried to persuade me to have his father, then my employer, taken into care. The young Dr Brownlow had been worried about the fact that his father was spending his inheritance and he hadn't been pleased when I had refused to help him.

'You know him?'

'Our paths have crossed.'

'He's a very influential figure. Besides, he plays golf with our advertising director.'

That really seemed to sum it all up. 'I take it you want to stop the column?'

'Well, I'm afraid that's about the size of it. Apart from our other problem I'm afraid that you've been undercut.'

'Undercut?'

'Another doctor has offered to write a column for us for less money than we're paying you.'

'Would that be the young Dr Brownlow?'

'Well, I don't suppose there's any harm in telling you. After all you'll see his column in the paper. Yes. It's Dr Brownlow.'

'Can I ask you what you're paying him?' I asked, out of idle curiosity.

There was a momentary pause. 'He's writing the column for nothing,' said Mr Lister. 'I think he rather sees it as a public service.'

'I don't think there's any danger that anyone else will under-cut him,' I said drily. 'I hope your publisher doesn't get any phone calls from people prepared to edit the paper for nothing.'

'I don't think there's any need for that sort of attitude,' said the editor, rather sharply. He put his receiver down and I found myself listening to the sound of a disconnected phone, wishing I'd put my receiver down first. I stood up.

'What on earth was that all about?' asked Patsy, standing up and moving over towards me.

'I've been sacked,' I told her, rather bluntly.

Patsy didn't say anything but just put her arms around me and gave me a big hug. In a way I was rather sad. I had enjoyed writing the column. And although I wasn't paid very well we needed every pound we could find to help pay for the renovations at Bilbury Grange. But in a way I was, I confess, rather pleased. I quite liked the idea that I had been sacked because I had made people think.

*　　*　　*

After that the day went a little more according to plan for a while. Miss Johnson telephoned to let me know that the drug company representative had turned up with a bottle of pills and that the district nurse, Kay Wilson, had taken them round to Miss Phillips.

In between visiting and stitching up a farm labourer who had cut himself while trimming a hedge and visiting Mrs Petti-grew who had, as usual, waited until she had completely run out of her high blood pressure pills to telephone and ask for help, I wrote some referral letters for patients who needed to see specialists at the hospital, filled in a lengthy and almost incomprehensible questionnaire from an insurance company which wanted to know whether a patient of mine was likely to drop dead before they had made a decent profit out of him, and tried to keep up to date by reading the comprehen-sible bits of a couple of medical journals.

Meanwhile, Patsy started work clearing the vegetable gar-den, the roofers carried on tearing slates off our roof and Thumper and young Ernie carried on replacing bits and pieces of rotten wood. Living at Bilbury Grange was a bit like living

61

on a building site but I was getting used to having a great crowd of builders around. I had an awful feeling that when they had all gone I might even miss them.

Thanks to Miss Johnson, who agreed to babysit the telephone for us and to ring me immediately at the restaurant if there were any calls, Patsy and I did manage to go out for our celebratory meal.

We shared a plateful of wild mushrooms with a tomato salad and a mountain of garlic bread and drank half a carafe of white wine between us. We couldn't stay out late because we had to get back to give the lambs their ten o'clock feed (I already knew how tying it can be to be a general practitioner having to be available to patients for a full 24 hours in every day, but I was now beginning to discover just how tiring and tying a farmer's life can be) and so we were back at Bilbury Grange at approximately a quarter to ten.

At half past ten, just after Miss Johnson had gone back home and we had given the lambs their feed, the telephone rang. Patsy answered it but handed it over to me straight away. She looked pale and anxious and her hand shook slightly as she handed me the receiver. 'It's Anne,' she said. 'The police have arrested Thumper.'

I felt cold inside as I lifted the receiver to my ear. My mother always used to say that bad things happen in threes.

By the time Patsy and I had driven round to the cottage where Thumper and Anne live, and I'd taken Anne to Barnstaple, Thumper had been released. As Anne and I walked towards the police station we saw him leaving and heading in our direction.

'I was just going to find a telephone box to call you!' he said. He kissed Anne and smiled at us both, but underneath the smile he looked grey and worried. In a strange way he looked younger than I'd ever seen him look before. And for the first time he looked vulnerable.

'What happened?' I asked him.

'I drove over to the river on the way home from your place,' answered Thumper. 'I thought I'd pick up a couple of trout for tea.'

I frowned. 'But what's wrong with that?'

'I don't have a fishing licence,' explained Thumper. 'And

I wasn't using a rod.' I remembered that when Thumper talked about 'picking up a couple of trout' that was exactly what he meant. Thumper was the only person I had ever met who could walk up to a river bank with nothing more than his bare hands, find a trout, use his fingers to hypnotise it and then pull it out of the water with hardly a splash.

'And they arrested you?'

'The Bilbury bailiff saw me tickling a trout,' said Thumper. 'He came up behind me and jabbed his stick in the back of my neck. I didn't know who it was or what the hell was going on so I rolled to one side and brought him down. He fell into the river.'

'So what did they charge you with?' asked Anne.

'Where's the baby?' asked Thumper suddenly.

'Patsy is looking after him for us,' answered Anne. 'What did they charge you with?' she persisted.

'I don't know,' said Thumper. 'Poaching and assault I think.' He shivered. 'I really hate those places,' he said, looking behind him at the police station. 'They put me in a cell!'

'But did you explain to them what happened?' asked Anne.

'Of course I did!' said Thumper. He shrugged. 'But the bailiff said I'd attacked him and deliberately thrown him into the river.'

'I still don't understand,' I said. 'If the bailiff fell into the river how did he catch you?' I'd seen Thumper run and I knew that there was no way a sodden water bailiff could have caught him on the tracks that run alongside the river.

'I fished him out of the water and then took him home,' said Thumper, rather shamefacedly. 'He was wet and looked really miserable.'

'And he still had you arrested?'

'He must have telephoned the police before he changed into dry clothes,' said Thumper. 'The police had two cars waiting for me at the top of our lane.'

'Let's get you home,' I said. 'Do you want to drive yourself and I'll follow. Or do you want to come with me and leave your truck here?'

'They've confiscated the truck,' said Thumper. 'Together with everything that was in it.'

'What for?' I asked him. I couldn't believe what I was hearing.

'If you're caught poaching they can confiscate all your equipment,' Thumper explained. 'I didn't have any guns or rods or anything so they took the truck. They said that was equipment.' He stopped for a moment. 'Look!' he pointed to the car park just behind the police station. 'There it is!' His truck was parked in between two police patrol cars in the police car park.

'When do you get it back?' asked Anne.

Thumper shrugged. 'If I'm found guilty I don't get it back at all.' He swallowed hard. 'But that's not the worst of it.' He put his arm around Anne. 'They said that if I'm found guilty I could go to prison!'

* * *

CHAPTER SEVEN

Thumper's arrest cast a huge black cloud over everything.

He borrowed an old Ford van from a friend who ran a small haulage business in Ilfracombe and carried on working at Bilbury Grange as though nothing had happened. And he tried to act as though he wasn't worried. But I knew that he was.

It wasn't the possible loss of his truck that worried him (though he was extraordinarily fond of it) and even though he didn't have much money I don't think it was the prospect of being fined that disturbed him.

It was, I knew, the fear of being sent to prison that had put the grey into his cheeks and the hollow look into his eyes.

Some people worry about going to prison because they are frightened of the shame or the damage it might do to their standing in the community, or because they are frightened of the people they would come into contact with. Thumper wasn't frightened by any of these things. He wasn't worried about his standing in the community because he didn't have one; at least, not one that would be affected by a spell in prison. He knew that the people he cared about wouldn't give a fig for the fact that he had a prison record. He certainly wasn't worried about whether or not he would be able to look after himself physically in prison. And shame was not a concept to which he gave any credence. And even though I know that he loved them both dearly I don't think he was even particularly worried about Anne or his baby. He knew that Anne could look after herself, and he knew that his friends in the village would see that she did not want for anything.

Thumper was frightened of prison for the very simplest of reasons: he was frightened because it would mean a loss of freedom. I had never before met anyone who was so completely at ease with nature as Thumper was. He was more at peace on the moors or along the river banks or in the woods than anyone I knew or had ever known. He could look at a patch of woodland and tell you which animals had passed through, which direction they had gone in, how long it was since they'd been there and what they had been planning to do. He could look at the river and tell you where the fish would be hiding and he could look at the sky and tell you, with far more accuracy than any professional forecaster, what the weather was going to be like for the next few hours.

It was the prospect of losing his freedom and the idea of being locked away from nature that had taken the steel from Thumper's soul. And I knew without him telling me that it was the waiting for his case to come to court, the uncertainty, that gave his fears strength and added vigour to his nightmares.

Some people need to talk about their fears and their anxieties in order to lessen the damage they do. Thumper didn't want to talk. But he didn't need to. All of us who knew him knew how he felt and what agonies he was enduring. There are probably some people who would say that by going poaching Thumper was breaking the law and was, therefore, exposing himself to whatever penalties the law might see fit to offer. But, for the first time in my life, I was beginning to have my doubts about the law and, in particular, doubts about the relationship between the law and its parent, justice. The problem was that I had always thought of prison as a place for bad people. And I knew that Thumper was not a bad person.

*   *   *

Meanwhile, life went on and occasionally there were bits and pieces of good news.

Our eleven bottles of wine were sold in London for slightly more than the wine expert had forecast, and far more than any sensible person would have paid. Patsy and I now had enough money to pay for our new roof and to replace the worst of our rotten window and door frames. Our four lambs had all survived the most difficult and most dangerous early days and had acquired quite definite personalities of their own. Sarah-Louise was coy and shy and loving; Lizzie was aggressive and playful and a born leader - it was she who would always start the others playing games; Petula was thoughtful, sensitive and very occasionally depressed and would look at us with huge brown eyes that were full of trust; Cynthia was full of mischief and seemed to get great pleasure from being difficult with us and with her half sisters. We loved them all.

There were, inevitably, many minor but annoying frustrations and disappointments too.

The work on our roof had come to a temporary standstill and for three whole days we didn't see the roofers at all. Then, while out visiting patients, I saw their lorry outside a hotel on the road to Combe Martin and found that they had started another job. They promised that they would be back with us within a couple of days and they seemed to mean it and I believed them and was afterwards quite charmed by my own naivety.

We discovered that the shop which had promised to deliver a cooker, but which had ended up by delivering nothing more substantial than a record number of excuses, was by no means unusual. A firm of electricians made three appointments to come and give us a quote for putting in some extra sockets but didn't keep any of them. The manager of a shop from which we had tried to buy a bed rang and said that there would be a five month wait and then seemed quite hurt when Patsy told him that we would like to cancel our order.

*   *   *

When Patsy and I had first bought Bilbury Grange we had hoped to increase our income by letting out rooms to holiday makers during the summer months. Most of the people who live in Devon are, directly or indirectly, dependent on the tourist trade for a living and we did not think we would have too much difficulty in finding tourists ready to come and stay with us.

Frank and Gilly Parsons at the Duck and Puddle told us that they often had more guests than they could cope with and said that they would be very happy to send us their overflow.

In my experience, very few things in life ever work quite as well as expected, and if there is one thing that fate doesn't like it is something that is well planned. The more precise the plans you make the greater the chances that something will go very badly wrong. Our plans to let off rooms in Bilbury Grange were, therefore, doomed from the start.

Our main problem was a very simple one. We had a limited amount of money available and so, inevitably, we had to repair the essential fabric of the building – the roof, the walls and the windows – before we could start spending money on decorating inside the house and buying luxury furniture such as beds, tables and chairs. We had known all this when we had bought Bilbury Grange, but it had quickly become apparent that we had not been quite pessimistic enough in our expectations. The cost of the new roof we had needed had, of course, been covered by the profit we had made from the wine but there had been no such windfall to cover the cost of repointing essential brickwork and replacing woodworm infested beams and floorboards. The cost of all these repairs had been enhanced by the fact that nothing in the house was of a standard size. Every piece of wood seemed to need to be specially cut by hand.

After a month of hectic building work had resulted in making the Grange less rather than more inhabitable we had decided that in order to try to boost our income we would convert the rooms above the coach-house into a self contained holiday flat. We knew that it would be at least another year before the main house would be in a fit condition to accommodate visitors, but we thought that a small holiday flat would enable us to improve our cash flow dramatically.

The rooms we chose had been unoccupied for a long time (the drawers in an old dressing table which we found in the bedroom were lined with a newspaper dated 1924), but although dirty and dusty they were light and airy and the rooms were undeniably spacious. Two of the main rooms, the kitchen and the living room, overlooked the courtyard while a third, the bedroom, had a lovely view into the walled garden. The flat was approached by a sturdy, iron spiral staircase, though it was possible to move large items into and out of the flat through a door sized hatch on the first floor which was still equipped with a working hoist. Surprisingly, the woodworm had left the coach-house more or less alone and there was no major repair work to do. All we needed to do was to clear out the straw, old cardboard boxes and other miscellaneous bits and pieces of discarded rubbish, give the rooms a lick of paint and then fill them with furniture.

So that Thumper could continue to work on the main house, Patsy decided to do all the necessary decorating herself. Once she had started work she refused to let me go into the flat at all.

'I want it to be a surprise!' she insisted. And so I grew accustomed to finding Patsy, dressed in jeans and an old tee shirt and with her hair pulled tightly back away from her face in a pony tail, covered in dust and cobwebs, and exhausted from washing, cleaning, polishing and, eventually, painting. The jobs seemed endless, and for a while I worried that she had taken on too much.

*   *   *

Within thirty six hours of re-starting her pills Miss Phillips made a fairly spectacular recovery. But she still wanted to try and stop the tablets.

Once again I rang the Medical Director of the drug company which made the pills, and once again he insisted that since the drug was not addictive and did not produce any noticeable withdrawal side effects there was absolutely no need for patients to come off the tablets slowly or, indeed, with any special care at all. With scepticism born of experience, Miss Phillips and I decided to begin a month long reduction programme with her taking slightly smaller doses on successive days in an attempt to get her body accustomed to life without the tablets.

One evening, two days after the reduction programme had begun, Miss Phillips and Miss Tweedsmuir arrived on our doorstep entirely unexpectedly. I was busy cutting down brambles and nettles in a corner of the vegetable garden that had still not been reclaimed and so Patsy answered the door. She left the two spinsters in the reception hallway (where we still didn't have any carpets or furniture) and then ran through the house, through the courtyard and into the vegetable garden to fetch me. My heart fell when Patsy told me who had arrived for my only thought was that something else had gone wrong. Wearily, and with a heavy heart, I followed Patsy back into the house. I was wearing a pair of tattered and stained jeans and an old and rather threadbare shirt that most tramps would have turned up their noses at. I had been wearing thick leather gardening gloves (our only really clothing extravagance had been to buy one another really good quality gardening gloves, and when I looked at how badly torn and tattered they had already become I thought they were worth every penny) but my hands were still filthy dirty. I had bits and pieces of bramble sticking in my hair and I knew that I must have smelt of bonfire.

'Oh, I'm sorry!' said Miss Tweedsmuir when I walked into the hall and apologised for my appearance. 'You're gardening, aren't you?'

'Taking advantage of the light nights,' I explained. 'We've got a lot to do.' I frowned. 'Is there something wrong?' I asked. 'Has something happened?'

'No. There's nothing wrong. Can we look?' asked Miss Phillips, clearly genuinely interested.

'At the garden?'

She nodded.

'It's still a terrible mess. I'm afraid there really isn't anything to see yet.' said Patsy. 'It's been overgrown for years.'

'Please!' begged Miss Tweedsmuir. 'We both love gardening.' She bent down to pat Ben who had followed us back into the house. Ben closed her eyes, rolled over onto her back and let Miss Tweedsmuir tickle her tummy. If she had been a cat she would have purred.

'She's really a guard dog,' I said. 'But she's in plain clothes.'

We led the ladies through the house and the courtyard, which they loved, and into the walled vegetable garden. Miss Tweedsmuir actually clapped her hands together in girlish delight when she saw it. 'Oh, how wonderful!' she said. 'How absolutely wonderful.' She turned to Miss Phillips. 'Isn't it going to be beautiful?' Miss Phillips looked just as excited and nodded. 'What a lovely greenhouse!' she said, pointing to the old Victorian greenhouse in a far corner of the garden. It badly needed painting and had several panes of glass missing.

'I'm afraid there isn't much else to see yet,' I said. 'We haven't bought any plants or seeds.'

'Would you like to see our lake?' asked Patsy. 'It's actually very small for a lake. But that's what it's called on the house deeds.'

We took them along the path we had partly cleared which led down to the still weed-clogged lake. We showed them where we had found a small stone bridge over the stream which fed the lake and where we had begun to explore the other side of the lake and we told them that we thought we'd found the front of an old summerhouse hidden under the brambles and nettles and we pointed out the statue of the little girl that was just poking up above the bulrushes on the tiny island in the middle of the lake and we talked about what we wanted to do and how we wanted to restore the garden and how we wanted to grow all our own vegetables and maybe make a little money to help pay for the restoration and replanting by selling vegetables to some of the local hotels.

We were walking back up towards the house, through a small copse of beech trees, when Miss Phillips suddenly stopped and dropped to her knees.

'Oh my heavens!' she said.

'What's the matter?' asked Miss Tweedsmuir.

'Look at this!'

Miss Tweedsmuir bent down beside her friend to examine a small red flower. 'It's a red helleborine!' she said, in awe.

'That's what I thought!' said Miss Phillips. 'Cephalanthera rubra.'

'What's a red helleborine?' asked Patsy.'

'It's an orchid and it's very, very, very rare!' whispered Miss Phillips. 'I didn't think there were any in the South West.'

'There were only thought to be two red helleborine plants in the whole of England,' said Miss Tweedsmuir.

'There are lots of them over here,' I said, unimpressed by this discovery. 'Look!' I pointed to a small, shady area where there were dozens of bright red flowers

'Oh, good heavens!' said Miss Phillips. And she fainted.

*　　*　　*

'Would you like to take a few of the orchids back for your garden?' I asked her when she had recovered.

Miss Phillips was obviously very touched by this offer. 'That is so very kind of you,' she said. 'But the red helleborine will only grow in beech woods and it adores deep shade. We haven't got anywhere that would be right for it.'

'Well, any time you want to come and look at ours you'll be very welcome!' said Patsy. 'Should we tell anyone what we've found?' she asked. 'What about the conservation groups? Do you think we should tell them?'

'Oh, I don't think so,' whispered Miss Tweedsmuir. 'If you do you'll have all sorts of people traipsing over your garden looking at them and they'll do far more damage than good. The only reason for telling people about a plant is if its habitat is threatened in some way. And your red helleborine are perfectly safe.'

'Aren't they sweet?' whispered Patsy, as we walked back up the path to the house behind Miss Phillips and Miss Tweedsmuir. They had both been so excited by the discovery of a rare orchid in our wood that they had seemed reluctant to tear themselves away. They were now walking up the path arm in arm and they too were whispering about something.

When we got back into the courtyard Patsy asked them if they wanted a drink of anything but they said they didn't want to drag us away from the garden any longer.

'Would you let us give you some plants?' asked Miss Tweedsmulr. 'We've got quite a collection and we could easily take some cuttings for you.'

'That would be wonderful!' said Patsy.

'We'll start some cuttings as soon as we get back,' prornised Miss Phillips. 'It'll be a joy to help you restore your garden.'

'When would it be convenient for you to come and choose your kitten?' asked Miss Tweedsmuir, quite unexpectedly, as they left. 'Tomorrow?'

Patsy looked at me, slightly puzzled. I was puzzled too. I'd forgotten that they had offered me a kitten.

'He's forgotten!' said Miss Phillips, smiling at her friend.

'We asked if you'd like a kitten!' Miss Tweedsmuir reminded

72

me.

'Of course!' I said. I felt embarrassed. 'It was very kind of you.'

'We'd love to come round tomorrow,' said Patsy, who was clearly excited at the idea of offering a home to a kitten. 'What time would be convenient?'

'Any time you like,' said Miss Phillips, reaching out and touching her on the arm. 'We'll be in all day.' She turned to me. 'What a beautiful wife you have, doctor!'

* * *

When, at the end of the next morning's surgery, Miss Johnson told me that there was a policeman waiting to see me my first thought was that it was something to do with Thumper. But it wasn't.

'Sorry to bother you, doctor,' said a policeman I'd never seen before. He was surprisingly short, rather stout and looked very young. He had his helmet tucked underneath his arm. We used to have a village policeman, a transvestite married to the district nurse, but he committed suicide after an accident in which he had knocked a local boy off his bicycle, and we now relied upon policemen from Ilfracombe and Barnstaple. It was a pity that we no longer had our village bobby. 'I'm looking for a Mr Keith Burrows.'

I knew who he meant straight away.

Keith Burrows is about sixty years old and lives in a ruined cottage on the road out towards Lynton. In the summer and early autumn he makes a living collecting elderberries and blackberries from the hedgerows and selling them to local greengrocers. In the winter he makes an even smaller living running errands for villagers who want bits and pieces fetching from the shops in Barnstaple. He rides a bicycle and tows a tiny cart behind it and can frequently be seen riding along the local lanes.

'What's he done?' I asked.

'I'm afraid he's wanted for non payment of fines,' said the police constable.

'What were the fines for?'

'I'm not sure I can tell you that, sir.' said the policeman rather officiously.

73

'I won't tell you anything if you don't tell me what the fines were for,' I told him firmly.

'He's been fined twice for riding a bicycle without a light,' said the policeman.

'And you've come out hunting him for that?'

'The court takes a dim view of people not paying their fines,' said the policeman very officiously. 'If you are cognisant of his whereabouts I must tell you that you're legally obliged to pass on the information.'

It may not have been a wise thing to do but I couldn't help it. I laughed at him. 'Are you telling me that if I don't tell you then you'll arrest me? For aiding and abetting a bicycle rider without lights?'

The policeman began to look just a trifle uncomfortable.

'How much does he owe the court?' I asked.

'I beg your pardon?'

'What were the fines?'

'They come to two pounds in all.'

I reached into my trouser pocket, found the appropriate coins and put them down on the desk between us. 'There you are. Case closed.'

The policeman looked at the coins and then looked at me.

'I'm not sure I can accept this,' he said. 'It has to be paid into the court.'

'Take it,' I told him.

And to my surprise and my relief he slid the coins off the desk and put them into his pocket. Then he insisted on writing out a receipt. 'This is very irregular, sir.' he said, with a weary shake of his head. 'Very irregular indeed.'

*　　*　　*

Miss Tweedsmuir answered Patsy's knock on their cottage door. 'You've come about the kittens, haven't you?'

We confirmed that that was, indeed, why we were there.

'Come on upstairs,' said Miss Tweedsmuir with a twinkle in her eyes. 'You'll love them. They look absolutely adorable.' She called to Miss Phillips who appeared from the kitchen, wiping her hands on a pale green hand towel, and the four of us, in single file, then climbed up the narrow staircase to the bedroom at the front of the cottage. A large double bed,

74

covered in a pale pink bedspread dominated the room. There was just about enough room left for a pine wardrobe, a pine dressing table and a pine bookcase that was packed with neat rows of paperback books. There were two nightdresses, one white and one in a floral pattern, neatly folded on the two pillows. Laid out neatly on the bottom half of the bed there was a large, fluffy white towel and on top of the towel there was an old fashioned wicker cat basket. Inside the basket lay, asleep, a large mixed tabby cat and the two most beautiful little kittens I had ever seen.

'How old is the mother?' Patsy asked.

'She's seven,' replied Miss Phillips. 'She's lived with me since she was a tiny, tiny kitten but I don't think she's ever been happier in her whole life. I got her from a friend who lived in the Bayswater Road. In London I never dared let her out of the flat so she'd never been outside until we came here.'

'She loves the garden here,' said Miss Tweedsmuir.

'Oh, she does!' agreed Miss Phillips. 'I wish you could have seen her when we first came to Bilbury. She was so excited!' She smiled at us and the memory of it all made her so happy that tears appeared in her eyes.

'What's her name?' I asked. I knew she'd told me but I'd forgotten.

'Ophelia!' replied Miss Phillips. 'Don't ask me why I called her that because I really don't know any more.' She pulled a handkerchief out of her sleeve and blew her nose almost silently.

'It's a lovely name,' said Patsy.

'She looks like an Ophelia,' I agreed.

'Oh, do you think so?' said Miss Phillips. 'That is nice. So do I.'

One of the kittens, a mixed tabby with a white ruff around her neck, a white splash down her chest and white paws, noticed us, miaowed loudly and stood up. She shook slightly and then hesitated before backing away and cuddling up against her mother.

'That one's a bit nervous,' explained Miss Tweedsmuir quietly.

Patsy very slowly reached out and stroked the kitten's head

with two fingers of one hand. The kitten, at first suspicious, tilted its head to one side. Then, very quietly, it started purring.

'Have you given them names yet?' I asked.

'No,' replied Miss Phillips. 'We thought that the people who take them would want to give them names so we just call them Kitty One and Kitty Two. She nodded towards the mixed tabby, 'That one is Kitty One.'

'They're both girls,' said Miss Tweedsmuir.

'Don't you want to keep them both?' asked Patsy.

'Don't tempt me!' said Miss Tweedsmuir with a tinkly, nervous little laugh. 'I'd love to keep them both but we've already got two cats and two is enough.'

The other kitten, a mackerel tabby and just as adorable, had a head that seemed far too large for its body. It woke up suddenly, pricked up its ears and clambered to its feet. Like its sister it stood unsteadily for a moment or two but, unlike its sister, then moved forward towards us instead of backwards towards its mother.

'She's ever so curious!' said Miss Tweedsmuir. 'A real bundle of mischief.'

I tentatively held out my hand and the mackerel tabby kitten moved its head forwards and sniffed at my finger tips. Then it miaowed very loudly, jumped out of the basket and walked unsteadily across the towel towards me. When it reached the edge of the towel it stood still for a moment and then jumped onto my lap, catching its tiny claws on my long suffering flannel trousers.

'What do you think?' asked Miss Tweedsmuir. 'Which one would you like?'

'Oh this one!' said Patsy, pointing to the mixed tabby.

'This one!' I said, holding the mackerel tabby.

'That one!' said Patsy and I simultaneously pointing to the other's choice.

'Would you like a cup of tea?' asked Miss Tweedsmuir, suddenly and quite unexpectedly.

Patsy looked at me. 'Well, I'm afraid I mustn't stay too long,' I said. 'Just in case Miss Johnson is trying to get hold of me. But a cup of tea would be very nice.'

'I'll go and put the kettle on,' said Miss Tweedsmuir. 'Edith will you come and put some of your home made biscuits out onto a plate?' Miss Phillips obediently followed Miss Tweedsmuir out of the bedroom and down the stairs.

'Aren't they gorgeous?' said Patsy, playing with the mixed tabby kitten.

'Miss Tweedsmuir and Miss Phillips?'

'The kittens, silly!' giggled Patsy. Reluctantly, she turned away from the kitten she was playing with. 'We'll take the one you chose.'

'No. Let's take the mixed tabby.' I said. 'I'm sure Miss Tweedsmuir and Miss Phillips will make sure that they both go to good homes.' The mixed tabby kitten, the one with the white paws, had huge eyes and it looked around at the world in wonderment.

The mackerel tabby kitten suddenly leapt off my lap and landed on my jumper. It then recklessly climbed upwards, miaowing loudly. Ophelia lazily opened an eye, saw that all was well, and then closed it again. Not to be outdone the mixed tabby kitten stood on the edge of the bed and looked across at her sister. She clearly wanted to jump too but she didn't quite have the courage. Patsy picked her up and put her down on my lap and she climbed rather slowly upwards.

'Tea's ready!' called a voice from downstairs.

'What shall we do with the kittens?' Patsy called back.

'Just leave them in their basket. They'll be fine.'

Reluctantly, we went downstairs.

'We've been thinking about it,' said Miss Tweedsmuir. 'And if you'd like to have both the kittens we'd like you to take them both.'

And so, half an hour later, we drove away with two beautiful kittens purring on Patsy's lap.

'What shall we call them?' asked Patsy.

'I think the mixed tabby should be Emily,' I said.

'And can we call this one Sophie?' asked Patsy.

As we drove home along the narrow Bilbury lanes the sun was slowly setting at the end of a beautiful, warm summer's day. The hedgerows were thick and lush in a thousand different shades of green. Sprinkled among the grasses and the brambles and the dock leaves were buttercups and foxgloves. There were thick clumps of grass growing in the centre of the lane and there was barely room to drive the car in between the hedgerows. Suddenly, a huge adult buzzard with his wings tucked tightly into his body dropped out of the sky in front of us heading straight for the tarmacadam. He pulled up with no more than a yard to spare, levelled out and then flew so that he was heading straight for our car. I braked to avoid crashing into him but I was wasting my time for he knew exactly what he was doing. No more than a dozen feet in front of us he swerved sharply to his right and disappeared into the undergrowth at the base of the hedge. Moments later, as the Morris Minor shuddered to an ungainly halt, he fell back out of the grass and onto the road clutching a rabbit in his beak. Taking just a moment to regain his composure he transferred the rabbit from his beak to his talons and then took off in a single, smooth, accomplished movement and soared effortlessly up and over the twelve foot high hedge at the side of the lane. The whole incident lasted no more than a few seconds and neither Patsy nor I had time to speak. Nature in the raw can sometimes be breathtaking.

*   *   *

CHAPTER EIGHT

It was early in the morning and I could already hear a thrush hammering a snail on a stone in order to break open its shell.

The day was still cool but the sun was already bright and it promised to be another untypically hot summer's day; the sort of day that makes living in the English countryside such a real treat, and the sort of day that all country dwellers survive on during the long, hard, cold, wet winter months that seem to drag on for ever.

Awakened by shafts of sunlight lighting up our bedroom, I had crept out of bed early, leaving Patsy to sleep for a few more minutes. A few yards away from me Emily and Sophie, our two new kittens, who had followed me out from the house, were playing hide and seek in and out of the greenhouse while Ben, lying sprawled out on one of the gravel paths, was watching them with a motherly eye. I had been worried about how Ben would take to the kittens but I need not have been. She loved them from the moment she saw them.

I had already watered the lettuce and left the wooden tops of the cold frames wedged open a few inches to allow a little air in, and although I was dressed ready for the morning surgery I couldn't resist pottering around in the vegetable garden, pulling out weeds that were about to start spreading their seeds and trying to decide exactly which part of the garden we should try to rescue next. I looked around, and although there was still a lot to do and a long way to go I was proud of what we had managed to achieve.

I stood for a few moments watching the butterflies: admirals and peacocks, blues and tortoiseshells as well as cabbage whites. I know a lot of gardeners dislike butterflies (or, rather, their plant eating predecessors) but both Patsy and I considered it a privilege to have them in our garden, and we were happy to accept as just payment the damage we knew they would do to our crops.

Although we still hadn't had the time or the money to repair the greenhouse, which had numerous broken panes of glass and a lot of rotten woodwork, and which was almost completely filled with an overgrown and totally out of control old grape vine, we had, after seemingly endless hours of work clearing away brambles and nettles and docks and couch grass and a thousand other species of weed, at last managed to clear a small area of ground in the walled vegetable garden so that we could start planting our first vegetable crop.

The walled garden had been built in Victorian times and it had clearly been designed by someone who had thought first and foremost of quality, convenience and style. Cost had clearly not been regarded as an influence of any significance. Although they were covered with a mixture of ivy, cultivated raspberries, yellow and green lichen and a wonderful pink climbing rose, the grey stone walls still seemed solid and sound. At its base, the wall around the vegetable garden was over two feet thick and at the top, to provide protection against the elements, the wall was covered by two double rows of grey slates topped with faded red coping stones.

The walled garden extended to about half an acre and included, in addition to the greenhouse which was attached to part of the garden's south facing wall, three large, wooden cold frames, a stone potting shed, a wheelbarrow and tool shed and, although the orchard (now consisting of elderly, unpruned trees which were almost entirely overgrown with the ubiquitous brambles and nettles) was outside the vegetable garden, a room that Patsy said was almost certainly an apple store.

Every building in the garden was equipped with cast iron guttering and downpipes which fed into water butts, and just in case that supply ever ran out there was a tap just outside the greenhouse which did not seem to be connected to the private water supply which fed the house, but which seemed to have a supply from some other source which we still had not identified. There was a stone seat built into an alcove in a shady corner of the wall, a small pond overgrown with lilies but teeming with tadpoles and a sundial on a small brick plinth. Everything in the garden had been so well built that it had survived years of neglect.

We did not have the time to plant the garden properly but we desperately wanted to grow something, and so while Patsy had resurrected an old cultivated strawberry bed, ruthlessly throwing out the old plants and rescuing only the younger, healthier looking plants I had sown three whole packets of lettuce seeds in the cold frames which still had unbroken glass. We thought it might be rather nice to at least be self sufficient in strawberries and lettuce for our first summer.

Suddenly, there was a splash and a loud miaow from somewhere behind me. I turned and saw Emily, the mixed tabby kitten, floundering in the lily pond. Sophie, our other kitten, was standing on the edge of the pond where Emily had fallen in and was miaowing loudly and plaintively for help. I dropped the pair of secateurs I had been using to prune a climbing rose which was so heavy that it was threatening to pull itself away from the wall and raced to the rescue. Even so Ben got there before me. She leapt into the water without hesitating and gently took hold of Emily's neck so that she could hold her above the surface of the water. I knelt down at the edge of the pond, reached out and took Emily from her.

While Sophie continued to miaow and Ben clambered out of the pond, stood next to me and shook herself dry, I tried to dry Emily on my handkerchief. But even when I had done this she was shivering and she still looked very bedraggled, miserable and sorry for herself. So, I unbuttoned my shirt and slipped her down next to my skin where it was warm and dry. She soon started to purr.

As I walked back to the house, with Ben ambling along beside me and Sophie scurrying to keep up with me, I could hear the sharp 'knock knock' of a woodpecker in a nearby tree and I thought for the thousandth time how lucky I was to live in Bilbury. Many of my student colleagues would, I knew, still be working in hospitals struggling to acquire more and more academic qualifications, ingratiating themselves with elderly, cynical and exploitative consultants, growing to hate every moment of every day, wondering if this was all

81

there was to life and constantly promising themselves something better sometime in the future. There was not a morning when I did not wake up wondering how and why I had been so fortunate to find myself living in such a wonderful, quiet village, in such a beautiful house and surrounded with good friends, a growing menagerie of animals and so much hope for the future. Every morning I would see and hear an endless variety of birds and wild animals. Best of all, of course, there was Patsy, and as I walked into the courtyard I could see her laying out breakfast on an old wooden table outside the back door. She was wearing a thin, sleeveless white cotton summer dress and a pair of white sandals. We had found the table in the stable where the lambs had been kept when they were being bottle fed. (They had begun to supplement their bottled milk by nibbling on grass and were now spending their days in the small paddock closest to the house.)

Patsy and I kissed. 'What on earth have you got inside your shirt?'

'Emily. She fell into the pond. Ben rescued her.'

Patsy, gently pulled at the front of my shirt and peeped inside. 'Oh, the poor thing!' Emily, looked up and miaowed loudly.

'She's drying off,' I explained.

'How long have you been up?' asked Patsy, letting go of my shirt front.

I looked at my wrist and shrugged. I'd forgotten to put my watch on. 'About an hour.'

'Why didn't you wake me?' Patsy poured me my first cup of coffee of the day. It smelt good. I could smell bread toasting in the kitchen. Why do all drinks and foods smell so much better out of doors?

I smiled. 'You looked too peaceful to wake.'

I frowned, remembering that I had to be at Dr Brownlow's to start the morning surgery. 'Do you know what time it is now?'

'It's well after eight. But you've got time for breakfast. I'll get the toast.' She went indoors.

I sat down, with Emily in my shirt, and Ben at my feet and sipped at my coffee. Using her claws as crampons Sophie climbed up my trouser leg and settled down on my lap. Somewhere in the distance I could hear the roofers arrive and start work. It was going to be another glorious day.

* * *

If I hadn't started the day realising just how lucky I was, I would have quickly been reminded of my good fortune shortly after I had arrived at the surgery to start the day's work.

Mrs Blossom was the first patient I saw and I don't think I have ever seen anyone look less like her name. Although she looked as though she was still only in her middle thirties she already had that glum, dark, sour look around her mouth that so often mars even the prettiest of faces. I had only met her a couple of times before, and although I didn't really know anything at all about her as an individual I had unfairly labelled her in rny mind as one of life's whingers, a dour pessimist for ever looking for, and inevitably finding, the worst in everything. She looked sour and miserable, and I had unjustly assumed that this was her natural demeanour. With out much interest or enthusiasm I waited for her to tell me what she wanted from me.

(It is sadly true that the way doctors treat their patients is very often unfairly influenced by appearances. A patient who walks into the surgery with a smile on her face will gain a weary doctor's sympathy far more speedily than the patient who walks in gloomy and bad tempered. It isn't fair and it isn't just, but it happens.)

Mrs Blossom slumped into the chair on the other side of my desk and stared glumly at me as though I had insulted her.

I smiled at her and asked how I could help her. The consulting room had no natural light and it was cool and gloomy. I struggled hard to acquire an interest in Mrs Blossom for a large part of me wanted to get through my patients as quickly as I could so that I could get back to the garden at Bilbury Grange.

'I want a tonic,' said Mrs Blossom.

She spoke in a dull monotone voice and it was neither a request nor a demand. She seemed angry and bitter and I didn't understand why.

83

'What symptoms do you have?' I asked, a little hastily perhaps.

Suddenly, and quite unexpectedly, Mrs Blossom stood up. 'You don't understand what it's like,' she snapped at me. 'It's all right for you, sitting behind your big desk. You don't know what real life is like. You don't have any problems. You're lucky. I wish you could have some of my worries for a day. That would take the damned smile off your face.' She turned and started to march towards the door.

I felt uncomfortable and did not understand what I had done to provoke this attack. But, perhaps justifiably, I nevertheless felt guilty and I knew that I had missed something. Somehow I felt that I had failed.

'Come back, sit down and tell me what's worrying you,' I said quickly. No one had ever prepared me for this. Medical schools train doctors to deal with symptoms and illnesses not with the patients who have them.

Mrs Blossom looked over her shoulder at me and I realised that what I had mistaken for hatred and anger was in fact nothing more than sadness fuelled by despair. There were tears in her eyes.

'Please!' I begged. I stood up and with my left hand indicated the chair she had vacated. 'Please, sit down. Talk to me.'

Mrs Blossom hesitated for a moment and for a few seconds I thought she was simply going to walk out of the consulting room. But she didn't. She turned round again, came back and slumped down into the chair I had indicated. I too sat down. I didn't speak because I didn't know what to say without offending her. She didn't speak, though this was probably because she was trying not to cry and knew that if she spoke she would not be able to hold back the tears. I waited and tried not to move, frightened lest any movement I might make be interpreted as a sign of impatience or boredom or not caring.

'I'm sorry,' she said at long, long last. She looked across at me and I wondered if the sourness of her mouth was simply a result of the fact that she had spent too little time smiling and too much time screwing up her face and trying not to cry.

'That's O.K.,' I said. 'Talk to me.'

But she didn't talk, she burst into tears. The dam opened and the tears flooded out of her and her body shook with great sobs and she looked at me with a deep sadness and overwhelming unhappiness that I had never seen before. I pushed a box of paper tissues across the desk towards her but it was like offering someone a paper handkerchief to stem the flow of the River Thames.

'I'm sorry. I'm sorry. I'm sorry.' she repeated, time and time again. It was as though it were a litany; an oft repeated prayer. She held a sodden, screwed up tissue so tightly in her fingers that her knuckles were white. And then she started to talk.

She told me that she had got married at seventeen not because she was in love but because she desperately wanted to leave home and knew of no other escape. She had three children in as many years and then her husband, a labourer, had gone out one night saying that he was going to the pub and had never come home again. For weeks she was frantic, convinced that he had had an accident but then she had discovered that he had left her to live with a barmaid in Ilfracombe. To keep her children she had taken a job as a store assistant but after three years of that she had left suddenly. The manager had assaulted her one night when the store was in darkness and they were closing up. Unable to get a reference she had worked briefly as a maid in a hotel, a waitress in a seaside cafe and a counter assistant in a fish and chip cafe. But then her mother had died and her father had announced that he was coming to live with her. She had never liked nor got on with her father and had always found him rude and overbearing. Now that he was living with her and constantly critical she found his presence intolerable.

'I would rather be in prison,' she told me, and I could see that she meant it. 'When I was eight my mother used to make me do the housework and by the time I was fourteen I was doing the cooking and the shopping. I've spent my life looking after other people, not because I want to but because I have no choice. I don't like my kids and they treat me like dirt and I hate my father, but I spend my life looking after them. I've never done anything because I wanted to do

85

it and never done a job I've enjoyed.' She stopped and looked straight at me. 'I don't feel like I'm a person any more,' she said.

I listened to her and felt the tears forming in my eyes. I thought how different our lives had been, were now and promised to be in the future. 'Are your children still living at home?' I asked her, quietly. I had worked out that since the oldest had been born when she was seventeen or eighteen they must be nearly grown up by now.

She looked at me, puzzled. 'Of course,' she said. 'The oldest is only nine.'

I realised, with horror and some embarrassment that she was ten years younger than she looked. She was hardly any older than I was although I'd thought of her as belonging to a different generation.

'Of course,' I said, hurriedly. 'I wasn't thinking.'

'I look older than I am, don't I?'

'No!' I said, too quickly.

She smiled at me for the first time. She looked almost pretty when she smiled, though it wasn't a proper smile, the cracks were still there underneath it. 'I'm sorry,' she said. She stood up again. 'I shouldn't be telling you all this. There isn't anything you can do. You've got a room full of sick patients to look after.'

'Please, sit down!'

She looked at me, hesitated, and then sat down. 'I should go,' she said. 'Thank you for listening to me.'

Just then the telephone rang. It was Miss Johnson, the receptionist. 'Are you all right, doctor?' she asked. 'You've had that patient in with you for twenty five minutes now and the others are getting a bit restless.' She wasn't being critical but thought I might have been trapped by a loquacious patient and needed an excuse to end an interminable conversation.

'Tell them I'll be as quick as I can,' I told Miss Johnson, and put the phone down. 'Please sit down a minute,' I said to Mrs Blossom.

'You're in trouble, aren't you?'

'The natives are getting restless,' I smiled at her. 'It's O.K. It doesn't matter. Anyone who is ill will wait.' I instinctively knew that if she left now I would probably not be able to get her to talk again. But she needed help. And I wanted to help her.

She talked to me for another fifteen minutes, told me things she said she had never told anyone else before, told me that she had always wanted to be a painter and that she had been good at it at school but that she'd never had a chance to try again, told me that her father had abused her when she was a child, told me that she got through the days only by thinking of the different ways in which she could kill herself, told me that for her death was a friend, the only hope she had.

In the end I didn't know what to do to help her. I told her I would arrange an appointment for her to see a psychiatrist and made her promise me that she would keep the appointment, although in my heart I didn't know what any medical specialist could do to help her. I wanted to help but I felt desperately useless and I finished the rest of the surgery in a mood of deepening sadness and despair.

Deep down I knew that there would always be such patients, and I would always be unable to help them and I didn't know how I would be able to cope with this aspect of general practice.

* * *

When I got back home Patsy had left a note to tell me that she had caught the bus into Barnstaple to try to find someone prepared to sell and deliver us a cooker and so I went round to the Duck and Puddle to get some lunch.

I was waiting for Gilly to cook the egg and chips I had ordered when Keith Burrows appeared as if from nowhere.

'I've got a bone to pick with you, doctor!' he said, rather aggressively. 'Am I right in believing that you paid a fine for me the other day?'

'That's right!' I agreed, slightly puzzled at Keith's attitude. I hadn't really expected him to be grateful but nor had I expected him to be so upset.

Keith shook his head as though exasperated by my stupidity. 'What's the matter?' I asked him.

'They were about to arrest me!' complained Keith.

'Exactly!'

'If I'd been lucky I'd have been given two weeks in Exeter gaol,' moaned Keith.

'But . . . did you *want* to go to prison?'

'Of course I did! I've got some good mates over there and the gaol is the coolest place I know of in the summer. All those thick stone walls.' Keith sighed. 'Besides,' he said,'I can't stand the roads in the summer. They're always full of grockles in caravans and cars. It's far too dangerous.'

I didn't really know what to say. I don't think I had ever come across anyone who actually wanted to be sent to prison. 'I'm sorry!' I said in the end.

'I should think so,' muttered Keith. 'Next time you see a policeman with a warrant for my arrest just tell him where he can find me, will you?'

'I will,' I agreed. I apologised again. 'Can I buy you a drink? To make up for it?'

'I'll have a malt whisky,' said Keith without hesitation. 'A Macallan preferably. Make it a double, please, Frank.' he added. When the whisky came he raised his glass. 'Here's to a life of crime!' he said, with a toothless grin.

*   *   *

The evening surgery seemed to go on for ever.

Although there were a few villagers calling in for prescriptions and advice, most of the patients were holiday makers who were in the area for no more than a few days. Most of them had nothing more wrong with them than mild sunburn or insect bites. By the time I had finished I was exhausted, desperate to get back home, to have something to eat and to then spend an hour or so working in the garden. I had never before been a very keen gardener but since Patsy and I had moved into Bilbury Grange I had found it to be the most relaxing and soothing of hobbies. I found myself anxious to see if any of Patsy's strawberries had started to redden or if any of my lettuce had started to grow.

When I got back to Bilbury Grange, keen for a quiet evening, I was dismayed and surprised to find the driveway blocked with cars I had never seen before. All of them were old, once expensive, covered in rust and clearly well past their best. My first thought was that they must all belong to campers who had taken the wrong turning and driven into our driveway by mistake. I had to park at the bottom of the drive and then walk up to the house through the wood.

'What on earth is going on?' I asked Patsy, who I found in the walled garden tending to yet another magnificent bonfire.

'The cars?'

I nodded.

'They belong to Thumper,' explained Patsy. 'He asked me if he could leave them here for the night.'

'Did he say what he was up to?'

Patsy shook his head.

'When is he going to move them?'

'He said he'd have them all towed away tomorrow,' said Patsy. 'A friend of his from Ilfracombe is coming with a pick up truck.'

'Won't they go under their own steam?' I asked, horrified.

'Well they were all mobile when they got here,' said Patsy, 'Because I saw Thumper driving them. But he says that they've all got water in their petrol tanks now.'

'*All* of them?'

'That's what he said.'

'But how? How have they come to get water in their tanks?'

'I don't know,' said Patsy. 'Do you want some tea? I bought a French loaf in Barnstaple. It smells lovely. I could make you tomato sandwiches.'

I forgot about Thumper's cars and ate a pile of the best tomato sandwiches I'd ever tasted.

'Did you find a cooker in Barnstaple?' I asked Patsy, when I had finished.

She shook her head. 'Well, I did and I didn't,' she confessed. 'I found one but it's only an old one and the man in the shop wants too much money for it. I looked again at the new ones but the prices are just horrendous.'

'So what are we going to do?' I asked her. 'It's not so bad now but we're going to need one for the winter.'

'The man at the shop said we should go to an auction if we are prepared to take a chance,' explained Patsy. 'He said that at house auctions they sell all that sort of stuff at knockdown prices. He said they virtually give away the sort of things we need.'

'That's just as well,' I said, gloomily. 'We can't afford to buy them.'

* * *

As soon as I heard Thumper arrive the following morning I rushed downstairs to catch him before he disappeared up a ladder. I was, I confess, extremely curious to find out why he had bought so many old and apparently useless motor cars. I also wanted to know how long he intended to leave them parked in our driveway.

'Don't worry about a thing!' Thumper grinned. Although his case still had not come up in court Thumper had recovered much of his previous cheerful confidence.

'What are you up to?' I asked him. 'How illegal is it?'

Thumper sauntered over looking rather sheepish. 'That's not a very nice thing to say!' he said, pretending to be hurt.

I laughed. I could never be cross with Thumper for long. 'How many are there?'

'Seven.'

'And how long are they going to be here?'

'A mate of mine is coming over from Ilfracombe about lunchtime,' Thumper replied. 'They'll be gone by this afternoon.'

'But if they don't work why did you buy them?'

'They were working when I bought them,' said Thumper.

'All of them?'

'All of them.'

I must have looked very puzzled. Thumper laughed. 'Did you hear about that garage just outside Bratton Fleming?'

I shook my head. 'No.'

'They had a petrol delivery yesterday morning but by mistake the tanker that did the delivering wasn't full of petrol it was full of water. Every car driver who stopped there for petrol got a tank full of water.' Thumper grinned at me. 'Someone screwed up at the depot.'

I still didn't understand.

'The petrol company immediately announced that they'd pay for any damage done to customers' cars and for any inconvenience caused,' explained Thumper. 'It was the least they could do to avoid bad publicity.'

I was beginning to understand. 'So you bought a pile of old crocks and filled their petrol tanks with water?'

'Exactly!'

'And now you're going to claim that all these cars were ruined when they were filled up at the petrol station?'

Thumper nodded. 'My mate owns a tow truck. He'll just tell them that he had to pick these up from where they'd broken down in the lanes.'

'But won't they get a bit suspicious when they discover that you took seven cars along to the same garage and had them all filled up with water?'

'They would if my name was on all the claim forms,' admitted Thumper.

I stared at him. 'Whose names have you used?' I asked him.

'Don't worry,' he said. 'I only put your name down on one of them.'

*　　*　　*

CHAPTER NINE

Two days later I arrived home for my lunch and found Patsy standing on the doorstep waiting for me and holding a copy of the local paper.

'There's one this afternoon!' she said, excitedly.

'One what?'

'A house auction. In Kentisbury. It's only a couple of miles away.'

'What time does it start?'

'Two o'clock.'

I looked at my watch. 'It's nearly half past one now,' I said. 'And I'm starving.'

'I've made you some sandwiches,' said Patsy. 'And I rang and checked with the auctioneer. There's a phone at the house and if Miss Johnson needs you they'll take a message.'

I started to say something because, in truth, I was nervous about going to my first auction and would have been happy to find an excuse to enable me not to go, but Patsy, who was already beginning to understand me well enough and was only too prepared for me to make excuses, was ready. 'I've spoken to Miss Johnson and given her the number. She says you only have one appointment this afternoon – for a life insurance medical – and she's sure she can move that to tomorrow.'

Realising that I had lost I picked up the basket full of sandwiches and the flask of coffee that Patsy had prepared, waved goodbye to the roofers who were now getting close to completing the re-slating and were cheerily working through their lunch hour, told Thumper and his assistant, who were both sunbathing on the front lawn, where we were going, opened the door for Patsy to get into the car, joined her and drove to the house auction in Kentisbury. I ate my sandwiches as I drove and drank a cup of coffee from the flask too.

Even Patsy nearly let me turn back when she saw the rows of cars that were parked on the verges around the house where the auction was being held. It looked as though everyone in Devon had turned up.

'There are a lot of dealers here,' whispered Patsy, as we climbed out of the Morris and followed the flow of potential buyers walking down the lane towards the house. I didn't bother locking the car doors because the hood was down.

'How do you know?' I asked her.

'Just look at all the vans and estate cars,' Patsy replied. I looked around. A good half of the vehicles which had been parked were vans, trucks and estate cars. Many were equipped with huge and sturdy looking roof racks. 'Do you think it's still worth going?' she asked me, beginning to lose her nerve. 'With all those dealers bidding?'

'If we're bidding against dealers we will at least know whether or not we're getting a bargain!'

Patsy looked at me and frowned. 'What do you mean?'

'Well, when a dealer bids he knows he's got to make a profit when he resells. So if we just outbid him we're almost certainly getting whatever we buy at below the retail price.'

'But it means we're not likely to get any real bargains,' countered Patsy who had, I think, harboured hopes that we would be able to repeat our success with the bottles of wine. 'Not with all those dealers around!'

The house where the auction was being held was an old and rambling Victorian vicarage. The former owner, a farmer and local businessman who had made a considerable fortune out of cattle and sheep, had died in his nineties and had left his estate to his housekeeper.

A young man from the auctioneers sat behind a wooden trestle table just outside the front door to the house and sold us two neatly printed catalogues listing the items for sale.

Inside the house it was clear that the former owner had not spent too much of his money on doing any repair work. Even though it was a warm and sunny day the rooms were all filled with a musty, damp smell that seemed to cling to

93

everyone who entered, and numerous damp patches on the walls showed where the roof was leaking. The paintwork was brown and the walls were covered in paper that had been past its best at least a decade earlier. The old farmer had, however, filled his house with well built, antique furniture, and it was easy to see why the auction had attracted so many antique dealers. There were bookcases, display cabinets, desks, wardrobes, dressing tables and pieces of furniture which I didn't even recognise. He had clearly been a hoarder of Olympic standard too, and every single room in the house was packed with bric-a-brac: old magazines, sporting programmes, stuffed birds in glass cages and bits and pieces of classic motor cars. In one room I spotted a radiator from a 20/25 Rolls Royce. In another I saw a mascot from an old Bentley. In addition to being a hoarder, the old farmer had clearly also been something of a collector and every available surface was covered with clocks, porcelain cows and, rather surprisingly, old telephones. There were prints and water colours hanging in vast numbers on every wall. There were also half a dozen shotguns on display. The auctioneers clearly regarded some of the items as valuable for they had stationed at least one representative in every room.

'Don't forget!' whispered Patsy, as we shuffled around among the crowds, 'Don't scratch your nose or sneeze during the bidding!' I felt her fingers reaching for mine and held her hand tightly.

I looked at her. 'Don't! I'm already terrified of moving. I'll be too nervous to breathe! What happens if we buy one of these expensive pieces of furniture by accident? Can they make you pay for it even if you don't want it?'

'If something is knocked down to you then you own it,' said an unshaven man in a pair of dirty jeans and a grubby tee shirt who was carefully examining a china cow that had a spout for a mouth and a hole in the middle of its back. He had a pony tail tied back with a small red ribbon. 'If you make the winning bid then it's a legally enforceable contract.' He turned and smiled. 'You're the new doctor from Bilbury, aren't you?'

I admitted that I was but I didn't recognise him. I didn't like to confess this, however. Not unreasonably, most patients are offended when their own doctor doesn't recognise them.

'You don't know me,' he said, with a grin. He had clearly read my discomfort accurately. 'My name is Fogg. You've treated my aunt. She thinks you're wonderful.' I felt myself blushing with embarrassment. He put the cow down carelessly. 'Fake.' he said.

'Fake? How do you know?' I was impressed.

'The maker's mark on the bottom is too neat.' He shrugged. 'And the piece doesn't feel right.'

'Is there enough money in those things to make faking worthwhile?'

The stranger looked at me and raised an eyebrow. 'Are you joking?'

I shook my head.

'If that had been real it would have been worth £700–£800.'

'What is it worth?'

'£20 to anyone who knows it's fake.'

'But if someone didn't realise it was a fake?'

'They'd probably pay £700 to £800 for it.'

I gulped and felt myself going cold.

'The old bloke who lived here thought it was real. He probably paid top price for it.'

'How do you know?'

'Because he's got real and fake stuff all mixed up. He didn't know which was real and which was made in Taiwan.' He looked at me. 'What are you looking for?'

'Cooker, fridge, washing machine – that sort of thing. We're furnishing a house.'

The stranger laughed. 'Really? Is that all?'

'Yes.'

'Have you looked in the kitchen?'

'No. We haven't even found the kitchen.'

He looked at his watch. 'Come on. I'll show you.'

'Don't you have things you have to look at if you're going to bid?'

'I've looked at the stuff I want to bid on. I've been here since ten this morning.'

We followed him along a dimly lit corridor and into a huge kitchen that looked as if it had last been decorated at the end of the nineteenth century. There were far fewer people in the kitchen than there had been in the reception rooms. I looked around but couldn't see any of the things we were looking for.

'The old man has his cooking done on the Aga,' said the stranger. He pointed to a huge cream coloured monster.

'They're wonderful,' said Patsy. 'My mother uses one.' She looked at me. 'I'm surprised there isn't one at Bilbury Grange.'

'Maybe someone had it taken out.' I suggested.

The stranger laughed. 'Unlikely,' he said. 'It's easier to move the house than to move one of those things.'

'So, no cooker,' I said sadly. I looked around. There was an old fashioned washboard standing in a corner, a wooden clothes airer hanging from the ceiling and a meat safe standing on a pine table. 'And no washing machine and no fridge.'

'In here,' said the stranger, disappearing through a plank door into a stone floored scullery. We followed him. There, still wrapped up in the plastic in which they had been delivered, were a brand new cooker, washing machine and refrigerator. 'Any good?'

Patsy pulled at the plastic so that she could look at the cooker properly. 'It's never been used!'

'None of it has. The old man finally allowed his housekeeper to order these things a couple of weeks before he died. They never had time to have them installed.' He pointed to a lot number stuck onto the top of the cooker. 'No one will be interested in any of this stuff. You should be able to get it for a song.' I checked my auction list and saw, to my surprise, that all three items were in the same lot.

'The auctioneer doesn't want to waste his time with that stuff,' explained the stranger. I had been desperately trying, without any success, to decide whose nephew he was. He looked at his watch. 'Better get back,' he said. 'They'll be starting any minute now and there's some good stuff fairly near the top of the auction.' He moved towards the door. 'Why don't you come and watch? The things you want won't come up for at least an hour and a half.'

The three of us hurried back along the dimly lit corridor to what had been the living room and squeezed into a space between a massive dark oak book case and a long, mahogany sideboard. Patsy, who was standing on tip toes to try to see, clambered onto a pile of old farming magazines from which vantage point she seemed to have an excellent view of the proceedings.

The auctioneer, a tall fair haired man with a ruddy complexion and a luxuriant moustache, the ends of which had been waxed and twirled into neat curls, was already standing on a box giving last minute instructions to a couple of his assistants. He had a clipboard in his left hand and a small wooden hammer in his right. He was wearing a red and white striped shirt with a plain white collar and a red and white spotted bow tie. His grey trousers were held up with a pair of wide, scarlet braces. His jacket was draped neatly on a wooden hanger that was dangling from the picture rail.

Without warning the auctioneer slammed his small wooden hammer down against the back of his clipboard.

'Ladies and Gentlemen,' he announced in a loud, clear voice.'Let's start the auction!' He read out a short list of rules and regulations giving his firm's commission rates and, confirming the stranger's comment about the legality of any bid, told us about another auction that was due to take place in a few days time and then, without any more warning, asked for bids for the first lot – a water colour print which was held up by one of two burly men whose job it was to identify and then display the items for sale.

'Cheap rubbish,' whispered the stranger. 'They always start auctions with something fairly cheap just to get things going before the big stuff comes on.' The print was bought by a thin man in a light grey suit who looked pleased with his purchase and carefully made a note on his catalogue. The auctioneer asked him his name and one of the assistants wrote it down on a sheet of paper.

The first half a dozen items were all fairly inexpensive. But when the auctioneer announced the seventh item the mood and atmosphere in the room changed noticeably.

'This is where the good stuff starts,' whispered the stranger. I was making a real effort not to make any discernible movement that might be mistaken for a bid. The auctioneer's burly assistants were pointing to a tall display cabinet and although I couldn't see where they were coming from the bids were coming thick and fast. Within a minute the bids, which had started at £100, were into four figures and rising rapidly.

'Come on now,' said the auctioneer, cajoling his audience. 'This is an excellent example of the period and in perfect condition.' One of his assistants stood on tip toes and whispered something to him. 'I'm told that there is one knob missing from the cabinet,' said the auctioneer. He frowned. 'Though I didn't notice it missing yesterday,' he added. The absence of a knob seemed to cool the enthusiasm for the piece and the bidding slowed. Eventually, the auctioneer lifted his hammer, slammed it against his clip board three times and then pointed it straight at me! I felt my mouth go dry and my heart missed at least two beats. I was waiting for him to ask me my name when he turned to the assistant who was writing down the buyer's names and said simply 'Fogg.' I looked to my left, to the spot where the stranger was standing and caught his eye. He winked once but showed no other sign of knowing what was going on.

'Was that you?' I whispered.

He nodded.

'I didn't even see you bid!'

He half smiled.

'What about the missing knob?' Patsy whispered between us. 'Doesn't that affect the value?'

The stranger didn't say anything but slipped his hand into the left pocket of his jeans and pulled out a small wooden knob. 'Saved me at least two hundred quid,' he whispered, slipping the knob back into his pocket and allowing his smile to broaden a little.

I felt my palms sweating and I had to swallow hard.

The auctioneer didn't pause.

As soon as each item was sold his assistant wrote down the details and the auctioneer moved immediately onto the next lot. The man standing next to us bid on half a dozen items and bought three of them. Several times he smiled and whispered 'Fake!' as the bidding soared upwards.

Eventually, the auctioneer had sold everything in the living room and he and his entourage moved off speedily towards the next part of the house.

'It's you next!' said the stranger. 'They're doing the stuff in the kitchen now.'

'How much shall we go to?' Patsy asked me as we filed along the dimly lit corridor in company with the other potential purchasers. Many of the dealers had stayed behind in the main part of the house since they realised that there was nothing of interest to them down in the kitchen and scullery.

'I don't know,' I said firmly. 'What do you think?'

'I'm not sure.'

Nervousness and the cup of coffee I'd drunk in the car were beginning to have an effect on my bladder and as we shuffled past a lavatory I slipped inside in order to relieve the pressure and discomfort. I had, in my innocence, thought that it would be easy to rejoin Patsy afterwards but I hadn't allowed for the narrowness of the corridor and the reluctance of other would-be buyers to let me through. To my horror I found myself standing in the doorway to the scullery, listening to the auctioneer announce the lot number that included our new cooker, fridge and washing machine. I couldn't even see Patsy or the stranger in the pony tail and I had no idea where they were.

'I have one bid only for this lot,' said the auctioneer clearly. '£2.' He paused. 'Is that all I'm bid?' I heard him slam his small wooden hammer down onto his clip board for the first time.

'£3.' I shouted as loudly as I could. My voice was hoarse and dry and I didn't recognise it. But that didn't matter. The auctioneer heard me.

'The bid is with the gentleman in the doorway,' he said. '£3. Do I have £4?'

Something happened out of my sight.

'£4.' said the auctioneer. 'Are you still in, sir?'

'£5.' I shouted back.

There was a moment's silence. 'I've got £6 here, sir.'

'£7.' I could feel the sweat pouring down my back. I knew that this was still a ridiculously cheap price but bidding still made me nervous. Oddly enough I had found bidding for Bilbury Grange far less stressful, even though a much larger sum of money had been involved.

'£8 here, sir.' said the invisible auctioneer. 'Are you still in?' The auctioneer sounded amused and several people in the audience were beginning to giggle.

'£9.' I shouted back. We really needed a cooker.

There was a longer interval now. 'I've got £10 in here, now,' said the auctioneer.

Desperately I searched the sea of faces for Patsy. I didn't know what to do. I didn't have the faintest idea what these things were worth. '£11.' I shouted.

Another wait. '£12, I'm afraid, sir.'

'£13.'

'£14.'

'£15.'

'£16.'

I panicked and this time I kept silent.

'Going now for £16.' said the auctioneer out of my sight. I heard him slam his wooden hammer down onto his clipboard. I had lost. Ours was the last lot in the kitchen. I stood back and let the people stream out of the scullery. The auctioneer and his colleagues shot past me, heading back up the corridor towards the study.

Suddenly I saw Patsy standing alongside our pony-tailed friend. I hurried towards her. She was blushing and looked hot and flustered.

'Where were you?' she asked.

'I got stuck outside,' I told her.

'I didn't get them,' I said miserably. 'I'm sorry. I lost my nerve.' I explained.

Patsy held out her hands to me. I took them and pulled her to me. 'I got them,' she said quietly. She sounded exhausted, as though she'd been running.

'You were bidding against one another,' grinned the pony tailed stranger. 'I thought you were. But I couldn't be sure.'

'You mean we were the only two people bidding?'

'We could have bought them for £2?'

'Don't worry about it,' said the pony tailed stranger. 'You still got a bargain.'

*   *   *

CHAPTER TEN

'It's someone called Harrison,' said Patsy, holding her hand over the mouth piece of the telephone. 'He says he's from the Sunday News.'

I had never heard of anyone called Harrison but I had heard of the Sunday News. It was a tabloid west country newspaper with a wide readership throughout Devon and Cornwall. 'What does he want?' I whispered.

Patsy shrugged. 'I don't know,' she whispered back. She held the telephone receiver out towards me. 'You'd better speak to him.'

I took the receiver off her. 'Hello?' I said, rather tentatively. 'What can I do for you?'

'My name is Harrison,' said a rather brusque voice at the other end. 'I'm editor of the Sunday News. Am I right in thinking that you are the doctor who used to write a column for the Herald?'

'That's right,' I admitted, rather cautiously.

'Have you got an agent?'

'An agent?' It seemed an absurd question. Why, I wondered, would I have an agent?

'A literary agent?'

'No.'

'I can deal with you direct?'

'Yes.'

'Good. You've left the Herald now?'

'Yes.'

'Can I ask you why?'

I thought about it for a moment. It was a cheeky question but I didn't see why I shouldn't tell the truth. 'I was sacked,'

I told him. 'They complained that I made people think too much.'

The man at the other end of the telephone laughed loudly. He had a good, solid laugh and I warmed to him. 'Did he really tell you that?'

'Yes.'

'Our readers like a bit of controversy with their Sunday cornflakes,' said Mr Harrison. 'Would you like to write a column for me?'

I hadn't been expecting it and I didn't reply for a moment.

'Are you there?'

'Yes!' I replied. 'That's very kind of you,' I mumbled. 'Every week?'

Patsy, who had been busy washing salad ready for our evening meal, turned round and looked at me. She raised a thumb and asked the question with her face. I held the telephone receiver between my head and my shoulder and opened both palms upwards, indicating that I wasn't sure.

'That's the usual arrangement with a column.'

'I don't know,' I said cautiously. 'What sort of column?'

'Same sort of thing that you were doing for the Herald. Some advice. Comment. Straight talking. Good honest opinion.'

'The Herald complained that they were getting lots of letters of complaint from doctors,' I warned him.

'Wonderful!' said Mr Harrison. 'I love getting letters of complaint. How much were they paying you to write for the Herald?' Patsy stopped what she was doing and wiped her hands on a towel. Then she walked across the kitchen to where I was sitting.

'Eight pounds a week.' I said, without thinking.

'God, you are honest, aren't you!' said the Sunday News editor. 'I knew you were getting that but I thought you'd tell me twice as much. I'll pay you twenty.'

'Twenty?' I said, astonished. It seemed a lot of money.

'Plus half of whatever we make from syndication rights.'

I hesitated. I had no idea what he was talking about. I said so.

'We'll try to sell your column to other papers round the country. And you'll get half of what we get.'

I was astonished. 'Do you think other papers will want to take it?' I asked, uncertainly.

'I should think so,' said the editor. 'Our syndication man sells stuff all round the world.' He laughed again. 'We could make you famous!''

'I'm not sure that I want to be famous!' I said quickly.

'But you like writing?'

'Yes.' I admitted. 'I do.'

'Well there isn't much point in writing if no one reads your stuff,' said the editor. 'I can promise you a big audience.'

'Right.' I said, rather hesitantly.

'Will you do it then?'

'Well, it sounds quite exciting.'

'Great. I'll put you a letter of contract in the post. Twelve weeks contract O.K. for you to start with?'

'Yes, fine.'

'I'd like to start a week on Sunday. Twelve hundred words.'

'Er ... yes. When does that mean you'd need the copy?'

'Tuesday morning. You can post it or phone it in.'

'I'll try and post it,' I said.

'Great. I'll get someone from our picture desk to give you a call and fix up a time when they can come and take some mug shots.'

'O.K.' I said, though I hated having my photograph taken.

'Good to talk to you. I'm sure you'll enjoy working with us.' I was about to say something back when I realised that the editor had put the telephone down. Gently, I lowered the receiver.

'What on earth was all that?' asked Patsy. 'It sounded pretty exciting. Have they offered you a job?'

I nodded. 'A weekly column. Twenty pounds a week and half of everything they make from selling syndication rights!'

Patsy frowned. 'What does that mean?'

I explained.

'That's terrific!' said Patsy. 'Are you excited?'

'I suppose I am,' I agreed. 'Yes, I think I am!'

*   *   *

After we'd eaten our evening meal Patsy and I went out into the vegetable garden. The strawberries were beginning

103

to ripen, the gooseberry, raspberry and blackcurrant bushes that we'd freed a little of the nettles and brambles which had been choking them were spreading their branches gratefully and were already laden with fruit. The garden was beginning to look much more like the productive, working garden it had once been. The lettuce which I'd planted in the cold frames were growing rapidly too.

'I think you were a bit overenthusiastic with the lettuce,' laughed Patsy.

'What do you mean?' I asked her, indignantly. There were at least a hundred lettuce plants growing in the cold frames and they all looked very healthy.

'The lettuce are all going to be ready at the same time,' Patsy pointed out. 'We won't be able to eat them before they start to wilt.'

'Oh,' I said, rather sadly.

'We should have put them in a few at a time,' Patsy pointed out. She started to giggle. 'It looks as if we've started a lettuce farm.'

Patsy's light hearted comment set me thinking.

'Maybe we could sell the ones we don't need?' I suggested.

Patsy frowned. 'Who to? Do you mean we should have a stall at the bottom of the drive?'

'We could try the village shop!' I suggested. 'Peter Marshall sells lettuce. Maybe he'd buy them from us instead of from the wholesaler?'

Patsy looked at me thoughtfully and then nodded. Then she walked over towards the strawberries. 'What about these?' she said. 'Do you think he'd take some strawberries too?'

'Why don't we ask him?'

*   *   *

The rumour that a construction company intended to start building houses in Bilbury had not gone away. Indeed, instead of going away it was gaining ground and credibility. I had been trying for days to find out more without any success. In the end it was Patsy who brought us news.

When I got back home for lunch the following day I knew at once that Patsy had something exciting to tell me. But I couldn't tell from looking at her face whether she had good news or bad. That was not, perhaps, too surprising since it turned out that she had both good and bad news for me.

First, she was desperate to tell me that Peter Marshall had agreed to take as many strawberries and as much lettuce as we could supply him with. Patsy said he hadn't offered a lot of money but had said that he knew of two hotels in Ilfracombe and one in Combe Martin which would happily buy fresh produce from us.

'He wanted to know if we used any chemicals on our crops – fertilisers and weed killers and so on,' said Patsy. 'And when I told him that we didn't he seemed very excited. He said that there was a growing demand for fruit and vegetables that were free of chemicals and told me that if he could describe our produce as 'organic' he could charge a higher price for it.'

'That sounds like Peter,' I laughed. 'Charging more money for stuff that hasn't cost as much to grow!'

'It's not that simple,' Patsy told me. She explained that if we had used chemicals on our crops we would have undoubtedly produced an even bigger harvest. I had forgotten that her father was a farmer, and that although he specialised in sheep and cattle she would know about such things. 'It's not difficult to double the yield per acre if you use the right fertilisers and pest control chemicals,' Patsy pointed out.

'How much did he offer?'

'Three new pence each for lettuce and seven new pence a punnet for strawberries,' Patsy told me. 'He'll provide us with the punnets. I know it doesn't sound much but I worked out that we could make a good profit next year if we used the whole of the vegetable garden and concentrated on the right crops. Peter said that the hotels were desperate for things like beans and peas and parsley and radishes. He's going to give me a list of the produce the hotels want most so that we can make sure that we grow the right things.' Patsy had worked out the size of the crops she thought we might be able to grow, and the sort of prices we might expect for them.

'So we could probably grow all our own fruit and vegetables free of charge and make a small profit out of the garden too?'

Patsy nodded.

'So, what's the bad news?' I asked her. I knew that despite

this wonderful news there was something worrying her.

'Peter also told me that he'd heard more about those plans to build houses in the village,' said Patsy. 'Apparently, the builder who has applied for planning permission has got some very good contacts locally. Peter says he's very confident that he'll get permission to start building.'

'Does Peter know where he's planning to build?'

'The nearest house will be less than a mile away from here,' said Patsy. 'Peter says they're also planning a shopping precinct.'

The news that Peter had agreed to buy our produce delighted me but this latest news about the plan to expand Bilbury depressed me enormously. In a way I felt guilty for I knew that it was selfish of me not to want Bilbury to grow. I wondered how many of the villagers would welcome the jobs and the increased prosperity that the development would bring, and I wondered how I could find out exactly what was planned for the village.

Strangely, I wasn't going to have to wait long, for I had a visitor later that day who told me more than I really wanted to hear.

*　　*　　*

'My name is Sherlock!' said the taller of the two strangers who Miss Johnson showed into the consulting room at the end of the evening surgery. He was broad as well as tall and brought with him an enormous, seemingly unshakeable sense of self confidence. He didn't so much enter the room as take it over, and within seconds of his arrival I felt as though I was the visitor and he the host. He wore a lightweight summer suit made of beige silk, an open necked silk shirt and dark brown moccasins, and as he came into the room he slipped a pair of expensive looking sunglasses into his top pocket. He was hugely overweight but he was light on his feet, and in some strange way he didn't actually look fat. Behind him there walked a man of about my age. He was thin, immaculately dressed and carried a leather document case.

I stood up and took the fat man's outstretched hand. He gripped my fingers so tightly that they hurt. He didn't introduce his companion who was, I assumed, an assistant.

'Have you got anything for hay fever?' he asked me, as he sat down. The joints of the chair creaked in protest at his weight.

I asked him what symptoms he had, how long he'd had them and what he'd tried. Then I started to write out a prescription for a suitable anti-histamine.

'What's your full name?' I asked him.

'Sherlock,' he replied 'Jack Sherlock. I'm the managing director of Sherlock Homes,' he added. 'I'm going to revolutionise your life!'

I was rather taken aback by this. I didn't really want anyone to revolutionise my life. 'Oh.' I said rather baldly. I carried on writing out the prescription. But Sherlock did not detect my lack of enthusiasm and was certainly not deterred by it.

'I want a few words with you,' he said.

I handed him the completed prescription form and nodded.

Sherlock folded the prescription form twice and placed it in the breast pocket of his jacket. 'I'm going to build five hundred new houses in Bilbury,' he told me with pride. 'I'll more than double the size of the village.' He took a cigar case from the inside pocket of his jacket, took the top off the case and offered a cigar to me.

I shook my head and held up a hand. 'No, thank you.'

He took a cigar from the case and examined it carefully.

I hesitated. 'If you don't mind I'd rather you didn't,' I said.

Sherlock stared at me in disbelief.

'This is my consulting room,' I explained. 'I'd rather it didn't smell of cigars.'

Sherlock returned the cigar to its case and then carefully slipped the case back into his jacket pocket. The assistant, standing behind Sherlock's chair, looked surprised and even slightly amused. 'I'm going to build a shopping precinct, a community hall and a health centre,' he said. 'I'm going to offer you the chance to take over the health centre.'

'Have you got planning permission yet?' I asked him.

'It's just a formality,' said Sherlock with a shrug.

'How on earth can you be so sure?' I asked him. I'd heard of people waiting years to get planning permission to build another bedroom over their garage.

Sherlock touched the tip of his right index finger on the

tip of his nose and winked. 'In this world it's not what you know or what you own but *who* you own,' he told me. He paused. 'I'll get planning permission,' he said confidently. He raised his chin and stared at me as though challenging me to defy him or doubt his confidence.

'Where are you going to do all this building?' I asked him.

'On the west of the village,' replied Sherlock. 'Between here and Kentisbury.'

'Around Softly's Bottom?'

He nodded.

'And Bluebell Wood?'

Another nod.

'I thought Lionel Francis's widow owned that land?'

Sherlock shrugged. 'She used to.' He stared at me. 'So ...' he said, after a moment or two. 'What's your answer?'

'It's very generous of you,' I told him. 'I'm very flattered.' Lionel Francis had died a few months earlier and I wasn't surprised that his widow had been willing to sell some of the land he had accumulated. She had probably needed some cash to pay his death duties. But it was a pity she'd sold out to Sherlock. I wondered how much he had paid her.

'So you should be,' said Sherlock quickly. 'But I had you checked out and the villagers seem to like you.'

'I'd like some time to think about it,' I said. 'I'd like to talk it over with my wife.'

Sherlock stared at me for a moment without speaking. He seemed surprised that I hadn't jumped at his offer. 'I'll give you a week,' he told me. 'Then I'll withdraw the offer and find another doctor.' He glowered at me. 'You'll never make a go of it with another doctor in the village.'

It was my turn to shrug. I didn't say anything.

Sherlock stood up, noisily pushing his chair back so aggressively that his assistant had to catch it to stop it falling over. He then turned and walked towards the door. He left without looking back. His assistant, who hadn't spoken a word, followed him still clutching the leather document case.

*   *   *

Patsy and I talked over Mr Sherlock's offer when I got home. It didn't take us five minutes to decide that I would not have anything to do with his plans to destroy Bilbury. I telephoned his office and left a message on his answering machine telling him of my decision.

*   *   *

CHAPTER ELEVEN

I came home one cloudy lunchtime and, failing to find Patsy anywhere in the house, went out into the courtyard and called to her.

'I'm up here,' she called, from an open window on the first floor. 'Come on up!'

'Are you sure?' For weeks Patsy had not allowed me into the coach-house flat, insisting that she wanted the restoration work to be a surprise.

'Yes!'

I climbed the spiral staircase, entered the coach-house and found Patsy sitting on the window seat in the living room looking rightfully proud and ever so slightly pleased with herself. The difference in the flat was extraordinary. The walls and the woodwork were painted white and the flat looked extremely smart and gloriously welcoming.

'It's marvellous!' I told her, looking round.

'All it needs now is some furniture,' said Patsy. 'And then we can start letting it!'

I looked around, making a quick mental inventory of the things we would need to buy: cooker; refrigerator; table; chairs; three piece suite; bed; wardrobe; dressing table. Most of these were, of course, items that we still had not bought for the house.

'We can get everything we need at an auction,' Patsy pointed out. 'It needn't cost the earth and there's still quite a lot of the summer left.'

She was right, of course. If we could let the flat to holiday makers for the rest of the summer we should be able to cover the cost of the furniture and make a small profit as well. I hadn't really needed Sherlock's visit to remind me of our financial vulnerability.

'O.K.!' I agreed. 'When's the next auction?'

'There's one next Friday!' replied Patsy, enthusiastically.

* * *

Mrs Blossom came into the surgery that evening, but for a moment or two I hardly recognised her. She came with a stout man in a suit. I had never seen him before but guessed that he was her father. He was almost bald but had a few long strands of dark hair combed right across the top of his head in that absurd way that vain men use to try to hide their baldness from the world. The last time I had seen her she had been agitated, nervous and tearful. Now she looked calm and at peace but she also looked even older than before. She had a look in her eyes which I knew I had seen before though I couldn't quite think where. I had, I remembered, arranged an appointment for her to see a psychiatrist.

'How did you get on?' I asked her.

There was a long pause before Mrs Blossom replied. 'Very well, thank you,' she answered, choosing each word carefully as though she were at a buffet and only had a small plate. She tried to smile but it was a thin, weak shadow of a smile that made her look haunted rather than happy.

'Did the psychiatrist prescribe anything for you?'

'He gave her some pills,' said Mr Blossom. 'She's got to go back in a week's time to collect some more.' I wondered why the psychiatrist didn't want me to write out the repeat prescription for him. Hospital consultants usually like to get general practitioners to do their routine work for them whenever they can.

I nodded my thanks to Mr Blossom and then turned my head towards his daughter. 'What are they?' I asked her. She looked at me blankly. 'What's the name of the pills he gave you?'

'I don't know.'

'Have you got them with you?'

'Yes.'

'Can I look at them?'

She opened her handbag, took out a small brown bottle

111

and handed it to me. She seemed reluctant to let it go. The bottle had a small white label stuck to one side and the name of the drug was scrawled on the label. The pills were the same as the ones that Miss Phillips was taking. I knew now why the psychiatrist had not asked me to write out the prescription - he knew that the pills were not available at the ordinary chemist's shop and could only be obtained directly from the manufacturer.

'Did the doctor at the hospital tell you that the pills are very new?' I asked Mrs Blossom.

She looked at me for a few moments and then, very slowly, shook her head. 'No.' she said.

'They're very special,' said Mr Blossom. 'The consultant said that only a few selected doctors are allowed to prescribe them.' He said the word 'consultant' as though it began with a capital letter.

'So I believe,' I said.

'The consultant said we should come and see you for a sick note,' said Mr Blossom.

'A sick note?' I was puzzled. 'I didn't think that Mrs Blossom went out to work.'

'She doesn't. The sick note is for me. I'll have to stay at home for a few days to look after her.'

'Ah.' I said, nodding. A thought struck me and I frowned. 'Why didn't the consultant give you a sick note?' I asked him.

'I did ask him for one,' said Mr Blossom. 'But he said that sort of thing was your job.'

'Very kind of him,' I said drily, pulling my pad of sick notes towards me and muttering an unspoken, unheard curse on consultants who regarded themselves as too important to spend fifteen seconds writing out sick notes, thereby wasting everyone else's time.

'How long is this likely to go on?' Mr Blossom asked me. He inclined his head towards his daughter as he spoke.

'Do you mean how long will it be before your daughter gets better?' I asked him.

'Yes.'

'I'm afraid I don't know.' I told him.

'It's damned inconvenient,' muttered Mr Blossom to no

one in particular. He took the sick note I held out, carefully read it, folded it into two, creased it sharply between the thumb and forefinger of his right hand, took out a wafer thin leather wallet and slipped the sick note inside it. Then he put the wallet back into his inside jacket pocket.

As Mrs Blossom stood up to accompany her father out of the surgery I remembered where I had seen the dull and lifeless look that was in her eyes. I had seen it on the faces of the patients in a geriatric ward in a hospital where I had once worked; described by a cynical young hospital consultant as the ante room to death. And I had seen it more recently than that. I had seen the same dull, half dead look on Miss Phillips' face too.

*   *   *

That afternoon Thumper was due to appear in court in Barnstaple, charged with whatever fancy word cocktail the judiciary chose to use when describing the unusual twin crimes of poaching and self defence.

Patsy and I picked Thumper and Anne up and drove them into town. Anne and Thumper left their baby with Miss Johnson whom I told where I was going and Dr Brownlow, who had a soft spot for both Thumper and Anne, had promised to look after any urgent problems which came up while I was out of the village. Barnstaple is only ten miles away from Bilbury but in summer the heavy holiday traffic means that the journey can take as much as half an hour. We had arranged to meet Thumper's solicitor, a Mr Suffolk, at the entrance to the court.

There were just five minutes to go and we had just decided that the solicitor wasn't going to turn up when a tall, gangling young man wearing a suit that was several sizes too large for him around the waist and chest and several sizes too short for him in length came rushing up to us in a rare state of excitement.

He had a bulging brief case in his right hand and a huge sheaf of papers and textbooks stuffed under his left arm.

'Mr Robinson?' he called, breathlessly.

We all turned to stare at him. Thumper frowned. 'Yes?'

'I'm Mr Colter of Mountfield, Briggs and Stratton. I'm

113

afraid Mr Suffolk has been unavoidably detained.' He brushed his long hair away from his eyes and smiled nervously. 'But he's handed your case to me.' He suddenly realised that the smile wasn't appropriate and banished it quickly. As he did so he looked at his watch. 'We'd better get a move on!'

'Right,' said Thumper, drily, moving off.

I put my hand on the solicitor's arm as we all walked towards the court. 'You do know what Mr Robinson is charged with?'

'Oh, absolutely!' replied the young lawyer. 'Mr Suffolk told me all about it this morning.'

'That was the first time you heard about it?'

'Half an hour ago.'

'Shouldn't you ask for a postponement or whatever you call it?' I asked him, horrified. 'Surely you need time to prepare a good legal case?'

'No need to worry about that!' insisted the young lawyer. One of the textbooks started to slip out from underneath his arm. I removed it before it fell and carried it for him. I had absolutely no experience of the British legal system, and despite all this I still had faith that somehow justice would be done.

Somewhere between the entrance to the court and the court itself Thumper was separated off from the rest of us. Patsy, Anne and I were sent along a dull and dingy corridor and after opening two wrong doors by mistake eventually found ourselves sitting on uncomfortable chairs at the back of the courtroom. Moments later Thumper appeared in the court, accompanied by his youthful solicitor. The three undistinguished looking magistrates sat high on their bench scowling down at the court as though anxious to hand down punishments and get away to do something more interesting and profitable. They looked the very essence of smug, self satisfied and sanctimonious middle class England.

I don't know what I had expected but the next ten minutes seemed more like something out of Kafka's imagination than any attempt to offer genuine justice. The absurdity and unfairness of it all became instantly apparent the moment the clerk had read out the charges. Thumper, when invited to tell the court whether he admitted his guilt or intended to defend himself stood up and in a clear and unshaken voice declared his intention to plead guilty to poaching but not guilty to assault. The young and nervous Mr Colter was clearly surprised by this for he whispered urgently to his client. He was obviously trying to persuade him to change his mind. But Thumper was adamant that he wanted to plead not guilty to the assault charge. He did not, he insisted, mind being punished for the poaching. He was guilty and he had been caught and that was fair. But, he insisted, the assault charge simply was not right.

The prosecuting solicitor, a dour faced man in his middle fifties who didn't look as if he had done anything enjoyable for at least twenty years, stood up and said such terrible things about Thumper that it was all I could do to stop myself from rushing up to him, taking him by the lapels and shaking some of the spite and malice out of his voice.

'This man is clearly a menace to human society,' said the solicitor who had never met Thumper before, pointing a finger directly at him. 'A nasty, evil and dangerous man who takes the law into his own hands and who has no respect for authority.'

The prosecution's only witness, the water bailiff, told such a sad and pathetic story that one would have had to have a heart of stone not to feel sorry for him. He did not bother to mention that when he had fallen into the water Thumper had rescued him.

Thumper's solicitor made a brave hash at offering some sort of defence but it was clear that his heart was not in it; he had panicked and lost control when he had discovered that the case was not as simple or as straightforward as he had been led to believe and the result was that he produced an inelegant stream of such unconvincing and irrelevant nonsense that in the end even Patsy, Anne and I would have found Thumper guilty.

After passing an urgent note down to the solicitor I managed to persuade him to let me give evidence as a character witness, though by then I suspected that it was probably too late.

I explained that Thumper was a good friend, a reliable workman, a devoted husband and a caring father. It may have sounded a little over the top but, in essence, it was the truth. We were in the end relieved that Thumper did not get a prison sentence but was simply fined and put on probation. He was told that when his fine was paid he would be allowed to have his truck back.

'Thank you!' said Thumper, shaking my hand firmly as we met outside the court. 'I owe you.' He looked pale but relieved. His solicitor hovered nearby looking quite pleased with himself. 'If it hadn't been for you I think they would have sent me down.'

'I think that went quite well,' said the solicitor, with a nervous and hopeful smile. He was carrying his bulging briefcase in his right hand and clutching his sheaf of books and papers under his left arm. I hadn't seen him refer to any of the books while in the courtroom though he had shuffled the papers about quite a lot.

'You didn't even know Thumper wanted to plead not guilty to the assault charge!' I said to him, angrily.

'It was a little unfortunate that Mr Suffolk couldn't be here,' said Mr Colter. I couldn't help wondering if Mr Colter had ever appeared in court before by himself.

'Where is he?' I demanded. 'Mr Suffolk?'

Mr Colter looked embarrassed and shuffled his feet nervously.

'Why couldn't he come?' I persisted. Patsy, Anne and Thumper had stopped and were waiting for an answer too.

'He had to go on a course,' muttered Mr Colter, defensively. He looked uncomfortable.

I knew instantly what he meant. I had heard the excuse too often before. 'He's playing golf!' I said angrily. 'Thumper could have gone to prison!'

'But he didn't!' said Mr Colter. He smiled thinly and waved a hand at Thumper. 'He's here, isn't he?'

'No thanks to you,' said Anne.

'Come on,' said Thumper quietly. We all turned and looked at him. 'Let's go home.' Mr Colter, looking relieved to have been let off so easily, scurried off.

We set off walking towards the car park and as we did so the prosecuting solicitor came out of a side door. In strange contrast to Mr Colter his suit was too tight for him. Because they were anchored around his hips instead of his waist his trousers were too long for him in the legs. But whereas Mr Colter's suit had never fitted him, the prosecuting solicitor's body had probably once been the same size and shape as his suit.

'Do you sleep at night?' I asked him angrily. 'Are your parents proud of you?' I was feeling very angry about what had happened in the courtroom. It seemed to me outrageous that a man could say things about another human being without having any idea about whether or not they were true. The prosecutor stopped, looked at me and instinctively backed away. He seemed nervous and looked around. 'I advise you not to say anything you're likely to regret,' he told me. He tried to walk away but I moved around and stood in front of him.

'Come on,' whispered Patsy. She took hold of my hand. 'He isn't worth it.'

'I doubt if your advice is ever worth taking,' I told him. I don't think I had ever before been so angry. 'How dare you describe a man as evil when you don't know anything about him?'

'I was just doing my job,' he said. Perspiration had formed on his brow.

'That's what the concentration camp guards said at Auschwitz,' I told him.

'That's an outrageous comparison!' said the lawyer. He looked around. 'Any more of that and I'll sue you for defamation.' His face had gone red and a vein on his forehead was bulging. (Two months later he died of a stroke).

I looked around. 'Don't you need witnesses for that?'

He looked at Thumper, Patsy and then Anne and unsuccessfully tried to walk round me again.

'You're worse than a prostitute,' I told him. 'You'll do anything for money, won't you?'

The lawyer blanched and pulled himself up to his full height. 'How dare you?' he remonstrated.

But I'd had enough of him. Still holding Patsy's hand I turned and walked away. Thumper and Anne followed behind and I could hear Thumper chuckling. After a few yards I started to smile. And by the time we were in the car driving back to Bilbury we all felt much better. We had all learned a lesson about the law. But at least Thumper wasn't in prison.

'Can you drop me off by the river?' Thumper asked, as we were about to turn off the main road and take the turning to Bilbury.

'O.K.' I said, puzzled.

'I just want to pick up a couple of trout on the way home,' said Thumper, laughing. Anne, who was sitting beside him on the back seat, hit him as hard as she could and that made him laugh even more.

*　　*　　*

CHAPTER TWELVE

As we approached the site of the auction Patsy and I recognised a number of the vehicles that were parked. We had seen them outside the house where we had attended our first auction.

Unlike that auction, which had been held in a private house, this one was being held in a village hall. As we drew closer to the hall we recognised many of the would be buyers too. Among them I spotted Mr Fogg, the man who had befriended us at our first auction. He was dressed in exactly the same clothes.

We entered the hall and started to walk around. The larger items of furniture were all arranged around the outer walls of the hall. In the middle, piled in neat rows on top of wooden trestle tables, were the smaller items. The more valuable small items, silver spoons, old watches and bits and pieces of ivory, were laid out neatly in a glass fronted cabinet which was guarded by a broad shouldered man dressed in jeans and a thick, fisherman's sweater. He had his arms folded and did not look like a man who liked a laugh. The least valuable items, and things like stepladders and gardening tools, were lined up outside in the tiny car park. A hot dog van was also parked there, presumably to provide refreshments for those attending the auction.

'Hello!' I said, as we passed Mr Fogg. 'Fancy seeing you here!'

Fogg, who was carefully examining a particularly ugly toby jug, turned sharply when he heard my voice and then visibly relaxed when he saw who it was.

'Looking for more stuff for your house?' he asked us. He

shook my hand and smiled at Patsy.

I nodded and said we were.

'The people who owned the house where all these things came from must have been very odd,' said Patsy. 'I've counted at least five complete sets of cutlery.'

Fogg laughed. He put down the toby jug and picked up a small porcelain model of a thatched cottage. 'All this isn't from *one* house!' He explained that the auctioneers had collected together furniture and belongings from three or four small cottages and had put all the bits and pieces together into one auction to save money.

'I keep seeing the same faces,' I said. A short, vaguely familiar man wearing a bright green jumper and a pair of shabby brown corduroy trousers walked past and nodded to Mr Fogg.

'At least half the people at an auction will always be regulars,' explained Fogg. He turned the thatched cottage upside down and carefully examined the maker's stamp. 'Antique shop owners looking for stock, junk shop people looking for bits and pieces and dealers looking for things they know they can turn round quickly and fairly easily at a profit.' He sniffed and put the thatched cottage down.

'No good?'

'Pardon?'

'The cottage.'

Fogg shook his head. 'Looks older than it is,' he explained. 'Made in Hong Kong sometime in the 60s.'

'What about the other half?'

Fogg looked at me, puzzled.

'The other buyers at an auction. You said half of them were professionals.'

'Oh, a few of them will just be vultures who have come for a nose around. When someone dies the neighbours want to see what they've left behind and how much it fetches. But most of the rest will be people like you – people furnishing a house and looking for a few bargains. You can furnish a house for next to nothing and make a decent profit on it if you're careful.'

Patsy, puzzled, looked at him. 'How?'

'Buy good, solid furniture that isn't old enough to be antique but isn't new and made of cardboard. By the time you're ready to sell it there's a good chance that some of it will have become antique. But even if it hasn't it will probably still be worth more than you paid for it because the next generation of house owners will be looking for good, solid furniture of their own.'

Fogg pulled out a large grubby handkerchief and blew his nose noisily. 'I can't imagine why anyone buys new furniture,' he said. 'It's mostly made out of hardboard, it loses ninety per cent of its value the moment you take it out of the showroom, it's got no character, and when you find you can't sell it you won't even be able to turn it into firewood.' He turned his attention to an old mains radio in a Bakelite case. He fiddled with the four control knobs on the front of the set and then used a penknife to open the back. He sniffed, seemed satisfied, quietly slipped one of the knobs into his pocket and moved on to something else.

'Is that worth anything?' I asked him.

Fogg shook his head.

'Why do you want to get it then?'

He looked at me, puzzled.

'I saw you take the knob,' I pointed out.

'I'm going to listen to it,' he explained. He wasn't in the slightest bit embarrassed about my having seen him steal the knob. 'It's not worth much anyway but with a knob missing it's virtually worthless. I should get it for a couple of shillings. These old radios have beautiful tone and they're so cheap that when they go wrong you can just chuck them away and buy another one.'

The auctioneer, a short, stout man in a three piece tweed suit, climbed up onto the village hall stage. He was smoking a huge cigar and ash had dropped down both the lapel of his jacket and the front of his waistcoat. He was as bald as a billiard ball, and nearly as round. A heavily perspiring assistant in a grey woollen suit with a thin white stripe hurried to the back of the stage, found a lectern and put it at the front of the stage. The auctioneer rested his elbows on it, placed his catalogue on the lectern and then put his wooden gavel on the small flat area at the front of it. Moments later the auction started.

An hour and a half later Patsy and I had bid for and bought

all the furniture we needed for the flat. We paid slightly more than we had expected, but that drawback was more than offset by the fact that we had managed to buy better furniture than we had expected.

We had arranged for a man with a removal van to transport our purchases back to Bilbury Grange and were standing by the hot dog stand drinking steaming hot mugs of tea when Mr Fogg hurried out of the back of the village hall. He stood there for a moment, clearly looking for someone or something. As soon as he spotted us he came straight over.

'I thought you must have gone,' he said. He looked agitated and relieved to have found us. 'Did you get what you wanted?'

'Yes, thank you.' said Patsy. I had a large chunk of chocolate biscuit in my mouth and did not attempt to say anything.

'Would you do me a favour?' asked Mr Fogg. He spoke quickly and confidentially. 'Of course,' said Patsy. She looked at me. I nodded. 'If we can,' she added rather cautiously. I swallowed the chocolate biscuit and washed it down with a swig of tea.

'There's a piece of furniture I'm rather keen to buy,' explained Mr Fogg. 'A burr walnut davenport. Victorian. Would you bid for me?'

I didn't have the faintest idea what a davenport was.

'Of course!' said Patsy. 'Do you have to go somewhere?'

'What's a davenport?' I asked.

'No. I'll be here,' said Mr Fogg, answering Patsy first. 'But if the other dealers see me bidding they'll know what I think the piece is worth and they'll go higher than they might have done.' He looked at his watch and hopped from one foot to the other. He was clearly anxious and impatient.

'What's a davenport?' I asked again.

'It's a writing desk,' Mr Fogg replied, speaking hurriedly. 'It's got a retractable writing surface, a couple of drawers and a secret compartment for hiding money and love letters.'

It sounded rather exciting.

'How do we know how much to bid up to?' asked Patsy.

'Go up to £750.' said Mr Fogg. 'Not a penny more.'

Patsy looked at me and I looked at her. It was a lot of money. 'Er ... ' I began, not quite sure how to say what we were both thinking.

'Don't worry,' said Mr Fogg with a reassuring smile. 'I know what you're thinking. You're worrying that if I disappear you'll be left having to pay £750 for something you don't want.'

Patsy and I, who had been thinking exactly that, protested that the thought had never crossed our minds. Mr Fogg held up a hand and took a thick roll of notes out from his jeans pocket. Without blinking an eye he counted out £800 in fifty pound notes and handed it to Patsy. 'If you're successful pay the auctioneer £750 and if you're not give me £750 back,' he said. 'Either way you keep £50 for your trouble.' Patsy handed the money to me. I put it into my trouser pocket and kept my hand on it. I had never handled that much cash before and it made me very nervous.

We both protested that we didn't want paying but Mr Fogg was insistent. He looked at his watch. 'I'm sorry to rush you,' he said. 'But its lot 137. And they'll be there any minute now.'

We followed him back into the village hall. The auctioneer was taking bids for lot number 136.

'Who's going to bid?' whispered Patsy.

'You can,' I answered. Even though I had just drunk a pint of tea my lips were dry and my throat felt parched. The £50 commission we were being paid would more than cover the cost of the furniture we had bought.

'I'd rather you did,' Patsy whispered back.

'The next item, lot 137, is a rather fine davenport,' said the auctioneer. 'Who'll start me off with £300?' One of his assistants pointed to a piece of furniture that looked like a cross behind a school desk and an old fashioned writing bureau.

I licked my lips and looked around for Mr Fogg. He was standing several yards away. I raised an eyebrow. He shook his head almost imperceptibly. I did nothing.

'Come on now!' said the auctioneer. He had a friendly, cajoling style which had worked well. 'Who'll give me £150?'

Still there was no response. Again I looked at Mr Fogg. Again he shook his head almost imperceptibly. I still did nothing.

'£100 then,' sighed the auctioneer. 'Let's do this the hard way.'

A voice from on my right shouted 'Here.'

'I have £150,' said the auctioneer, though I hadn't heard the second bid. 'Do I have £200?'

'£250,' said the voice from my right.

'£300,' countered the auctioneer.

I waved my hand to indicate that I wanted to join in the bidding. I was frightened that the davenport would be sold but not to me.

The bidder on my right must have responded in some way though I didn't hear or see anything.

'£350,' said the auctioneer. 'I have £350. Do I hear £400?'

I raised my hand as high as it would go and waved it about like a small boy trying to catch the teachers attention but the auctioneer didn't seem to see me. I had always worried that I would end up buying something by mistake. Now I had discovered that it sometimes possible not to buy something you want. The key to successful bidding is, I learnt later, simply to catch the auctioneer's eye.

Slowly the bidding crept up to £500 and still I hadn't made a bid. Then the bidder on my right pulled out.

'I have £500,' said the auctioneer looking around the room. 'Do I have any advance on £500?' The room had gone very quiet. This was by far the biggest bid of the day so far.

I had not lowered my hand and this time the auctioneer saw me. 'Are you bidding, sir?' he asked me.

'Yes.' I croaked.

'£550,' said the auctioneer. It seemed that everyone in the room was looking at me. Some of the dealers were whispering among themselves. I tried to catch a glimpse of Mr Fogg but I couldn't see him anywhere.

I nodded.

'I have £600,' said the auctioneer. He looked at me and raised an eyebrow. I nodded again.

'£650.'

And so it went on. Every time I made a bid the auctioneer met it with a higher one. I still couldn't see who I was bidding against but there was clearly at least one other dealer around who was convinced that the piece was worth buying. Eventually I reached my limit of £750. But it wasn't enough.

'£800,' said the auctioneer. He looked at me, expectantly.

For a moment I was tempted to carry on. I did, after all, have £800 in my pocket. I could see how people could get carried away at auctions. But common sense prevailed and, rather sadly, I shook my head. I felt I had failed Mr Fogg and I could almost taste the disappointment. I turned away, as sad as if I had failed to buy something I wanted for myself. Mr Fogg had reappeared. He nodded his head slightly towards the exit at the back of the hall and while the auctioneer continued with the next lot Patsy and I followed him out of the hall and back into the car park.

'I'm sorry,' I said to Mr Fogg, handing him his roll of notes. He didn't seem in the slightest bit disappointed.

'Have you taken your £50?' he asked.

I shook my head.

He grinned, peeled off a £50 note and handed it to me. 'Thanks,' he said. 'You did brilliantly.'

'I'm sorry I didn't get it for you,' I said.

'That's O.K.,' he said. And he disappeared back into the hall again.

'He took it very well,' said Patsy.

'We've got £50 we didn't expect!' I said, showing her the note that Mr Fogg had given me. 'Is there anything else you want to bid for?' I'd been bitten by the bug and I was keen to get back into the bidding.

Patsy laughed and shook her head. But we did bid. Twice.

First, the auctioneer held up an old wedding gown which no one seemed to want.

'Oh it's beautiful!' sighed Patsy.

'Buy it if you like it,' I told her. No one was prepared to bid and it was obviously going to be very cheap.

'Oh I don't know,' said Patsy. She hesitated. 'I could alter it and turn it into a lovely dress, though.' The auctioneer was getting desperate and was now offering the dress for anyone prepared to make an offer for it. I knew we had to act fast and so I put up my hand and offered five shillings.

'You mean 25 pence, sir!' said the auctioneer sternly. The nation's currency had gone decimal the previous year and I still sometimes forgot.

'Yes, 25 pence!' I agreed.

'Done!' said the auctioneer, banging down his gavel. 'Sold

125

to the gentleman over there. You'll look lovely in it, sir!'

There was a ripple of laughter, but when Patsy took my hand and whispered 'thank you' I didn't care.

Then, right at the end of the auction, the auctioneer's assistant held up a tin bath full of all sorts of bits and pieces of assorted rubbish and, encouraged by me, Patsy bought the lot for 50 pence. It was hardly the big time, but not knowing exactly what we had bought added a considerable frisson of excitement to the deal.

As I queued in a small back room to pay for the furniture we had bough for the flat, for Patsy's dress and for the tin bath we had bought in a moment of wild extravagance, I felt someone tapping me on the shoulder. I turned round and saw the auctioneer standing behind me.

'Excuse me, sir,' he said quietly. 'Could I have a word with you?'

'Of course,' I said. I left Patsy to pay our bill and walked with the auctioneer to a quiet corner.

'I'm sorry you didn't get the davenport,' said the auctioneer.

I looked at him slightly puzzled.

'The davenport,' repeated the auctioneer. 'Lot 137.'

'Oh yes,' I said. I remembered the lot number but I had forgotten that it had been called a davenport.

'You were very keen to buy it,' said the auctioneer.

'Oh yes.' I said. I felt uncomfortable and hoped that he wasn't going to tell me that the higher bidder had dropped out and that I could now have it for £750. I wondered where Mr Fogg was and what my legal responsibilities were. Did unsuccessful bids still count?

'I hope you won't mind my asking,' said the auctioneer. 'But just for my own curiosity do you mind telling me if you were bidding for someone else?'

'Is that illegal?' I asked him anxiously.

'Oh good heavens no!' said the auctioneer. 'If it was I doubt if we'd ever sell anything.'

'Well then yes I was,' I said.

'For Patchy perhaps?'

'Patchy?'

'Patchy Fogg,' explained the auctioneer. I laughed. What a wonderful nickname.

'Yes,' I agreed. 'That's right.' I lowered my voice confidentially. 'I don't suppose there's any harm in telling you,' I said. 'But he was worried that if other dealers saw him bidding the price would go up.'

The auctioneer smiled. 'I thought he might have told you something like that,' he said. 'But the funny thing is that Mr Fogg was the seller.'

I didn't understand and I suspect that my confusion was quite apparent.

'No,' I said. 'You must be wrong about that. He gave me instructions to bid up to £750 for him. He wouldn't do that if he was selling it, would he?'

The auctioneer put a hand on my shoulder, as though comforting an innocent in a harsh world. 'He might,' he said. 'If he knew that a London dealer had telephoned in giving me instructions to bid up to £800 for it.'

It took a moment or two for this to sink in. I remembered that the last bid I'd heard had been for £500. Without my bids the seller of the davenport would have received £300 less – the same £300 that the London dealer would have saved.

'But how would Mr Fogg – Patchy – know what the dealer had bid?' I asked.

'I don't know,' said the auctioneer quietly. He paused and then nodded at me. 'I'm sorry to have bothered you with this,' he said. 'I hope you didn't mind?'

'No.' I said, still rather shocked by it all.

'It's not that you've done anything illegal,' he said soothingly. 'But I always like to know what is going on at my auctions.'

'Of course.' I agreed.

The auctioneer melted away and after a few moments I wandered back to join Patsy who was now busy paying our bill and obtaining the necessary receipts. I didn't tell her about Patchy Fogg, the auctioneer, the davenport and the London dealer until we were in the car and on our way home.

*   *   *

When we got back to Bilbury Grange we were both in a slightly subdued mood. Not even the sight of the roofers dismantling their scaffolding cheered us up.

We didn't know how Patchy Fogg had found out what the London dealer's top price was, but it wasn't difficult to hazard a guess. Mr Fogg could have paid one of the auctioneer's own staff a few pounds for the information. Or since the telephone bids had to be written down somewhere maybe he managed to sneak a look. Whatever he'd done, it was fairly obvious why he needed us to bid for him.

'I'll put the kettle on,' said Patsy as Thumper and I staggered into the house behind her carrying the tin bath and its contents. The removal man had promised to deliver the furniture either that afternoon or the following morning. I couldn't help noticing that Thumper was moving cautiously and slowly. He put his end of the tin bath down and put his hand in the middle of his back.

'Are you O.K?' I asked him.

He nodded. And then immediately held his head.

'I take it you had a little celebration last night?'

'The human body has got a design fault,' he said, speaking quietly and very slowly.

I stared at him and waited. It is difficult not to feel self righteous and pleased with yourself when you're talking to someone who has a hangover, but I tried.

'How are you supposed to know when you've had enough to drink?' he asked me.

I shrugged. It didn't seem like the sort of question I was expected to answer. It wasn't. Thumper answered it himself.

'You only start to notice that things are going wrong when you've had too much and you only *really* notice that you've had too much the next morning when it's far too late!'

I grinned at him. 'Give me a hand with this tin bath,' I said. 'Or I'll start whistling – loudly!'

'You should have been in the Gestapo,' he said, screwing up his face in misery. He bent down and picked up his end of the tin bath again.

'What the hell have you got here anyway?' he asked.

I explained that I didn't know yet, but that Patsy had bought the lot as a sort of lucky dip for 50 pence.

'You both seem a bit miserable,' said Thumper. 'What's gone wrong?'

I started to tell him the story of Mr Fogg and the davenport and by the time I had finished we were indoors. We put the tin bath down.

Thumper laughed out loud and then held his head in regret. 'Not old Patchy!' he cried.

'You know him?'

'Of course I know him!' said Thumper. 'He plays in our football team. He's a great guy.'

'But he cheated a dealer in London out of £300!' I protested.

'Don't be silly,' said Thumper. 'The dealer was prepared to pay £800 so he was, presumably, convinced that he could get more than that from some other customer. Do you feel sorry for the customer who's going to buy it from the dealer?'

I thought about it for a moment. 'I suppose not,' I admitted.

'There you are then,' he said. Patsy handed us both mugs of tea.

'But I do feel used,' I said, after sipping at mine.

'Ah, now we're coming to it,' said Thumper with an admonitory shake of a finger and a muted laugh. He reached for the sugar bowl and dropped half a dozen lumps into his mug. He stirred it with a pencil he took from behind his ear and winced at the noise the pencil made when it came into contact with the sides of the mug.

I had to nod and grin. He was right, of course.

'Are you going to send your £50 to the London dealer?' asked Thumper. He took a noisy slurp from his mug.

I looked at Patsy. She looked at me. 'No.' we said simultaneously.

'Well then,' said Thumper. 'Don't begrudge Patchy his profit.' He paused. 'Don't forget he had to lay out money to buy the damned thing in the first place. He probably spent a few quid having it restored. He was taking the risk.'

'But the auctioneer was very upset,' I reminded Thumper.

'No he wasn't,' said Thumper. 'He might get a bit upset if someone on his staff is giving away information. But he won't mind the dealer in London getting ripped off for a few quid. And don't forget that the higher the selling price the bigger his commission will be.'

Auctions were clearly more complicated than I had thought.

'Oh, by the way,' said Thumper turning to Patsy and finishing his tea in one great gulp, 'Your father called and asked me to give you his love.'

'My father?' said Patsy, surprised. 'Did he come for anything in particular?'

'He picked up those lambs of yours,' said Thumper. 'He said he was going into the market so he'd take yours along with his to save you a journey.'

'What!' cried Patsy. 'When was this?'

Thumper looked startled. 'I don't know,' he said. 'About an hour ago I suppose.' He turned to me. 'What's the matter?'

'The lambs are pets,' I said, putting down my tea and picking up the car keys. 'Which market have they gone to?'

'Pets?' said Thumper, puzzled. 'Lambs?'

'Yes.' I said.

'Which market?' asked Patsy. 'Blackmoor Gate?'

'I guess so,' said Thumper.

Patsy and I left him standing in the kitchen as we ran out to the car to get to our second auction of the morning.

*   *   *

The livestock market at Blackmoor Gate was in full swing when we got there with thousands of lambs, calves and ponies for sale and scores of farmers standing around. I had to swerve to avoid a huge lorry leaving the market. We could see at least a hundred lambs inside. The ones that were closest to the walls the lorry were looking through the holes in the slatted sides and 'baaaaaing' and 'maaaaaing' unceasingly. Patsy and I looked at one another sadly.

The farmers all seemed to be dressed the same - in grubby faded jeans, checked lumberjack-style shirts with the sleeves rolled up and, despite the fact that it was sunny and had not rained for days, mud encrusted black wellington boots. Most of them carried wooden sticks of various shapes and sizes and nearly all of them wore flat caps. The sun was shining brightly but I noticed that none of them wore dark glasses. Several dozen dirty Land Rovers were parked haphazardly, and an almost equal number of empty livestock trailers were scattered about. There were nine or ten large lorries parked around the edge of the field.

There was a constant background of sound as lambs and sheep baaed and cows and their calves mooed, but above it I could hear the sound of the auctioneer shouting prices and taking bids from farmers, butchers and dealiers of various sorts. It seemed a sorry place to be and a sorrier place to work, and I was sad that I didn't have enough money to buy all the animals and put them into green fields where they could nibble grass unthreatened by humans.

'Hello Patsy!' said a farmer whom I vaguely recognised. He wore the usual unifrom of faded jeans, checked shirt and dirty wellington boots, but had no hat. 'It's a long time since I've seen you here!'

'Oh hello Uncle Charlie!' said Patsy. 'Have you seen my dad?'

'What's up sweetheart?' asked Charlie, frowning. I realised I'd seen him in the Duck and Puddle. He spole unhurriedly and leaned on his stick. He didn't look as if he had ever panicked in his life.

'I need to see him urgently,' said Patsy. 'Please, Uncle Charlie, have you seen him?'

'He was over by the selling ring a few minutes ago,' said Charlie. 'He's got some lambs coming up for auction.'

'Thanks!' said Patsy, racing off. I hurried off after her.

'Can you see him?' asked Patsy desperately looking around. I couldn't.

'Surely they won't do anything to them here?' I said. 'Won't they have to take them to the abattoir first?;

'But they could have gone already,' said Patsy. 'Once they get put into a lorry we'll never find them.' There were tears pouring down her cheeks. I took her hand as we both searched the sea of faces around the selling ring, looking either for Patsy's father or four our lambs.

'Dad!' shouted Patsy suddenly. She pulled at my arm and dragging me behind her pushed her way through the crowd of farmers which had collected around the metal bars of the selling ring. I could see her father. He was standing with two other farmers on the other side of the ring. Mr Kennett stood out for even though the temperature must have been in the 70s he was wearing his faded and torn coat tied with orange baler twine. I had never seen him out of doors without it. We left behnd us a trail of cursing and protesting farmers. Two men with large sticks opened a gate and let a flock of

131

fifty or sixty lambs out of a pen into the selling ring.

'Dad!' shouted Patsy again, stopping for a moment.

This time her father heard her. He looked up and waved.

'Where are our lambs?' shouted Patsy. I was desperately searching the faces of the lambs in the ring looking for our four. I had visions of having to bid for the entire flock if ours had got mixed up with some of Mr Kennett's lambs. But I didn't care. No one would outbid me this time.

But Patsy's father didn't hear and he wasn't even listening. He had turned back to the two farmers he was talking to.

Patsy started running again and I ran after her as quickly as I could.

'Dad,' shouted Patsy for the third time. Now that we were only a dozen yards away he heard her. He turned and looked and waved his stick. 'Where are our lambs?' she shouted.

Patsy's father excused himself and walked towards us. 'What's all the fuss?' he asked, frowning. He looked beyond us at the crowd of farmers who were all nursing their bruised shins and staring rather angrily in our direction.

'Where are our lambs?' asked Patsy again.

'Gone!' said Patsy's father, looking very pleased with himself. 'Sold 'em all half an hour ago. I'll pay you when I get paid.'

'Who to?' begged Patsy.

'What does it matter?' asked Mr Kennett. 'I got a good price for them. You can't go back on the deal now.'

'But dad!' cried Patsy. 'They were pets. We didn't want to sell them.'

'Pets?' said Mr Kennett, uncomprehendingly. 'But they were lambs.'

Patsy burst into tears and started to sob her heart out. I felt like sobbing with her and put my arm around her shoulders as much to steady myself as to comfort her. I could feel the tears in my eyes. I had helped rear those lambs and now they were going to end up on someone's dinner table surrounded by new potatoes and mint sauce.

'What's the matter with her?' Mr Kennett asked me, genuinely puzzled. 'You've turned my daughter into a right funny one.'

'I'm sorry Mr Kennett,' I said, trying hard to be as polite

as I could. 'But I'm afraid there's been a terrible mistake. We'd be very grateful if you could tell us who bought our lambs.'

Mr Kennett looked at me and saw that I was serious. 'Come with me,' he said, turning and heading towards the spot where the auctioneer was standing. 'I'll ask for you.'

*   *   *

We were told that our lambs, together with the others that Mr Kennett had sold, had been taken by lorry to an abattoir near South Molton, a village about ten or twelve miles to the south of Bilbury. The villagers call it a town but most townsfolk would call it a village.

Patsy and I leapt into the Morris Minor and set off southwards down the road from Blackmoor Gate. The road twists and turns and passes through some beautiful rolling countryside, but Patsy and I were concerned only with getting to the abattoir as quickly as possible. I thought for a moment of driving back home to try telephoning to tell the men at the abattoir that they had got four lambs by mistake but decided that this would probably be a waste of time.

We raced past Friendship Farm, across Bratton Down, through Brayford, down past the stone quarries at Charles, across the A361 at the roundabout near North Aller and down across the Common Moors to the village of South Molton. I stopped for nothing and no one, and drove like a man possessed. Fortunately God was with us. We left our stomachs and most of the rubber from our tyres on the road and took just under fifteen minutes for a journey that usually takes twice that long. When we got into South Molton I turned to Patsy in a panic.

'Where is the abattoir?' I shouted.

Patsy didn't know either so I screeched to a stop by an old lady trundling home with her weekly shopping in a small wicker trolley. She knew and gave me excellent directions though if she wondered why anyone needed an abattoir in a hurry she didn't allow her curiosity to show on her face.

The man on the gate at the abattoir had a clipboard and because we weren't listed on it he was reluctant to let us in. He listened to my explanation with no interest whatsoever but proved far more amenable when Patsy got out of the car and pleaded with him. Eventually, he agreed to let us park our car outside on the road and to walk into the abattoir on foot. Two huge lorries had already unloaded their live cargoes and a third was being emptied. The lambs which had been delivered for slaughter were crowded into tiny pens and they were clearly all terrified. The stench was terrible and the sounds coming from inside were blood curdling. Patsy gripped my hand so tightly that I felt my fingers going numb. Our four lambs had to be in one of those tiny pens.

'What do you want?' demanded a hugely fat man who wore a once white boiler suit that was covered with red splashes. Like the man on duty at the gate he carried a clipboard. The breeze rustled the sheets of paper that were attached to it and he smoothed them down with a blood stained hand.

'We're looking for four lambs,' explained Patsy.

'Not here you don't,' said the fat man aggressively. He held out a hand, rather like a traffic policeman on duty, and went as though to push Patsy backwards.

I moved in between them. 'Our lambs were taken by mistake,' I explained. 'They shouldn't have been sold to you.'

'Too late now,' said the fat man who was clearly uninterested in our predicament.

'You could be charged with dealing in stolen property,' I told him, clutching desperately at straws.

'Prove it,' sneered the fat man. 'One carcass looks much like another.'

Suddenly, and I don't know where it can from, I had an inspiration. I sighed. 'I didn't want to do this,' I told him. 'Because if it gets out I'll be in as much trouble as you will.' I turned to Patsy. 'Go and fetch the police,' I told her. 'And then ring the public health department and tell them that I want this place closed down immediately.'

The fat man stared at me, startled. I didn't want to give him time to think about what I was saying. I took out my small cardboard Bilbury Cricket Club pass and hoped he wouldn't recognise it for what it was. It had my name written neatly in black ink on the front cover and, fortunately, my title was written there too. 'I'm a doctor,' I told him. 'You've got four lambs here which have been used in a scientific experiment. They are infected with anthrax. Once those lambs get into your building you'll have to be closed down permanently.'

I was relying on the fact that if there is one thing that everyone involved in the meat trade is terrified of it is anthrax. And it worked brilliantly. The fat man paled and stepped backwards as though to distance himself as much as possible from Patsy and I.

'If you let us take our lambs away from here there won't be any problem,' I told him. 'They aren't infective while they're still alive. But if any of their blood is spilt this whole place will be finished.'

'Are they marked?' asked the fat man.

'We'll recognise them,' said Patsy.

The fat man led us across the courtyard towards the pens where the lambs were crammed together. For a brief moment I was worried that we wouldn't be able to recognise our lambs. But my worry was unjustified for the lambs recognised us. The moment they saw us walking towards them they began bleating noisily and desperately. They even struggled to climb out of their pen to get to us.

'There they are!' said Patsy.

The fat man waved to a colleague dressed in waders and a waterproof smock and pointed to our lambs. 'Get them out of there!' he shouted.

The man in the waders looked puzzled.

'Don't waste time!' shouted the fat man, now desperate to see the back of our lambs. 'Get them out of there.'

Seconds later they were bounding up to us like four puppies. They were wagging their tails and bouncing up and down like toys on springs.

'They don't look ill,' said the fat man suspiciously. 'If anything they look plumper and healthier than the rest!'

'It's the new test we're doing,' I lied. 'They've been injected with a drug which holds the disease at bay but unfortunately it doesn't kill it. They'll live but they're still infective.'

The fat man still looked doubtful.

I sighed and moved closer to him. 'We're working for Porton Down,' I told him. 'They want to breed apparently healthy sheep that carry anthrax.'

There was disgust in the fat man's face and for a moment

I feared that he was going to say that he didn't believe me. But he didn't.

'You people are disgusting!' was all he said, as he backed away from me again.

I shrugged. 'You have your job to do, we have ours.'

He just scowled at me. 'Anyway if you're from a government department how about some compensation?'

I stared at him but didn't say anything.

'We bought those lambs in good faith,' he told me, belligerently.

I reached into my trouser pocket to see what money I had and found the fifty pound note that Patchy Fogg had given me. I pulled it out and handed it to him. 'Will this do?' I said. 'I don't want a receipt and I don't care whether you tell your boss you got it.' Fifty pounds was a lot of money then. It was certainly more than the lambs were worth to a slaughterhouse.

I think it was the fifty pound note that finally convinced the fat man that my story was true. It certainly made him *want* to believe that my story was true.

Patsy and I walked out of the abattoir with our four lambs following us and I doubt if there have ever been four such gloriously happy lambs.

Farmers and butchers claim that animals are stupid and do not know what is happening to them when they are taken to the killing grounds of commerce, but my experience that day told me differently. Our lambs knew exactly what was going to happen to them, as did all the others that the abattoir had taken delivery of that day.

Outside the abattoir Patsy and I had the devil's own game to get our lambs into the back seat of the Morris Minor and we had to keep talking to them to calm them down and stop them getting agitated again.

As we drove back home, far more slowly than we had driven down to South Molton, I heard Patsy sobbing quietly beside me. I reached out a hand to comfort her and turned my head. Tears were running down her cheeks.

'It's O.K.,' I said quietly. 'We've got them back now.'

'It's not our lambs I'm crying for,' said Patsy sadly. 'It's the ones we left behind.'

*   *   *

CHAPTER THIRTEEN

I had to call in to see Miss Phillips on my way to the surgery the following morning. Miss Tweedsmuir had rung me just as I was finishing my breakfast.

'I'm sorry to call you so early,' she apologised, 'but would you be kind enough to call round to see Miss Phillips as soon as you can?'

'What's wrong?' I had asked anxiously. I knew that Miss Tweedsmuir wasn't a woman to panic unnecessarily.

'It's difficult to explain on the telephone,' whispered Miss Tweedsmuir. She had spoken so quietly that I could hardly hear her and I had guessed that she had been frightened of Miss Phillips overhearing.

I drove round there as quickly as I could.

As I reached out to knock on the front door the door opened.

'Thank you for coming, doctor,' said Miss Tweedsmuir quietly, standing back to let me in. She sounded relieved to see me but looked drawn and tired and clearly hadn't slept. She wore an ankle length red velvet dressing gown and fluffy, pale pink slippers which I guessed had been a present since they certainly weren't the sort of thing I would have expected her to buy for herself. She signalled for me to precede her into the living room and then closed the door behind us and stood with her back to it. I stood with my back to the empty fireplace, still clutching my doctors bag in my right hand.

'You must promise never to tell anyone what I'm about to tell you,' she said.

'Of course I won't!' I assured her.

Miss Tweedsmuir wet her lips and swallowed hard. 'Last

night Miss Phillips tried to kill herself,' she said.

Of the several dozen questions which sprang into my mind the first one that escaped was: 'Is she all right?'

'She's fine, now,' answered Miss Tweedsmuir. She pointed up at the ceiling. 'She's sleeping.'

'What did she do? How did she, er . . . ?'

'Pills,' replied Miss Tweedsmuir simply.

'The Angipax?'

Miss Tweedsmuir shook her head. 'I keep those,' she said. 'But I was very careless.' She blushed and looked embarrassed and started playing with the belt of her dressing gown. 'I have a small supply of barbiturates,' she said. The red flush on her cheeks spread to her forehead. 'I use them very occasionally when I can't sleep. I've had them for years.'

'She took those?'

Miss Tweedsmuir nodded.

'How many?'

'About ten. Less than a dozen.'

'I'd better have a look at her.'

'She's O.K. Really.' said Miss Tweedsmuir. 'I made her keep walking about the house for most of the night.' She did not move from her position behind the door and for a few moments did not speak at all.'I don't know what to do,' she said at last, 'I just don't know what to do'.

'Let me have a word with her,' I said to Miss Tweedsmuir.

We tiptoed up the stairs and I let Miss Tweedsmuir enter the bedroom they shared ahead of me. Miss Phillips was asleep and to my surprise looked angelic and carefree. Miss Tweedsmuir bent over her and gently put a hand on her shoulder. Slowly, Miss Phillips awoke and I could see the lines of care and worry gradually returning to her face as she regained consciousness.

'The doctor has come to see you,' said Miss Tweedsmuir quietly.

'Hello.' I said, standing still at the end of the bed.

Miss Phillips opened her eyes wide and looked straight at me. She knew who I was straight away. 'I'm sorry you've been troubled,' she said. And then, without warning, she began to cry. Miss Tweedsmuir sat on one side of the bed and I sat on other and together we tried to comfort her.

139

'It's those tablets,' said Miss Phillips a few minutes later when the tears had stopped and she regained her composure. She sounded more sad than angry.

Miss Tweedsmuir looked across at me. 'I think she's been trying to cut them down too quickly,' she said.

Between them they told me that Miss Phillips had accelerated the rate at which she had been cutting down her tablets. 'They make me ill when I take them and they make me ill when I try to stop them,' said Miss Phillips plaintively. 'I wish to heaven I'd never heard of them.'

'If I ever see that doctor who gave them to you he'll get a good piece of mind,' said Miss Tweedsmuir angrily.

'That won't help,' said Miss Phillips quietly, reaching out and taking her friend's hand.

'How long will this go on for?' asked Miss Tweedsmuir.

'I don't know,' I confessed.

'Did you tell him about my silly episode last night?' Miss Phillips asked her friend.

Miss Tweedsmuir didn't say anything but looked at me.

'I guessed,' I said quickly. The lie didn't worry me. 'I made her tell me. But I won't tell anyone else.'

I told them both that I'd see what else I could find out about the Angipax tablets and that I would return to their cottage later that day, then I got back into my car, drove to Dr Brownlow's house and started the morning surgery forty five minutes late. Miss Johnson didn't ask me why I was late and I didn't tell her.

* * *

'Would you have a look at these stitches for me?' asked Mr Yardley. 'I don't know whether they're ready to come out yet.'

He unwound a thick woollen scarf from around his neck and revealed the worst and most untidy piece of human repair work I had ever seen. A four inch long cut had been repaired with a series of stitches. Each stitch had been tied with a reef knot and the material used looked more like thick fishing catgut than anything I'd ever seen used in a hospital casualty department. The whole area around the cut was red and inflamed and clearly infected and there were trickles of yellowish fluid leaking out of each stitch hole.

'Who on earth did that to you?' I asked him.

'I fell on a fence,' said Mr Yardley simply. 'Barbed wire.'

'No,' I said. 'I mean, who did that stitching?'

Mr Yardley fingered his neck cautiously, touching each knot in turn with his finger tips. 'I did.' he said, with a smile of pride.

I stared at him. Part of me didn't believe him. But part of me knew that no professional could have ever done such a shoddy job.

'Didn't it hurt?' I asked him.

Mr Yardley looked surprised at the question. 'No.' he said. 'Not that I can remember.'

'Were you drunk?'

'I think so.' He grinned an almost entirely toothless grin. 'I can't remember.'

I got up, walked round the desk and looked closely at Mr Yardley's neck. He needed an antibiotic and the wound clearly needed cleaning and restitching. The smell that came from it was awful, overpowering even the smell of tobacco which emanated from his clothes. I noticed that there were several cigarette burns in his jacket.

'You need to go to the hospital!' I told him.

Mr Yardley frowned and shook his head firmly when I suggested this. 'My father went into the hospital once and came out dead,' he explained. 'I'm not going into no hospital.'

'But your neck needs resuturing!' I insisted.

'Can't you do it?' he asked me. 'You're a doctor aren't you?'

I sighed and swallowed hard. 'The hospital would be able to make a better job of it,' I told him. 'They've got better equipment and the doctors there are more skilled at surgery. They can give you a better anaesthetic too.'

'I don't mind you doing it,' said Mr Yardley firmly. 'But I'm not going to the hospital.'

I felt quietly flattered.

'You may be clumsier than they are,' said Mr Yardley with disarming honesty. 'But it'll be more embarrassing for you if you kill me. You live round here.'

My newly raised self confidence collapsed and I felt considerably deflated. 'Take your shirt off, please,' I said to him, getting up and walking over to the sink to wash my hands. It took me half an hour to cut through Mr Yardley's thick and clumsy stitches, to clean out the wound and to replace them with my own stitches, to give him a tetanus injection and a shot of penicillin. By the time I'd finished the sweat was pouring off the tip of my nose.

'I'll give you some penicillin tablets,' I told him. 'But you must come back and let me have another look at it tomorrow.'

'There's one other thing,' said Mr Yardley. 'While I'm here.'

'What's that?' I asked him. I was back at the sink washing my hands again.

'I keep getting nose bleeds,' he said. 'Have you got anything for that?'

As soon as I had washed and dried my hands I sat down and took a fuller history. Then, while Mr Yardley still had his shirt off, I took his blood pressure. It was very high.

'It's your blood pressure,' I told him.

'Why does that make my nose bleed?' he asked.

'When the pressure is too high it bursts open small blood vessels,' I explained. 'And the ones in your nose are the smallest there are. They act as a sort of relief valve. When your nose bleeds and some of the blood comes out the blood pressure comes down.'

'Are you going to give me pills?' he wanted to know.

'I can,' I said. 'But you could help yourself by giving up the cigarettes.'

Mr Yardley looked at me. 'I'll have the pills,' he said.

Sighing, I wrote out a prescription for a drug designed to bring down his blood pressure and handed it to him. 'If you have any unpleasant side effects with these you must come back and tell me.'

Mr Yardley looked at me suspiciously. 'What sort of side effects?'

'They do affect some people's sex lives,' I explained. 'They can occasionally cause impotence.'

Mr Yardley stared at me and frowned. Then he stood up and started for the door. Just before he reached it he turned round, a puzzled look on his face. 'How did you know I smoke?' he asked me.

I touched the side of my nose with my forefinger. 'I'm a doctor,' I said. 'We're trained to spot these things.'

Mr Yardley showed no signs of being impressed and left.

* * *

'I'm sorry to take up your time, doctor,' said Mrs Francis. 'But I had to come and see you.'

I asked her what was troubling her.

I liked Mrs Francis a lot more than I had liked her late husband. I know one should not speak ill of the dead but her husband had been a difficult, arrogant man. He had also been unfaithful and had died in the arms of another woman in Barnstaple. Mrs Francis, however, was a kind, patient and charming woman.

'It isn't my health doctor,' she said. 'I feel a bit of a fraud.' She hesitated. 'But it's something I had to say; something I had to tell you.'

I waited.

'When I sold Softly's Bottom and Bluebell Wood to that Mr Sherlock I didn't know he was going to build houses on it,' said Mrs Francis. 'He told me that he wanted to set up a nature conservation area there.' She bit her lip. 'I'm so sorry.'

I reached across the desk and held her hand.

'I desperately needed the money and I wanted to be sure that the land went to someone who would look after it,' said Mrs Francis. 'I never dreamt ... ' She burst into tears.

I let go of her hand, got up, walked around my desk, and put my arm around her. 'It wasn't your fault!' I told her.

'I love Bilbury,' said Mrs Francis. 'I feel so terrible.' She looked up at me. 'But he seemed so plausible. So nice.' She cried a bit more. 'I've always loved that part of Bilbury so much. It's always full of wild flowers at this time of the year.'

'He hasn't started building yet,' I said. 'We haven't lost yet.'

'Oh but you can't stop someone like him,' said Mrs Francis, sadly.

And I had an awful feeling that she was probably right.

* * *

At the end of the morning surgery I decided there was no

point in telephoning the drug company again about Miss Phillips' pills. Instead I rang Tom Parker, a friend I knew who ran the pharmacy at a large hospital in Bristol.

'What do you know about Angipax?' I asked him when we'd exchanged news and gossip.

'Never heard of it,' he told me.

I told him that it was new, told him the name of the drug company which made it, told him that it was being tested and told him that a patient of mine had become seriously addicted.

'You want me to see if I can dig out anything about it?'

'Yes, please.'

'O.K.' said Tom without hesitation. 'I'll see what I can find out and then I'll ring you back this afternoon.'

* * *

'How was Miss Phillips?' asked Patsy when I got home for lunch. Patsy had answered the phone when I had taken the call from Miss Tweedsmuir that morning.

'She's O.K.' I told her, with a smile. I didn't tell her about the suicide attempt. I didn't like not telling Patsy everything but we had talked about the problem of confidentiality before.

'Patients tell me a lot of things in confidence,' I had told her shortly after we had got married. Patsy understood instantly as I knew she would. 'You mustn't tell me anything confidential,' she had said. 'Apart from the fact that you shouldn't tell me it would put me in a difficult position. It will be much easier for me if I don't know anything I shouldn't know about and shouldn't talk about.'

'Good!' said Patsy, who, like me, was very fond of both Miss Phillips and Miss Tweedsmuir. She pulled apart a lettuce that she had clearly just taken from the garden. There were two small snails clinging to an inner leaf and she carefully lifted them off. Afterwards, I knew that she would take them outside and put them back in the garden. 'There was a telephone call for you from an administrator from Withymoor. Miss Johnson gave them our number.' She handed me a slip of paper with the details written on it.

I raised an eyebrow. 'Did he say what he wanted?'

Patsy shook her head.

I stuffed the piece of paper into my pocket and helped Patsy carry our salad lunch outside. After we had eaten we spent half an hour in the vegetable garden picking strawberries and lettuce. We were still selling to Peter Marshall at the village shop, and Peter had told us that the hotels were very satisfied with our produce and wanted to know what else we would have to sell them in the future.

Patsy spent at least two hours every morning working in the vegetable garden, and although there was a long way to go it was beginning to look more and more as it must have done in Victorian times.

As we carried our two baskets of produce back to the house Patsy tapped me on the arm to catch my attention. She pointed and I followed her outstretched arm. Emily was crouching down on the path and had clearly spotted something which she was now stalking. We both looked ahead of her and saw a young buzzard sitting on the bottom rail of the wooden fence around the meadow where our four lambs lived. The buzzard's head was poking through the fence on the field side and its tail was poking through on our side. It was watching something in the field. We stood in silence and watched as Emily carefully and quietly crept up towards the buzzard. We were both ready to pounce if either creature looked like harming the other.

When she reached the fence Emily raised herself up on her hind legs and sniffed at the buzzard's tail. Very, very slowly the buzzard turned its head, looked down, saw Emily and then, still moving slowly, turned its head back to the front. Emily was shocked by this. It was not the sort of behaviour she expected from what was very clearly a bird. She moved backwards a foot or so. Then, after a short delay, she moved forwards again and had another sniff at the buzzard's tail. This time the buzzard didn't even bother to turn round but ignored Emily completely. Poor Emily. She slunk away looking quite miserable about the whole thing.

Patsy and I quickly walked on, making sure that Emily had no idea that we had been watching her. She would, we knew, have been mortified if she had known that we had watched her being humiliated.

I only remembered the message from the administrator as

145

I was about to leave the house to go back to the surgery. I'd put my hand in my pocket to pull out the car keys and the piece of paper had fluttered to the ground.

The administrator, a miserable sounding man called Perkins who had an annoying, whining voice, wanted to know if he could make an appointment to come and see me. He wouldn't tell me what it was about.

'When would you like to come?' I asked him.

'As soon as is convenient.'

'I can see you this afternoon,' I told him. 'But not until the surgery finishes.'

'What time is that likely to be?'

'Seven or seven thirty.'

'Good heavens, no!' said the administrator. 'I finish work at 4.30. I couldn't possibly see you then.'

In the end I made an appointment to see him at 11.30 the following morning.

As soon as I put the telephone down it rang again. This time it was my friend Tom the pharmacist.

'I've been doing some checking,' he said. 'I hadn't heard of Angipax because it doesn't come through our pharmacy, but there are patients in the hospital here who are taking it.'

He explained that the drug company which made it had done a deal with a couple of consultants, offering them sizeable cash inducements to test the drug out on a number of patients.

'It must be costing the company a fortune!' I said to Tom. 'The only patients who seem to be taking it are getting it free.'

'Oh it makes sound commercial sense,' said Tom. 'Don't you worry about that!' He laughed, presumably at my naivety.

He explained that the company making the drug was using the clinical trial as a marketing ploy. 'Within a few weeks,' said Tom, 'all the doctors who have been giving the drug away free will have got into the habit of prescribing it.'

It occurred to me that the company's profits would probably be enhanced by the fact that since the drug seemed to be addictive the patients who were taking it would probably have to keep on taking it. But I didn't mention this. I didn't think any drug company could possibly be unethical enough to take

146

advantage of such a problem.

'One of the guys who has been prescribing it here has noticed that a couple of his patients do seem to have got hooked on it,' said Tom. 'He says he reported it to the drug company but they said no one else had noticed it and so he thought it must have just been an isolated phenomenon.'

That, I thought, was exactly what the drug company's medical adviser had told me. I thanked Tom and told him I'd buy him a drink next time I saw him. He told me not to bother about the drink but to make sure I let him know what I found out.

After I'd finished the surgery that evening I drove round to Miss Phillips' cottage. As I drove I realised how hungry I was. I suddenly had a mouth watering vision of egg and cress sandwiches. I swallowed hard and tried to suppress the image.

When I got to the cottage I told Miss Phillips what I'd found out, warned her and Miss Tweedsmuir that no one seemed to have any firm answers, but said that if she carried on cutting down the drug slowly she ought, eventually, to find that the withdrawal effects began to diminish.

Miss Tweedsmuir said that it made her very angry that a drug company was allowed to put a drug on the market that caused so much unhappiness. I said it made me very angry too and I told her that I had thought of a way in which I might be able to warn other patients of the problem.

*   *   *

When I got home it was well after nine and I found Patsy on her hands and knees in the kitchen surrounded by the most astonishing variety of junk.

'Where on earth did you find this lot?' I asked, stepping over the most eclectic assortment of artifacts I had ever seen. I could see at least half a dozen rusty rat traps, a pair of wooden boot trees, a dozen rusty spanners, three croquet balls, a wooden tennis racket with most of its strings either missing or broken, a metal money box with a large hole in the lid, a kite with a huge ball of string attached to it, a wooden box with no obvious purpose, half a dozen long playing records made by recording artistes who were popular during

147

the Second World War, a bundle of clergyman's collars held together with a piece of orange baler twine, a large wooden scrubbing brush and a small leather gladstone bag with a broken catch.

'They were in the tin bath,' replied Patsy. 'There's some wonderful stuff here!'

'What tin bath?' I asked, puzzled. I didn't remember seeing a tin bath.

'The one I bought at the auction.' She stopped what she was doing and looked up at me. 'You must remember! It cost fifty pence.' She nodded towards the far corner of the kitchen where an almost empty tin bath lay incongruously on the floor. It had a large red, rusty patch on one side and I wouldn't have bet on it being watertight. I remembered. The last lot Patsy had bought after I had earned £50 bidding for Patchy Fogg's davenport had been a 'tin bath and contents'.

'What have you found?' I asked, kneeling down beside her. Patsy was right. It did look rather exciting. The auctioneer had dumped all sorts of miscellaneous bits and pieces into the tin bath, turning it into a genuine lucky dip.

'This,' said Patsy, handing me an old photograph frame that looked as if it might be made out of silver and which contained a photograph of a stern looking old lady glowering at the camera. I examined the frame but couldn't see any sign of a hallmark. 'It might be silver,' I said.

' ... and this!' Patsy handed me a very elderly looking teddy bear with one eye missing and an arm hanging loose.

' ... and this!' She handed me a rusty metal toy car which had one wheel missing.

'I wonder if it's valuable?' I asked her.

'I don't know!' admitted Patsy. 'That's what makes it so exciting!'

'I like the Gladstone bag!' I told her, putting the toy down and reaching across for the bag. 'I wonder if the fastener can be repaired.' I had always wanted a genuine old fashioned Gladstone bag. I was surprised at how small it was.

'Probably!' said Patsy. 'There's an old fashioned cobbler in Barnstaple who mends bags and cases. I'll take it in to him.'

'What are those?' I asked her, pointing to a small pile of about a dozen books.

'Oh, just novels,' said Patsy. 'I don't think there's anything very valuable there.'

'And what's that?'

'I don't know!' laughed Patsy, picking up a large, weird looking metal gadget. 'I think it might be a doughnut making machine.' She wound a wooden handle round and round and a thin wire moved up and down.

'What are we going to do with all this?' I asked her.

'I thought I might take some of it into Barnstaple,' said Patsy. 'To one of the antique shops. To check if any of it is valuable. We might be able to make some money out of it.'

I remembered the wine and wondered if we might be lucky enough to strike gold again. It was certainly worth trying.

Suddenly, Patsy sat back on her heels and clapped her hands to her mouth. 'Oh, darling!' she said. 'I'm sorry!'

'Why?' I asked, suddenly alarmed.

'I forgot that you hadn't eaten,' she said. 'You must be starving!'

I had been hungry but I'd almost forgotten about food. Patsy's reminder brought back the memory of hunger. She blushed a little and tiptoed through the bits and pieces on the kitchen floor to get to the fridge. She opened the fridge door, reached in and brought out a plate that was covered with a shallow dish. She shut the fridge door and brought the plate over to me. Then she lifted the dish off the plate. There was a pile of egg and cress sandwiches.

'I hope you like them!' she whispered. 'I made these for you a couple of hours ago. I don't know why but I just felt sure that you'd like egg and cress sandwiches for your tea.'

*   *   *

CHAPTER FOURTEEN

If I had seen him in the street I would have known just from looking at him what Mr Perkins did for a living.

He looked just like all the other Health Service administrators I have ever come across.

He was of medium height, slightly overweight and with receding hair. He wore a cheap, off-the-peg suit that had probably never fitted him properly, a white nylon shirt and a badly knotted red nylon tie which was decorated with a number of stains. He had three pens clipped into his outside jacket pocket and a fourth clipped into his shirt pocket. He had a thick layer of dandruff on both shoulders and had the sort of pallid face which gives meaning to the word nondescript. He brought with him a cheap black briefcase and, even though it was a gloriously hot day, he carried a raincoat.

He looked like a man who had never followed a dream or taken a risk in his life.

He sat down, opened his briefcase and took out a thick cardboard file. Then he took a plastic spectacle case out of his jacket pocket, removed a pair of steel framed spectacles and put them on. Ben, lying underneath my desk as usual, sat up and growled. She had only ever done that once before and that had been when Mr Sherlock the builder had come into the consulting room. I reached down and stroked Ben's neck to reassure her that everything was all right. I wouldn't have minded having someone to stroke my neck to reassure me. I wasn't at all sure that everything was all right. I didn't like the look of Mr Perkins and I had a feeling I wasn't going to like what he was going to say.

'I'm from the Planning and Rationalisation Department,'

he told me in his annoying and whiny voice. 'We've been looking at your per capita throughput figures.' As he spoke he opened the file and pointed a stubby figure at a line of type. 'I'm afraid that your practice badly needs rationalising.'

I stared at him uncomprehendingly.

'Even allowing for the special circumstances of your rural position, the practice review group feels that there are clear indications for dramatically redefining your catchment area downwards.' Mr Perkins took a red pen out of his jacket pocket and pointed at another row of type. He made no attempt to turn his file around so that I could see what he was pointing at.

'I'm sorry,' I said. 'But I don't quite understand.' I stole a look at my watch. I had three home visits to do before I could get home and I wanted to spend a few minutes helping Patsy pick the day's strawberries. Our strawberry plants were producing fruit with reckless enthusiasm. I also wanted to see how Patsy was getting on with our new paying guests. Frank and Gilly from the Duck and Puddle had telephoned to ask us if we could provide accommodation for a family of four who were coming from Essex, and so we were about to start our career in the tourist industry.

'To put things bluntly, doctor,' said Mr Perkins with a sniff, 'our group feels that your practice should be merged with another practice in order to maximise resource utilisation.'

'Which practice?' I asked, startled.

'I beg your pardon?' He sniffed again.

'Which practice do you want me to merge with?'

'Well, the nearest suitable practice is one on the outskirts of Barnstaple. And it just so happens that Dr Brownlow and his colleagues are advertising for a new junior partner. It would make excellent administrative sense if you were to apply for the post and take your present list of patients with you.'

'I don't think that would be a very good idea,' I said.

'May I ask why not?'

'Firstly, I prefer working here by myself. Secondly, if I closed down this practice my patients would have to travel several miles to get to see a doctor. And thirdly, I wouldn't work with the young Dr Brownlow if you paid me in gold bricks.'

'Ah.' said Mr Perkins. He didn't seem particularly surprised.

'Why can't I just carry on as I am?'

'I'm afraid it is largely a question of resource allocation,' said Perkins. He sniffed again and I had to fight back the temptation to offer him a tissue so that he could blow his nose. 'Our advisers feel that, as it stands, your practice is too small to be economically viable, and they have recommended that under Rule 49, Clause 17c of your contract of employment with the Secretary of State we withdraw your basic payment allowance, rural inducement allowance and per capita support payment.'

'But if you withdraw those allowances I won't be able to make a living!' I protested. General practitioners working within the National Health Service are technically self-employed, and their income is made up of a vast number of allowances, fees and special payments. I knew that without the payments Mr Perkins had mentioned my practice income, already small because Bilbury was such a tiny village, would fall by well over half.

Mr Perkins looked very smug. 'That may be so,' he said. 'But there is another alternative which we are prepared to endorse and subsequently authorise.'

'What's that?'

'There is, as I believe you know, a proposal to build a number of new dwellings in Bilbury.' He looked at me and raised an eyebrow.

'I do know about it,' I said. I wondered what sort of person chose to say 'dwelling' instead of 'home'.

'In the opinion of our study group the number of new dwellings proposed would raise the per capita quotient to an acceptable level,' said Mr Perkins.

I was beginning to get a very uneasy feeling about all this, but to my own amazement I didn't feel particularly surprised or angry about any of it. 'Let me see if I've got this right,' I said. 'Either I agree to work at Sherlock's new surgery and to welcome the new development in Bilbury; I close down this practice and apply for a job as a junior partner with another practice or I carry on working here and go bust because you withdraw my Health Service payments?'

Perkins, who had listened carefully to this, put his pen back into his breast pocket, shuffled uncomfortably and sat back. 'That isn't how I would choose to summarise things,' he said.

'But you wouldn't deny that it is an accurate summary?'

'There are no immediately apparent inaccuracies,' he admitted. He spoke as though he had a sour plum in his mouth.

'Well, thank you for making things so clear,' I said, standing up.

Mr Perkins folded up his file, put it back into his briefcase and stood up. 'Will you let us know what you decide to do?'

'Naturally,' I said, coldly. 'You'll be among the first to know.'

*   *   *

Our first paying guests had arrived and moved into the coach-house flat no more than an hour before I got home for lunch. Patsy had laid the kitchen table for lunch. We normally ate out in the courtyard when it was sunny, but the coach-house flat overlooked the courtyard and Patsy thought it might be better to have our lunch in private.

'What are they like?' I asked Patsy anxiously.

'They seem quite nice,' Patsy answered.

I can't imagine why, because the coach-house flat was at least sixty yards away from where we were standing, but we were both whispering. 'They've brought a lot of luggage with them.' She told me that she had counted six suitcases being carried up the circular staircase from the Ford which was parked down in the courtyard.

'For the four of them?'

'Mr and Mrs Wakeham and their two teenage daughters,' replied Patsy. 'I don't know any of their first names.'

'How old are the daughters?'

'They look about seventeen but they could be thirteen.'

'I hope there's going to be room,' I said. There was only one bedroom in the coach-house flat, but the sofa in the living room did convert into a spare bed and we had told Frank and Gilly that the flat would accommodate two adults and two children.

'I thought we could perhaps take them some strawberries after lunch,' said Patsy. 'As a sort of welcome present.'

153

I said I thought that sounded a nice idea.

And then I told Patsy about Mr Perkins' visit.

'So it's true that they want to turn Bilbury into a small town?' said Patsy, sadly.

'I don't think the plans have been passed yet,' I said.

'But they want you to support it by agreeing to work with them?'

'Yes. And if I don't then they'll close the practice down.'

'That's a nice choice,' said Patsy. 'Either we help them ruin the village or else they'll ruin us.'

I hadn't thought about it like that, but Patsy was right, and several thoughts started to appear in my head. Why, I wondered, were the National Health Service administrators apparently helping Sherlock and his plans? Was it just a coincidence?

My thoughts were disturbed by a knock on the back door. I got up from the table where we had been having lunch and went to the door. A very large man and a very small woman greeted me. He was wearing a colourful short sleeved shirt and a pair of equally colourful Bermuda shorts. She was wearing a bikini top and a billowy, flimsy skirt.

'Wakeham,' said the man, holding out his hand. 'Call me Dicky.'

I took it and introduced myself.

'This is my wife, Doris.'

I introduced Patsy.

'Thought we'd just come over and introduce ourselves.' said Dicky.

'Would you like to come in?' said Patsy.

'Not just now, thanks.' said Dicky. 'We've left the girls unpacking.'

'It's nice to meet you both,' said Doris. 'What a lovely home you have.' She peered around us to peek into the kitchen.

'Thank you,' said Patsy. 'We've still got a lot to do.'

'I hear you're a doctor,' said Dicky.

I agreed that he had heard correctly.

'Very handy to have a doctor on the premises,' he laughed.

I laughed back, though my laugh was more forced than his.

'We thought we ought to let you know that there isn't a potato peeler in the kitchen or a toothbrush holder in the bathroom.'

'And there's no sharpener for the carving knife,' said Doris.

'Oh,' said Patsy. 'I'm sorry. Is the carving knife blunt?'

'I don't know,' said Doris. 'I haven't tried it yet. But I thought you'd want to know.'

'Thank you.' Patsy and I said together.

'Well. We'll be getting back over there before the girls wreck the place,' said Dicky. 'We'll be in most of the afternoon getting ourselves settled in so there's no hurry for those bits and pieces.'

'Right,' said Patsy. 'Thank you.'

'Maybe we could meet for dinner one evening?' suggested Dicky.

I looked at Patsy. 'That's a very nice idea,' I said. 'Unfortunately, it's not easy for me to get out. I'm usually on call for the practice.'

'That's O.K.,' said Dicky. 'We don't mind eating here.'

'Of course.' said Patsy.

'Oh, and we could do we with more coat hangers,' said Dicky.

'But not those wire ones, please,' added Doris with a smile. She kept her jaw clenched when she smiled, in that uncomfortable way that people do when they have ill-fitting false teeth.

'Right!' I said. 'We'll see what we can do.'

Dicky and Doris, smiled, said 'goodbye' and then turned and walked back across the courtyard. Patsy and I exchanged glances and wondered if all our visitors were going to be like this.

*   *   *

'You've got to do something to help her,' said Mr Blossom insistently. He sounded angry rather than sad, aggrieved rather than depressed. He had rung me and demanded that I visit his daughter immediately, though he admitted that it was he and not she who could no longer cope.

We both stood and looked at his daughter and if I had been in his position I would have said something similar.

Mrs Blossom was lying in bed, and although she wasn't

asleep she didn't really look as if she was awake either.

I sat down on the edge of a pale pink counterpane. 'Hello Mrs Blossom. How do you feel?' There were roses embroidered around the edges of the bed covering.

She slowly turned her head and stared at me. She tried to speak but although small bubbles appeared at the corners of her mouth no words came out. A look of recognition appeared on her face and in her eyes.

'She's hardly spoken for days,' said Mr Blossom. 'I think it's those pills that doctor at the hospital gave her.'

'I think you're probably right,' I said quietly. I couldn't help noticing that there was far less respect now for the consultant psychiatrist.

'So what are you going to do about it?'

'Would you like me to fix up another appointment with the consultant?'

'Certainly not!' said Mr Blossom, without hesitation. 'I want you to look after her.' His faith in the consultant had melted and the respect was but a memory.

'Then I think the best thing would be to stop the tablets.'

'Right,' said Mr Blossom emphatically.

'But not suddenly,' I said sharply. 'She mustn't stop them suddenly.'

Mr Blossom looked at me.

'The pills are new,' I told him. 'They seem to be addictive.'

I gave Mr Blossom similar instructions to the ones I had given Miss Phillips and told him that I would call in to see his daughter again the following day.

*   *   *

We had a considerable amount of lawn to keep trimmed at Bilbury Grange.

Cutting the lawns is, in some ways, a tedious chore but I confess that I find it a pleasing task in a simple sort of way. Nothing makes such a difference to the appearance of a garden as an expanse of newly cut grass.

Apart from the croquet lawn, which had once been an old tennis court, there were two large lawns at the front of the house and a number of grassy strips around the side of the house. There was also quite a lot of grass under and between

156

the bushes in the shrubbery which shielded the house from the driveway.

When we had first moved into Bilbury Grange I had tried to cut the lawns with a small petrol driven mower that I had found in an old wooden shed to the left of the croquet lawn. It had not been a great success. The mower had cut the grass without too many problems, and left it looking smart, but it took me over eight hours to finish the lawns. I realised that I had to get something speedier and more efficient. In the end I had purchased a ten year old ride on mower that Dr Brownlow needed to get rid of because his gardener found it too speedy and frightening for his taste. This may have had something to do with the fact that the mower had lost its two lowest gears and could now only be driven in reverse or at full forward speed. I drove the mower back to Bilbury Grange along the village lanes, and going up Bilbury Hill I travelled so fast that Dr Brownlow, who was driving behind me in his elderly Rolls Royce to make sure that I arrived home safely, couldn't keep up with me.

That evening was warm but there was just enough gentle breeze blowing to make it pleasant for working in the garden, and while Patsy picked strawberries I decided to cut the lawns. I slipped into my shorts and an old shirt, took the six, white metal croquet hoops and the coloured finishing peg out of the lawn, made sure that the mower was filled with petrol and set to work.

One of the things about the ride on mower is that it saves time. Instead of having a tiny grass box at the front that has to be emptied every few yards it tows a huge collecting box which holds an enormous quantity of grass cuttings and which only has to be emptied every quarter of an hour or so.

At that time I had not yet built a compost heap big enough to cope with the quantity of grass cuttings I was producing and so I simply dumped the grass cuttings in the field where our four lambs lived. This was a fairly tricky procedure. To get into the field I had to use a wooden, five bar gate which separated the field from the shrubbery, and every time I opened the gate the lambs tried to get through into the garden to eat our shrubs. I wouldn't have minded if the lambs had simply come into the garden and helped to keep the grass down. But they seemed to find fuschias, honeysuckle, hydrangeas, rhododendrons and flowers of all sorts far tastier than grass.

The theoretically simple procedure of driving the tractor into the field and unloading its cargo of grass cuttings was made infinitely more difficult by the fact that instead of running away whenever they heard me and the mini-tractor approaching (as normal sheep would have done), our four pet lambs would run towards the sound it made. They were as curious as cats and as reckless as kittens.

Despite this hazard, and the problem of keeping the lambs out of the garden, my first three grass dumping trips that evening were uneventful. The lambs sniffed and sneezed at the grass cuttings but I managed to stop them from squeezing through the gate.

By the time I arrived with the final load of grass cuttings it was almost dark and I had to switch on the mower's two headlamps. As I opened the gate and manoeuvred the tractor through into the field I peered into the half darkness looking for the lambs but could see no sign of them. They had, I guessed, either gone foraging for sweet grass in another corner of the field or, more likely, had settled down for the night in their favourite spot underneath a huge, old ash tree. I dumped the grass cuttings onto the enormous mound I had made, shut the gate firmly, put the mower away and then went into the house for a cool drink, a piece of Patsy's carrot cake and a long, warm soak in the bath. Patsy, who had been turning some of the strawberries she had picked into jam, had put the jam down in the cellar to cool and set and was already upstairs in one of our twin baths. I shut the cellar door which Patsy had left open, shut and locked the back door and then went upstairs to join Patsy in the bathroom.

*   *   *

Patsy and I still hadn't bought ourselves a new bed, partly because we hadn't had time to get one and partly because we didn't have any money to spare. But we did have something to sleep on and we were comfortable enough.

I was fast asleep and enjoying a dream, which at the time

158

seemed important but about which I can now remember absolutely nothing, when I suddenly awoke in a panic, unable to breathe. I tried to cry out but realised that there was a hand clamped firmly over my nose and mouth. As I struggled to free myself I heard Patsy's voice. I opened my eyes. It was pitch black but a tiny shaft of moonlight shone through a narrow gap in the curtains. Having spent the last couple of years of my life having to wake up suddenly and immediately to deal with medical emergencies I was quite good at waking up quickly.

'Sssshhhh . . . ' said Patsy. 'Don't make a sound!'

I touched her hand gently to let her know that I was awake. She moved her hand away from my mouth.

'What's the matter?'I whispered.

'I heard a noise!' whispered Patsy. 'Downstairs! There's someone downstairs.'

I had often wondered how I would react to such an event. Now I found out. I didn't panic. I didn't scream or shout. I didn't retreat under the covers. I simply froze for what seemed like a month.

'What do you mean?' I forced myself to whisper at long, long last. 'What sort of noise?'

'Just a noise,' murmured Patsy. She put her arm around me. 'Listen!' she said quietly, putting a finger over my lips.

We both lay there listening to the sound of our own hearts beating. It's surprising how much noise the human heart makes as it goes about its regular business. Mine had become so enthusiastic that it seemed determined to escape from my chest.

'Why would anyone want to burgle us?' I asked. 'We haven't got anything worth stealing!'

'Maybe they don't know that!' whispered Patsy. 'Sssshhhh! Listen!'

We continued to lie there, wrapped in each other's arms, lying in such total silence that I thought I could hear the hairs standing up on my arms.

'There you are!' whispered Patsy suddenly, holding me closer to her. 'Did you hear it?'

I had. Patsy was right. Someone was moving about downstairs.

'Maybe it's the people from the coach-house flat?' I suggested.

'The Wakehams? What would they want?'

'Perhaps they're looking for coat hangers?'

'They haven't got a key!' Patsy pointed out.

That was, I realised, the trouble. No one had a spare key. We had intended to give Thumper and Patsy's parents spare keys, just in case we ever got locked out, but we'd never got round to it.

'I'll go and have a look,' I whispered.

'No!' said Patsy. 'Stay here!'

'I'll be careful!' I promised. I don't know why I wanted to go and look. It certainly wasn't bravery. It was, I suspect, curiosity mixed with annoyance more than anything. I didn't want to go downstairs to see who was there but I couldn't stay where I was. In a funny sort of a way, going downstairs to see who was there required less courage than staying in bed. 'You stay here and lock the door behind me.' All the rooms in the house were equipped with huge, solid-looking old fashioned locks and keys.

'I'm coming with you!' said Patsy. 'I don't want to stay here by myself. Besides,' she added, 'I can help!'

Moving with exaggerated slowness I pushed back the bedclothes, as though the sound of sheets being moved would attract attention, and levered myself off the bed. My eyes had become accustomed to the dark, but even with the shaft of moonlight coming through the curtains I couldn't see very much. I tiptoed gently towards the door. We didn't have any carpets anywhere in the house and I knew from past experience that there were numerous nail heads sticking up through the floorboards. A loose board creaked noisily and I froze again.

'Aren't you going to put some clothes on?' asked Patsy. She had stood up and was busily trying to disentangle her underwear. It was only when I looked at her and saw how naked she looked in the moonlight that I realised that I was naked too. I tiptoed back towards the bed. I didn't want to confront a burglar without my trousers on.

'This might not be the most appropriate time to tell you but you're beautiful,' I whispered. 'And I love you.'

Patsy stopped what she was doing and peered through the

darkness towards me. 'I love you too!' she whispered. She blew me a kiss as she struggled to fasten her bra.

We dressed as best as we could, put on our shoes and then tiptoed towards the door again.

I opened it a few inches and peered outside. I couldn't see anything unusual. The large window on the landing had stained glass panels in it, and the moonlight was split into shafts of red, yellow and blue. But with the bedroom door open I could hear the sounds from downstairs far more clearly. They sounded indistinct and strangely muffled.

'It sounds as if someone is moving furniture!' I whispered.

'But we haven't got any furniture!' Patsy pointed out.

'Maybe we've got burglars who are bringing furniture in!'

I started to tiptoe gently down the stairs, stopping on every step to listen. The noises down below didn't seem to diminish at all, and whoever was there didn't seem to care whether or not we heard them. At last we reached the bottom of the stairs and moved into the hall.

'It sounds as if it's coming from the cellars!' whispered Patsy, who was right behind me.

I listened again. She was right. I crept to the kitchen door, which was open, and peered through. The kitchen was empty and the noise, much louder now, was definitely coming from the cellars.

'It sounds as if whoever it is who is in there is banging on the door to be let out!' I said, not bothering to whisper now.

'Maybe it's a trick!' said Patsy, holding onto my arm.

I picked up a broom that was standing nearby and crept towards the cellar door, motioning to Patsy to stay where she was. The door to the cellar steps opened inwards. Gently, I turned the door knob to release the catch. But whoever it was that was on the other side simply continued to bang on it and the door remained shut.

Suddenly, I heard a sound which I recognised.

I put down the broom and bravely pushed on the door.

'Be careful!' shouted Patsy, behind me.

There was a scuffling sound on the other side of the door and then, as a gap appeared, first one lamb and then a second, then a third and finally a fourth came rushing out of the cellar and into the kitchen.

'Our burglars!' I said.

After we had made a fuss of them and escorted them back to their field, we returned to the kitchen to make ourselves a pot of tea. By this time the moon had almost disappeared and the first rays of the day's sunshine were beginning to brighten the sky.

'How on earth did they get down there?' asked Patsy.

'They must have slipped through the gate into the garden when I was dumping the grass cuttings,' I explained. 'Then they found their way through the back door and down into the cellar.'

'You were very brave!' said Patsy. She put her arms around my neck and kissed me. 'My hero!'

*   *   *

CHAPTER FIFTEEN

'Your column on Angipax seems to have stirred things up a bit!' said the editor of the Sunday News.

I felt my stomach turning over. I'd had a busy morning and arrived back home to find that Patsy had spent two hours fielding increasingly excited telephone calls from the editor. I had written the column after Miss Phillips' suicide attempt, and although I had not mentioned him by name I had quoted my friend from Bristol too. I decided to telephone the editor before I had my lunch and was put straight through to his office.

'Oh dear,' I said. 'I'm sorry.' I felt certain I was about to be fired. It seemed a pity. Apart from the fact that we needed the money I quite liked writing a weekly column and having a chance to influence things a little.

'Don't apologise!' insisted the editor. 'It's great stuff!'

This was not what I had expected to hear. 'Oh!' was all I could say. 'Thank you,' I muttered after hesitating for a moment. Patsy, who was standing a few feet away waiting to hear what happened, raised a questioning eyebrow. I hesitantly lifted a thumb to suggest that everything might, after all, be all right. A smile of optimism lit up her face. We had had enough bad news.

'You've had a sackful of mail from readers,' said the editor, 'and we've had another sackful for the letters page.'

'Is that good?' I asked him, tentatively.

'Marvellous!' said the editor cheerfully.

I felt distinctly relieved at this.

'The really good news is that I've had two phone calls this morning from other editors who want to run your column in their paper.' He mentioned two quite large evening news-papers in the north of England.

'That's great!' I said, delighted. It was good to know that my column was gaining some approval from other editors. I liked the idea of having more readers and the additional income would be more than helpful.

We kept a notepad by the side of the telephone for recording details of patients who needed visits at home and I wrote a short message to Patsy: TWO OTHER PAPERS WANT TO BUY COLUMN! Patsy read the message and kissed me. I tried to hold onto the telephone but dropped it. The handset bounced off the wall and then dangled a few inches above the floor. I stooped and picked it up. Ben found it all very exciting and jumped around barking furiously.

'Are you there?' I heard the editor saying.

'I'm sorry,' I apologised. Patsy put her hand over her mouth to cover up the sound of her giggling.

'What do you want to do about your mail?' asked the editor.

'Can't you just post it up to me?' I asked him. I'd had one or two letters from readers in the past when I had been writing for the Barnstaple, Bideford and Bilbury Herald and they had usually been posted onto me.

The editor laughed. 'You obviously thought I was exaggerating,' he said. 'You really have got at least one sackful of mail.'

'What sort of sackful?'

'A canvas post office mail sack,' laughed the editor. 'Don't worry,' he said. 'I'll wait a couple of days and then get one of our delivery vans to bring the mail up to you.'

'But what am I going to do with that many letters?' I asked him.

'I would have thought that rather depended on what they say,' said the editor. 'What are you writing about next week?' he asked.

I had one or two ideas but had not really chosen the topic. I was still getting used to the fact that I could write about anything I chose and didn't have to worry about writing a column full of practical advice on how to deal with corns, colds and cystitis. 'I thought I might do a column on animal experiments,' I said.

'Are you for or against them?'

'Against!' I said, rather shocked that the editor should ask.

'Great!' said the editor.

'It may cause more trouble,' I warned him, hesitantly.

'That's good,' said the editor cheerfully. 'That's what I pay you for.'

*   *   *

If there had been any danger of us getting too excited by this news we were brought back to earth with a bump a few moments later when the Wakehams knocked on our back door.

Patsy had managed to borrow some extra coat hangers from Gilly at the Duck and Puddle and she had given the visitors our potato peeler but she had to drive ten miles into Barnstaple to buy a sharpening tool for the carving knife. Since then they had called at our back door at least twice a day with small requests, comments, complaints and suggestions; all of which had been delivered with unfailing courtesy. There was, they said, no brown shoe polish. Did we know, they asked with cloying niceness, that the tea towels had no loops on them and so could not be hung up securely on the hook we had provided?

'I'm sorry to bother you,' said Mr Wakeham, beginning with a familiar litany the honesty of which we were beginning to question, 'but the light bulb in the bathroom has gone.'

'Oh, I'm sorry about that,' I apologised. 'But there are some spares in the cupboard under the sink in the kitchen.'

'Oh good,' said Mr Wakeham. He paused. 'We'll be in for another half an hour. Would it be convenient for you to pop over now?'

It took me a moment or two to realise that he expected me to go over to the flat to replace the bathroom light bulb. I started to say something about being rather busy but at the last moment I weakened. I wasn't entirely sure about the responsibility of a landlord. 'Right,' I said. 'I'll come back with you now.'

'Jolly good,' smiled Mr Wakeham.

I followed him back across the courtyard, up the staircase and into the coach-house flat. Mrs Wakeham was in the kitchen washing up and her two daughters were sitting on the sofa flicking through pop music magazines, eating chocolates and listening to the radio. Mrs Wakeham turned and shouted a greeting when she saw me. Her daughters sat sullenly, looked up briefly and then carried on looking at the pictures in their magazines. I returned Mrs Wakeham's greeting, said 'Hello' to the two daughters, who continued to ignore me, walked into the kitchen and opened the cupboard underneath the sink. I picked up a spare light bulb and then carried it through to the bathroom where I took out the old, useless bulb and replaced it with the new one. Mr Wakeham followed me around as I did all this, though I was not sure whether he was watching in order to learn or watching to make sure that I did the job properly.

'All done!' I cried, more cheerily than I felt.

'Jolly good!' said Mr Wakeham.

Mrs Wakeham came out of the kitchen drying her hands on a towel and hissed something at her husband. I couldn't tell what it was but he seemed to understand.

'Would tomorrow night be all right?' he asked.

I turned, about to leave, and waited. I didn't know what he was talking about.

'Dinner,' explained Mr Wakeham. 'You invited us to dinner. Tomorrow would be convenient for us. We wondered if it would be suitable for you.'

'Oh, well, yes,' I said hesitantly. 'I suppose so.' I added, rather ungraciously.

'Wonderful!' said Mr Wakeham, rubbing his hands together. 'We'll all look forward to that.'

I looked around at them all. Mrs Wakeham was still drying her hands and still smiling her thin, denture retentive smile. The two daughters hadn't looked up. 'So will we,' I said, hoping that I looked more enthusiastic than I felt but comforting myself with the thought that the Wakehams were too concerned with themselves to notice how I felt about anything.

*   *   *

I called in to see Mrs Blossom on the way to the surgery. There wasn't much change, but Mr Blossom was less belligerent and seemed happier. He said that his daughter had spoken a little more and had eaten two small meals. I told him to continue with the withdrawal programme I had outlined. Because I knew I was calling at the Blossom's I had left Ben at home with Patsy. Mr Blossom had a large and very aggressive Alsatian which didn't like other dogs at all. The last time I had visited I had left Ben sitting peacefully in the car and had returned a few minutes later to find the Alsatian clawing at the paintwork and growling menacingly. I don't know which of us was most miserable about this enforced temporary separation. I liked having Ben lying at my feet and it seemed strange not to have her around. And she liked being with me. She barked furiously and angrily whenever I drove off without her.

*　　*　　*

Less than a quarter of an hour later I was sitting in Dr Brownlow's consulting room working my way through the evening surgery. Out of the first four patients I saw I knew only one; the other three were all holiday makers. The fifth patient was a stranger too. Or at least that was what I thought when I first saw her. She was tall, slightly on the plump side and pretty in a pouty sort of way and I guessed that she was probably about eighteen or nineteen years old. She had shoulder length brown hair, cut in a fashionable style, wore a white tee shirt with a cartoon character on the front and a pair of blue denim shorts with frayed bottoms. She had an unusually well developed chest and she wore a lot of make up. I didn't know why, but there was something vaguely familiar about her. I guessed I had probably seen her somewhere around the village. She continually looked behind her at the friend who had accompanied her.

'What can I do for you?' I asked her.

'Is this all private?' asked the girl hesitantly.

'Yes,' I assured her.

'You won't tell my mum and dad?'

'Not without your permission.'

'I want to go on the pill,' said the girl.

'The contraceptive pill?'

'Yes,' said the girl. She looked behind her at her friend and they both giggled.

167

'Are you taking any other medicines?'

'No.'

'Are you on holiday here?

'Yes.' There was a noisy snigger from the girl behind.

'What's your name?'

'Anthea.'

'Anthea what?'

'Anthea Wakeham.'

I had written the name down before I realised why it was familiar. I looked up at the girl. 'Where are you staying?'

'The coach-house at Bilbury Grange,' giggled the girl. She looked behind her and she and her friend both giggled uncontrollably.

I felt myself blushing with embarrassment. 'I'm sorry,' I said. 'I didn't recognise you.'

'That's all right,' said the girl, still giggling.

I peered past her. 'Is that your sister?'

There was more giggling and much nodding of both heads.

'How old are you, Anthea?' I asked her.

'Seventeen,' she replied quickly. Even through her make up I could see that she was blushing heavily.

I didn't say anything but just stared at her. She looked down at her lap and played with the cheap, gaudy ring which she wore on the third finger of her right hand.

'How old are you?' I asked her again.

'Nearly fifteen,' she told me, quietly.

'Fourteen.' I said firmly, writing her age down on the form I had taken out of my desk drawer.

'Have you asked your own family doctor to prescribe the contraceptive pill for you?'

Anthea shook her head.

'Why not?'

'He'd tell my mum and dad. I know he would.'

'And you don't want them to know?'

'Are you kidding?' she said. 'My dad would kill me!'

'Why do you want to go on the pill?' I asked her.

Anthea stared at me for a moment and then turned round and looked at her sister. They both started giggling again.

'Have you got a steady boyfriend?'

She shrugged but did not look at me.

'What does that mean?'

'Not particularly.'

'Do you have a sexual relationship with anyone?'

Anthea stared at me and frowned. 'What do you mean?'

I swallowed. 'Are you a virgin?'

'No!' she said indignantly. 'What sort of question is that?'

'When did you first have sex?'

Anthea turned round again and whispered to her sister. After a few moments she turned back. 'I was thirteen,' she said. She paused for a moment and played with her ring again. 'Nearly thirteen anyway.'

'How often do you have sex?' I asked her.

'Why are you asking me all these questions?' she demanded. 'You're just a dirty old man, aren't you?'

I'd never thought of myself as 'old' before. It was a unique experience to realise that in the eyes of these two young girls I undoubtedly was 'old'.

'No!' I said, probably rather indignantly. 'But before I decide whether or not to prescribe the contraceptive pill for you I need to know whether or not you really need it.'

Anthea didn't say anything but played with her ring again.

'What precautions do you take?' I asked her.

Anthea frowned and thought about this. 'I'll only do it in cars and at parties,' she said. 'I won't do it in doorways in case anyone sees us.'

It was my turn to think for a moment. I decided that as far as Anthea was concerned 'taking precautions' meant 'not getting found out'.

'Do you use a condom?' I asked her.

This caused another bout of giggling. 'That's up to the fella, isn't it?' said Anthea at last. 'Some do and some don't.'

'Don't you worry about getting pregnant?'

Anthea looked at me as though I was truly stupid. 'I'm here, aren't I?' she protested.

'Slip your things off,' I sighed. 'I need to examine you.'

'What?' said Anthea, blushing. 'Here?'

'I need to take your blood pressure and examine your breasts,' I told her. 'I can't do that unless you take your tee shirt off.'

Anthea still hesitated.

'Will it make you happier if I go out for a minute?' I asked.

She looked at her sister for a moment, looked back at me and shook her head. She stood up, turned away from me and pulled her tee shirt up over her head. There was then some frantic activity, during which the two girls stuffed a number of paper tissues into their pockets, and then Anthea removed her bra and turned round again. Her chest now looked far less impressive. I took her blood pressure, examined her breasts and asked her some more questions then I told her she could get dressed again.

'Have you met anyone in Bilbury?' I asked her.

Anthea stared at me uncomprehendingly.

'Are you having sex with anyone in Bilbury?'

'I'm not going to tell you who it is,' said Anthea defensively.

'I don't want you to,' I said quickly. 'I just wanted to know whether or not there was a risk that you could get pregnant while you're here.'

'That's why I'm here.'

I wanted to talk to her, to find out why she felt the need to have sex with virtual strangers and to try and help her, but I knew she wouldn't let me into her life in the few days she was staying in Bilbury. Instead I wrote out a six month's prescription for her to take to the chemist and then gave her careful instructions about how and when she had to take her pills.

'When you get back home you must visit a contraceptive clinic,' I told her. I looked up and then gave her the address of a clinic where they would, I knew, treat her request for help confidentially and where, I hoped, they might be able to help her tackle her sexuality with more maturity. 'What about you?' I asked her sister.

'Oh don't worry about her,' said Anthea, with a carefree wave of her hand. 'She's all right.' Anthea's sister, whose name I still didn't know, smiled demurely as though she'd been congratulated on winning a Sunday School prize.

I didn't think either of them were 'all right' but I didn't see what else I could do to help them.

* * *

Miss Phillips was the next patient and I was surprised to

see her at the surgery.

'I feel a lot better today,' she said, when I told her that I would have been happy to visit her at home. 'And I'm determined to get myself off those pills.'

'You'll have to do it slowly,' I warned her.

'I know,' said Miss Phillips quickly. 'I will,' she added firmly.

I was pleased to hear that she was being so sensible, but I did suffer a shiver of apprehension, for although I was eager to help I still hadn't been able to find anyone who could tell me exactly how to help a patient withdraw from Angipax tablets. I had, however, prepared a withdrawal programme which involved a gradual cutting down of the pills which I felt fairly confident would be safe. I carefully explained to Miss Phillips exactly what I wanted her to do.

*　　*　　*

Patsy had spent the whole afternoon preparing the meal to which the Wakehams had invited themselves. She had bought a box of locally picked mushrooms, two dozen tomatoes and a large hunk of locally made cheese from Peter Marshall and had prepared two huge pizzas as the main course. They smelt very good.

'I wish you'd told them that we were vegetarian,' she said, as she straightened the table cloth for the umpteenth time. We still did not have any dining room furniture and so we had to entertain our first dinner guests in the kitchen. And since we didn't have half a dozen chairs Patsy and I were going to have to sit at the two ends of the table on upturned tea chests.

'I didn't really have an opportunity,' I said. I was busy looking through the classified advertisements at the back of the British Medical Journal to see if I could find another job.

Neither of us wanted to leave Bilbury but we were getting increasingly anxious about our future. I didn't want to work in Sherlock's brand new consulting room on his new estate and neither of us wanted Sherlock to get planning permission to turn Bilbury into a town. However, it had become quite clear that if Sherlock was turned away, then the practice I had inherited from Dr Brownlow would either have to be

171

merged with another practice in Barnstaple or else I would be forced to close down. And so, with Patsy's agreement, I had reluctantly started hunting for another job.

'What about this?' I said, reading out an advertisement. 'Thriving practice seeks fourth partner. Wonderful countryside within twenty minutes drive. Congenial companions. Modern, well equipped consulting rooms.'

'It sounds very good,' said Patsy. 'Where is it?'

'In the Midlands.'

'Oh,' said Patsy, being careful not to commit herself.

'There's some lovely countryside around there.'

'Yes.'

'It is a long way from the sea, though.' I pointed out.

'That's all right,' said Patsy bravely. 'I've always lived near to the sea. It will make a nice change.' I knew that she didn't mean it, but I didn't say anything. She stopped tidying the cutlery and turned to me. 'I don't mind where we go,' she said very seriously. She moved closer and reached out and touched my hand. 'As long as we're together it doesn't really matter.' I put down the journal, stood up and held her close. 'As long as we have some land for the lambs,' I said. 'And are quite a way from the road.' We knew of too many cats which had been run over and we wanted somewhere where Emily and Sophie would be safe.

I had just put an ink circle around the advertisement I'd read out when Patsy suddenly let out a small angry cry.

'What's the matter?'

'I meant to pick some watercress but I forgot.'

'Do you want me to pop down to Peter Marshall's shop to see if he's got any?' Peter Marshall never closes his shop. Even if the front door is shut he will happily open up to sell a box of matches.

'There's no need,' said Patsy. 'There's some growing in the stream.' She picked up a large plastic carrier bag, walked swiftly to the back door and then hesitated for a moment. 'Do you think it's going to rain?'

I walked over to where she was standing and looked up. The sky looked heavy. 'I don't know,' I said. 'Probably.' I sniffed the air as I'd seen Patsy's father do. 'But not for ten minutes. Come on – I'll come with you!'

172

We darted out of the back door, through the courtyard, over the fence, across the field and down to the stream. I hadn't seen any watercress growing, but Patsy had and she went straight to it. We picked a couple of large handfuls and stuffed them into the plastic bag and then started back towards the house. It was at that point that the heavens opened and the huge black cloud that had been hovering over Bilbury decided to jettison its load of water. I don't think I've ever seen water come down so quickly.

Patsy was dressed in the wedding dress I had bought for her at the auction, though it was impossible to recognise it as the same dress now that she had altered it. It looked beautiful. We darted back under a huge ash tree for temporary shelter. But the leaves only provided shelter for a moment or two and the rain soon started to come through.

'We're going to get soaked!' said Patsy. 'And I haven't got anything else nice to wear. Oh damn these people!'

I took the plastic bag from her, tipped the water cress out onto the ground and held it open. 'Quick!' I said. 'Take your dress off and put it in here.' Patsy didn't hesitate and a few seconds later her dress was wrapped in a roll at the bottom of the plastic bag.

'Now you!' said Patsy, taking the bag off me.

I hesitated for a moment.

'That's your only jacket,' she pointed out unnecessarily. 'And your only half decent trousers.'

I didn't need reminding twice. I took off my sports jacket, rolled it into a ball and stuffed it into the bag. Then I took off my shoes and trousers and socks and stuffed them in too. 'Take off your shoes,' I told her. Patsy took off her shoes and popped them into the bag. It was now almost full.

The rain was still streaming down. The only good thing was that it was at least quite warm. I twisted the top of the plastic bag to stop the rain getting in and picked up as much of the water cress as I could carry. 'We might as well take what we came for!'

Patsy picked up the rest of the water cress and together we ran back across the field and towards the house. The rain stopped as suddenly as it had started as we climbed gingerly over the fence onto the path leading back to the house.

We were about fifty yards from the coach-house when Patsy put a hand on my naked arm to stop me.

'What's the matter?'

'Sssshhhh! Look!'

I looked. The four Wakehams were clambering down the spiral staircase from the flat on the first floor. Mrs Wakeham, who was wearing high heeled shoes, came down first, treading very gingerly on the wet metal steps, her two daughters followed and her husband brought up the rear. I shivered involuntarily. The rain had been warm but now that it had stopped it felt quite cold. We crept towards the hedge on our right and watched in horror as each of them stepped off the spiral staircase and then strolled casually through the gateway and into the courtyard.

'Give me my dress!' whispered Patsy, covering as much of herself as she could with her hands.

'No one can see you!' I assured her. 'You need to dry off before you put your dress on.'

'But how are we going to get back into the house without being seen?' asked Patsy.

'We'll have to get in through the front!' I told her. 'Quick! Follow me.'

I ran along the track towards the coach-house but instead of turning in through the gate and into the courtyard I ran straight past. When I was safely past the gateway I looked behind me. Patsy, naked and shivering, was standing on the other side of the gateway.

'Come on!' I hissed.

'They might see me!' mouthed Patsy. I suddenly began to see the funny side of things and had to struggle not to laugh. I peered through the stone archway, into the courtyard. The Wakehams were walking slowly across the courtyard and had their backs towards us. I waved a furious hand beckoning Patsy to join me. She closed her eyes and ran across to where I stood.

'Did they see me?' she asked me, breathlessly, as I caught her in my arms.

'No. Come on!'

We hurried around to the front of the house and went straight to the front door. It was, inevitably, locked.

'I'm going to get dressed!' said Patsy. 'I don't care whether I ruin my dress or not.'

'No, you're not!' I said. 'Look, there's a window open upstairs.'

'But it's on the first floor. How on earth are you going to get in?'

'Easy!' I said. I pointed to a ladder that Thumper had left lying on the ground, bent down and manoeuvred it into position. Then I put the plastic bag containing our clothes on the ground and handed my watercress to Patsy. A few moments later I was climbing up the ladder.

I hate heights, but in an emergency it is astonishing what you can do.

Less than a minute later I was inside the house, with nothing more to show for my efforts than a rather large splinter in a very embarrassing place. I could hear someone banging on the back door and someone, I assumed it was Mr Wakeham, was shouting to try and attract our attention. I ran down the stairs, opened the front door and let Patsy in and then took the ladder away from the house and laid it back down on the ground. I didn't see why burglars should have things handed to them on a plate. I ran into the house and shot upstairs to our bathroom. Patsy was already drying herself and when she had finished I took the towel from her while she dressed.

Three minutes later I raced down into the kitchen just as Patsy opened the back door and ushered the Wakehams into the kitchen. 'I'm sorry,' I said. 'I hope you weren't waiting there long?' I pointed to my still wet and tousled hair. 'I was in the bath and it's impossible to hear anything up there.'

'Oh, that's all right!' said Mrs Wakeham with a sweet smile.

Mr Wakeham was clutching a bottle of wine wrapped in tissue paper. He was wearing a beige suit, a dark brown shirt and a light green tie. He had a matching green handkerchief neatly arranged in the breast pocket of his jacket and had been rather too generous with a particularly pungent after shave. Mrs Wakeham, who followed him into the kitchen, was wearing a plain, navy blue pleated skirt and a tight blue jumper which had glittering sequins embroidered across the chest in the shape of a peacock. She wore pearl earrings and

175

a pearl necklace and had had her hair permed. She smelt strongly of hairdressers. Behind them came their two daughters. Both wore knee length summer dresses, white cardigans and sandals; neither wore make up and both looked five years younger than they had when I had seen them earlier that day. I recognised Anthea only by the sullen look in her eyes and by the ring she wore on her right hand. I Wouldn't have recognised her sister at all and, for all I knew, she might have been a stand in.

'Get the corkscrew out!' said Mr Wakeham cheerily unwrapping the bottle of white Californian wine he had brought with him. 'It's been in the fridge so it's ready to drink.'

Patsy took our corkscrew out of the cutlery drawer and handed it to him. Mr Wakeham took the cork out and stood there holding the opened bottle. 'Have you got any glasses?'

'I'm sorry,' said Patsy, blushing. She glanced at me. We both suddenly realised that we didn't have any wine glasses.

'It'll have to be tumblers,' I apologised. I opened a cupboard and took out first our two drinking glasses and then our two coffee mugs. I handed the two drinking glasses to Mr Wakeham and then put the two mugs down on the table. 'Would your daughters mind using these?' I asked.

'Oh, good heavens they don't drink wine,' said Mr Wakeham, slightly shocked. He poured two inches of wine into the two drinking glasses. 'You have these,' he said indicating the two coffee mugs.' Have you got a couple of cans of something fizzy for the girls?'

Patsy opened the fridge and produced two cans of Coca Cola which she handed to the girls. They took them demurely. 'The girls both go to a convent school,' said Mr Wakeham. 'They get taught proper values.' He smiled at them but they didn't smile back.

'I've made pizza,' said Patsy. 'I'm afraid we don't eat meat.'

'Oh how sweet!' said Mrs Wakeham. 'You're vegetarians!'

'How do you make pizza without meat?' asked Mr Wakeham. He sounded genuinely puzzled.

'Cheese, mushrooms, tomatoes, onions,' said Patsy. She turned and opened the oven. 'They're ready to eat,' she said. 'If you don't mind sitting down?'

The four Wakehams sat down on our four chairs and Patsy

served up the pizzas and a huge bowlful of salad. For a few moments there was silence as everyone helped themselves. 'Oh darn it!' said Patsy suddenly. 'I left the watercress in the bathroom.'

Mr and Mrs Wakeham both looked at her.

'We keep it in the bath to make sure it's kept fresh!' I explained. 'It's a spare bath,' I added quickly. I stood up, excused myself and raced upstairs to retrieve the watercress. It had caused a lot of trouble I wasn't going to leave it there to go yellow.

'Dickie is very proud of our girls,' said Mrs Wakeham when I returned a few moments later with the water cress. 'Aren't you dear?'

Mr Wakeham, who had a mouthful of pizza nodded and hurried to finish so that he could speak. 'You have to know just how far you let your children go,' he said, warming to what was clearly one of his favourite subjects. 'They need some space to spread their wings, but they also need barriers so that they learn what's right and wrong.' He beamed at his two daughters who were giving a passable imitation of a pair of angels. Anthea glanced at me to see if I was about to say anything. I took a sip of the wine her father had brought. It tasted terrible.

'We sent our girls to a convent school so that they would get the same strong standards at school as at home,' said Mr Wakeham. 'There are too many schools where the children are allowed to do and say whatever they like.' He cut off a large piece of pizza, pierced it with his fork and popped it into his mouth. There was silence for a few moments while he chewed and then swallowed it. 'There are schools near us where girls no older than our two have got boyfriends and are off out every night to parties and pubs and heaven knows what else,' he said. He leant across the table towards me and pointed an empty fork in my direction. 'I've heard that there are some girls not much older than ours getting the contraceptive pill from doctors!' he said.

I looked across at Anthea and her sister. They both looked perfectly innocent. Anthea looked at me, defying me to say anything. 'I think you're embarrassing your daughters,' I said.

Mr Wakeham looked down the table. 'They know how I

feel about this,' he said. 'And they know I trust them.' He now stabbed his fork in their direction. 'Mind you,' he said, 'they know what would happen if they ever started behaving like that!'

'Would anyone like any more pizza?' asked Patsy, who was, of course, oblivious of the real significance of all this. Her offer was accepted with enthusiasm.

The Wakehams stayed for two hours and ate every piece of food we had in the house.

As they left one of the girls whispered furiously to her mother. Mrs Wakeham shook her head and said 'No.' The daughter whispered again.

'What's the problem?' Patsy asked, smiling and trying to be helpful.

'Oh, it's nothing!' said Mrs Wakeham. She seemed embarrassed. 'It's nothing at all.' She hesitated. 'It's just that Anthea ... ' she stopped. 'No, really. It doesn't matter ... '

'Go on ... ' said Patsy, encouragingly.

'Well, is there a nudist colony anywhere near here?'

'A nudist colony?' Patsy was blushing bright red. 'No. How odd. Why do you ask that?'

'Oh, Anthea thinks she saw two nude people running around in your garden,' said Mrs Wakeham, with an apologetic smile. 'But you know what young girls are like! Vivid imaginations!'

Patsy and I both smiled and agreed that young girls did sometimes have very vivid imaginations.

*   *   *

CHAPTER SIXTEEN

The next morning I wrote out a letter of application to the practice in the Midlands and posted it on my way to the surgery. Neither Patsy nor I wanted to leave Bilbury but we both knew that we had to think seriously about it.

'It'll be a challenge to move somewhere different.' Patsy lied.

'We'll find somewhere just as lovely as this,' I lied.

'It will probably turn out to be a blessing in disguise,' lied Patsy. 'These things often do.'

'We'll find another garden to restore,' I lied.

'And we'll find someone we like to love this house,' lied Patsy.

The truth was that we both knew we would never again find anywhere half as wonderful as Bilbury Grange. And we would certainly never be able to afford anything like it. We'd been lucky to buy the house fairly cheap because it had been run down and more or less derelict when we had found it. The chances of finding another house in a similar condition were remote indeed. And even if we did find somewhere we loved as much how would we cope without a Thumper to help us and to protect us from greedy or dishonest builders? I suddenly realised that I had made a lot of good friends in Bilbury. Frank and Gilly, Peter Marshall, Miss Johnson, Miss Phillips and Miss Tweedsmuir and Dr Brownlow.

I didn't know whether or not Sherlock Homes was going to get permission to build in Bilbury, but from what I had seen and heard I strongly suspected that they were going to succeed. And even if they failed to get the permission they wanted it looked increasingly as though my professional future in

Bilbury was limited. Whatever happened it now seemed certain that our stay at Bilbury Grange would be a short one.

* * *

'I missed two of my tablets the day before yesterday,' said Mrs Blossom. 'I went out to a friend's wedding in Bideford and completely forgot.' She looked tired and pale. Mrs Blossom was trying to cut down on her Angipax and I had warned her that she had to do it very slowly.

'What happened?' I asked her.

'I went all sweaty and I had this terrible panicky feeling,' said Mrs Blossom. 'I could hardly breathe and I had this awful headache.'

'How long did all that last for?'

'Most of the afternoon,' said Mrs Blossom. 'I had to get a friend to take me home early and when I got back and took a tablet the symptoms gradually disappeared.'

'How do you feel now?'

For a few moments Mrs Blossom didn't answer. 'Tired,' she said at last. 'Very tired.' She sounded tired and she spoke carefully and deliberately as though each word was an effort. She licked her lips carefully and held her head for a moment. She looked at me for a few moments and frowned as though suddenly trying to remember who I was. 'I'm very forgetful,' she said. 'Could that be the tablets?'

I nodded. 'It could be.'

'A friend showed me your article in the paper,' said Mrs Blossom. 'Is that all true?'

'Yes.'

There was a long silence. 'I can't explain it,' said Mrs Blossom. 'But I feel ... ' she paused again and licked her lips. 'I feel as though I am thinking through cotton wool.' There was another silence. 'My problems haven't gone away,' she told me. 'But somehow I can't be bothered even to think about them. And I know that's not helping me.'

'I'll help you,' I promised her. I reached out and touched her hand. Her skin felt dry and papery. 'I'll help you. But you must remember to come off the pills very slowly to minimise the withdrawal effects.'

*   *   *

Despite the fact that we did not know how much longer we would be able to remain in Bilbury or at Bilbury Grange we had arranged for the carpet fitters to come that day.

To anyone brought up in a town the phrase 'carpet fitters' usually implies a team of skilled workmen who are sent by a well established firm, and who arrive in a large and well-equipped van. We had arranged something rather different.

When we had decided that we could afford to clothe one or two of our naked floors Patsy told me that she knew of a man called Mr Liveridge who didn't have a shop but sold and delivered carpets to remote farms and outlying cottages. He had, she said, fitted carpets for her parents and they had been more than satisfied with his work. She had telephoned him (or, to be more precise, left a message with his sister at the tea rooms in Kentisbury) asking him to call round.

When he arrived that same evening we had explained that in due course we hoped to carpet the whole of the house, but that we would like to start with the reception hall, the living room and our bedroom. Since each of these three rooms had more floor area than the average cottage, the amount of carpet involved was not insubstantial and Mr Liveridge was enthusiastic. He was also able to offer us an extraordinarily low price.

Mr Liveridge had long grey hair pulled straight back over his head and tied into a pony tail with an elastic band. He wore luxuriant grey side whiskers, was in his mid 50s and had not always been in the carpet business. For the first thirty years of his life he had been a teacher of English Literature at a large comprehensive school in London. Then, in one fateful year, his wife had left him for a young woodwork teacher, his only daughter had married an electrician and moved to Australia and he had walked out of his job after a row with the school's twenty eight year old headmaster who wanted the works of popular paperback authors to be introduced into the syllabus.

Enraged by what he considered to be an unforgivable erosion of standards, Mr Liveridge had left his chalk-stained grey suits in London and headed west.

181

For three months he had lived with his sister in Kentisbury and then he had taken a job as a carpet salesman at a store in Barnstaple. When the store went into liquidation just nine months later he had decided to go into business for himself.

These days he travelled the countryside in an elderly coach which had been built back in the days when such vehicles were known as char-a-bancs. This one had all except the front two rows of seats removed to make way for the storage of lengths of carpet, carpet samples, tacks, hammers and the other impedimenta of his trade. A piece of old carpet had been used to partition off and turn into living quarters the back six feet of the coach. The side windows had been covered with white paint in order to convince the licensing authorities that the vehicle had been turned into a commercial vehicle. The outside of the coach, which still had WESTON S'MARE on its destination board, was painted pale blue, as it had been, I suspect, when it was still being used to carry passengers, but Mr Liveridge's deliberately illiterate slogan 'U-CHUZE' had been painted on the side in maroon. Underneath this had been added, in script, 'In the comfort of your own home' but, for some reason, Mr Liveridge, who had done his own sign writing had made his 'f's look like 's's so that the message looked more like 'In the comsort os your own home' and as a result Mr Liveridge was known to his customers first as Os and, later, as Ossie.

In the winter Mr Liveridge lived in a small flat in Ilfracombe. In the summer, when holiday-makers could afford to pay a higher rent than he could, he lived in the back of his converted char-a-banc.

When not selling, delivering or fitting carpets, Mr Liveridge wrote poetry and stories, and although he would occasionally allow his customers to read some of them, nothing he wrote was ever published for the very simple reason that he would never submit anything to an editor or publisher.

Before I left home for the surgery I helped Patsy tidy up and move our few belongings out of the way so that Mr Liveridge could lay his carpets without too much delay. The tidying up didn't take long. Apart from our bed and an old wardrobe we had virtually no furniture.

'Do you think it's silly?' asked Patsy.

182

'What?'

'Having carpets fitted when we don't even know for sure whether or not we are staying?'

'No!' I said firmly. 'If we do stay then it makes sense to have carpets laid before we start buying furniture and if we can't stay then the house will be more attractive to potential buyers if its got one or two carpets in it.' I had no evidence for this optimistic assumption but it cheered us both up a little, and because I liked him I desperately didn't want to have to tell Mr Liveridge that we didn't need his carpets after all. I took one last glance at our naked floors, kissed Patsy goodbye and left for work.

* * *

Miss Johnson came into the consulting room at the end of the morning surgery with a very worried look on her face. She had been subdued all morning and I knew that something was worrying her. She was normally the most self-contained and self-confident of people, but today she seemed strangely troubled.

'What's the matter?' I asked her, after inviting her to sit down. 'What's worrying you?'

'I don't really like to mention it,' apologised Miss Johnson. 'I'm not sure that it's really my place.'

'If it's worrying you and it involves me then you should certainly tell me about it,' I told her.

'It's just ... ' began Miss Johnson confidently; she faltered and then she took a deep breath and took her courage in both hands. 'It's just this business over those Sherlock building people.' She looked across at me and swallowed. 'Is it true what I've heard?'

'What have you heard?' I asked her, gently.

'People are saying that the Sherlock people are planning to build over a large part of Bilbury and to turn it into a town.'

'That's true,' I nodded.

'It's very unpopular in the village,' she said.

I nodded. But I knew that that wasn't all that she had come to say.

Miss Johnson looked down at her hands. Whatever else

183

it was that she wanted to say was clearly the difficult part.

'Go on,' I said quietly, trying to encourage her to speak.

'That isn't all,' she said, clearly prefacing something that she knew I wouldn't like to hear.

I leant forwards a little and rested my arms on the desk. But I didn't say anything else.

'I think you should know,' she began. 'I don't know whether it's true or not and it isn't really any of my business.' She paused and looked up at me. 'I hope you don't mind my mentioning it?'

'Mentioning what?' I asked her, quietly.

'They are saying that you've agreed to work for Mr Sherlock and that he's building you a new health centre on his new housing estate.' Miss Johnson looked straight at me and her eyes were full of sadness.

'It's true that Mr Sherlock has invited me to work in a new surgery on his estate,' I said. 'But I don't approve of his plans to expand the village and I won't be involved in any way.' I looked down at my desk. 'I'll do anything I can to help stop him,' I told her. 'I think that if he does get permission he will ruin Bilbury. It will change beyond all recognition. I know people need houses, and I know that the holiday homes will provide employment, but Bilbury is a community and I want to see it remain unchanged.' I felt embarrassed when I stopped speaking. 'I'm sorry,' I said. 'I hadn't intended to make a speech.'

Miss Johnson's eyes said everything. One moment they were full of fear, suspicion and apprehension. The next they were filled with happiness, relief and tears.

I didn't want to spoil what was clearly a happy moment for her. But I knew I had to tell her the whole truth now.

'Unfortunately, there is a problem,' I said.

Miss Johnson looked across at me and waited expectantly.

'I don't know whether it is simply because Mr Sherlock has a lot of power or whether it is just a coincidence,' I told her. 'But if the plans to expand Bilbury don't get the go ahead then I think it is very likely that this practice will have to close.'

Miss Johnson frowned. 'Close?' she said. 'Why?'

'The administrators have decided that, as it stands, the village is too small to have its own practice,' I told her.

'But Dr Brownlow ... ' began Miss Johnson.

'I know,' I said. 'Dr Brownlow had a practice here for years. They say that now that he has retired it's an opportune time to reorganise the medical cover in the area.'

'But they can't just close the practice down!' said Miss Johnson indignantly. 'What are the villagers going to do?'

'The administrators say that the village will be looked after by a practice in Barnstaple,' I told her. I paused. 'They've said that I can apply for a job there.'

'But ... what will happen to the surgery?'

'The surgery in Bilbury will close. Patients will have to go into the surgery in Barnstaple.'

'But that's ten miles!'

'I suppose that they might do a temporary surgery once a week in the village hall,' I said. 'That's how it sometimes works with villages which are looked after by town practices.' I shrugged sadly. 'That would be up to the senior partners in the practice involved.'

'Will you take the job in Barnstaple?' asked Miss Johnson.

'I don't think I'd get it even if I applied for it,' I told her.

'But surely Dr Brownlow would have some influence?'

'I don't think so,' I said. 'The senior partner in the practice is Dr Brownlow's son. Neither he nor I get on very well with him.' I paused again. 'I'm afraid I don't know what all this will mean for you,' I told her.

'Oh, don't worry about me,' said Miss Johnson quickly. 'I have a little inheritance and I can always take my pension.'

'But you'll miss the work ... '

'Of course,' agreed Miss Johnson. 'But I'll find something else to do.' She stopped for a moment and swallowed. I looked at her and saw that there were tears in her eyes. 'What will happen to you and Patsy?' she asked. 'The house and the garden and everything?'

I shrugged. 'I don't know,' I said. 'I'm afraid I just don't know.' I paused. 'But if by any chance we do manage to stay in Bilbury I'd very much like you to carry on working with me.'

'I'd love to,' said Miss Johnson. She looked puzzled. 'But doing what, exactly?'

'I've started getting a lot of mail from readers of my column,' I told her. 'I need some help replying to them.'

'Oh yes!' said Miss Johnson, smiling. 'That would be very nice! Oh yes. I'd like that very much.'

*   *   *

When I got home Mr Liveridge had finished laying the carpet in the living room and was busy laying the carpet in the reception hall. He worked alone but quickly. Patsy was warming up some soup and some home-made bread rolls. I went to ask Mr Liveridge if he wanted some.

'No!' he said firmly. 'That's very kind of you. But I've got my flask and sandwiches. I'll eat when I've finished the carpet in here.'

'It's looking great!' I told him. He was a good workman.

'Thank you,' he said.

I sat down on the floor beside him.

'Do you ever miss teaching?' I asked him suddenly.

He stopped what he was doing and looked at me. Then he resumed the hammer stroke he had interrupted and put another tack into place. 'Never,' he said firmly. I believed him.

I watched him for a few moments.

'I like what I do now,' he said after a while. 'At the end of a day I can see what I've done. I know I've done a good job. And because I always do the best I can, and always make sure that my customers are satisfied before I leave, everyone is happy.' He smiled at me. 'I don't get much hassle or many complaints,' he said. 'If anyone does ever complain I just ask them what they want me to do about it. And then I do it.'

'Did you enjoy teaching?' I asked him.

He thought for a while. 'I was in love with the idea of teaching,' be said. 'But most of the children I taught didn't want to learn. And I was constantly under pressure from the bureaucrats and the philistines.' He smiled at me. 'I ended up hating the job.' He carried on fitting the carpet. I sat and watched him until Patsy called me to tell me that the soup was ready.

186

*   *   *

After lunch I had an hour and a half free so I telephoned
Dr Brownlow and asked him to stand in for me while I drove
Patsy over to Barnstaple. We wanted to see whether any of
the things we'd bought in our tin bath job lot was worth
selling.

The salesman in the antique shop, a man in his early thirties
whose two most noticeable features were thick blond hair
and a carnation in his button hole, did not hide his disappointment when we told him that we weren't looking for anything
to buy but simply wanted to know whether one or two things
that we had brought with us were worth selling.

'Do you think this is silver?' asked Patsy, taking the little
photo frame out of her bag and handing it to him.

'No.' said the salesman bluntly after a cursory examination
of the frame. 'It's silver plate.' He handed it back to Patsy
with what I can only describe as a sneer.

'What about this?' said Patsy, taking out the teddy bear.

'It's a teddy bear,' said the salesman. He did not take the
bear and Patsy was left holding it out to him. After a few
moments she lowered her arm.

'But surely old teddy bears can be worth a lot of money,'
I said.

'Sometimes,' said the salesman. 'But that one isn't.'

Patsy put the bear away and took out the toy car.

'What about this?' she asked, hesitantly.

'Scrap,' said the salesman impatiently. He waved an imper-
ious hand. 'All junk my dear.' He was a nasty little man.
I wanted to hit him. We left quickly.

'Never mind,' I said. 'We can't win them all. But it's worth
looking. And who knows what we'll find next time?'

'It's not the fact that they aren't worth anything,' said Patsy.
'But he was so hateful!'

I put my arms around her. 'Do you want me to go back
and hit him?'

Patsy laughed. 'No!' she said. 'Of course not!'

'Then let's forget all about him,' I said.

'Let's go and see the cobbler about your Gladstone bag,'
said Patsy, cheering up. She led me down an alley I didn't

187

even know existed and into a tiny courtyard where there were just four small shops. One of them was a cobbler's.

The cobbler put the smile back onto both our faces. He greeted the bag like a long lost friend.

'Wonderful!' he said, clearly delighted. 'I haven't seen one of these for years.'

'Can you mend it?' asked Patsy.

'Of course I can,' said the cobbler. 'It'll be a pleasure!' He fondled the cracked leather with the eye and finger of a craftsman.

'The lock has completely broken,' said Patsy.

'I can mend it,' said the cobbler with certainty. He smiled at her. 'You won't recognise it when I've finished with it.'

'How much will it cost?' asked Patsy.

'No more than you can afford,' said the cobbler. He looked at us and must have seen the apprehension on our faces. 'It won't be more than £2.' he promised. He smiled as our looks of apprehension were replaced by looks of relief. 'I told you,' he said. 'It'll be a pleasure to work on it.'

He told us to call back for it in a few days time. We left his shop with smiles on our faces and a bounce in our steps and walked hand in hand to a tea shop in Bear Street which made wonderful cakes and served large cinnamon scones smothered in butter.

*   *   *

When we got back to Bilbury Grange the carpet fitter had finished. He had done a wonderful job. It was starting to get late, but when Patsy called the cats in for their tea only Sophie appeared. Emily, our cute young mixed tabby with the pure white paws and the soft, faraway beguiling look in her eyes, didn't come.

'Don't worry,' said Patsy, who could see that I was worried. 'She's probably out hunting and too busy to come back for tea.'

I knew she was probably right. But it didn't stop me worrying.

*   *   *

CHAPTER SEVENTEEN

I woke up at six the following morning desperately hoping to find Emily asleep alongside us. Sophie was there, curled up by Patsy's feet, but of Emily there was no sign.

I climbed quietly out of bed, hoping that I could do so without waking Patsy. Sophie pricked up her ears and opened one eye.

'Is she back?' murmured Patsy, still half asleep.

'No.'

Patsy sat up and opened her eyes. Sophie jumped down off the the bed and sat, expectantly, on the floor. I drew the curtains and opened the window and blinked at the bright morning sunshine. Normally the view from our bedroom never failed to fill me with wonder and admiration but this morning I just peered out looking to see if I could see any sign of Emily. I saw a rabbit hopping along one of the paths and there were birds sitting and twittering on trees and bushes everywhere. I dressed quickly in shorts and a short sleeved shirt for since it was a Saturday morning I did not have to go to the surgery until an hour later than usual.

'Where do you think she can be?' asked Patsy. She too had dressed quickly in shorts and a short sleeved shirt, but the effect on her was far more dazzling. Her legs, arms and face had already been burned a rich, even brown by a summer sun which had also bleached her hair an even lighter shade of blonde. Her short white shorts and white shirt contrasted strongly with the brown of her body.

'I'm going to go through every room in the house and all the outbuildings,' I said. 'She might have got herself shut in somewhere.' I had checked everywhere the night before

189

but she could, I still hoped, have got herself shut in and fallen asleep somewhere.

'Maybe we should check the coach-house flat,' suggested Patsy. 'She could have wandered in there.'

'I'll have a look,' I said. 'But I don't think she would go in there.' Our two young kittens had already developed clearly defined personalities. Sophie liked people and would rub herself up against any pair of human legs. But Emily was shy and nervous and usually ran away and hid if she heard footsteps or voices that she didn't recognise. I didn't think for a moment that she would willingly have gone into the flat with a party of complete strangers.

'You do the cellars and the outbuildings,' said Patsy. 'I'll do inside the house.'

So we split up for our search.

The cellars, which were as always a cool and dark refuge from the bright summer sunshine (I had noticed that the temperature down there never seemed to change whatever the weather outside was doing, and understood at last why cellars were regarded as such a good place to store wine) took quite a long time to search because there were lots of small and secret places where a kitten could hide. I was worried that if Emily had injured herself she might have crawled into a dark corner in the way that animals do when they are ill. By the time I'd finished down there and had emerged, covered in dust and cobwebs, Patsy had just finished searching the house. Neither of us had had any luck at all.

Patsy came outside to help me search the outbuildings.

The sun was still low but it was bright and the day was clearly going to be warmer even than its predecessors, but to us it seemed flat, grey and glum. All we could think of was the fact that Emily could be lying somewhere frightened, cold, injured, hungry and alone. She had stolen our hearts since she had come to live with us and neither of us could bear the thought of her being in any sort of distress.

In one of the stables, the one where I kept the lawn mower, we found that a pair of swallows had built a nest where two cross beams met. I hadn't noticed it before. The tails of two baby swallows were sticking out over the sides of the neatly made nest and we closed the door of the stable quietly so as not to disturb them. I didn't know how they'd been getting in and out but there wasn't any point in leaving the stable door open now for they clearly had an entrance and exit of their own.

By the time we had finished searching the outbuildings around the courtyard nearly an hour had passed.

Patsy put her hand in my mine as we walked together out of the courtyard calling Emily's name. 'I thought we'd have found her by now,' she said. 'I keep having this vision of her lying somewhere cosy and comfortable and looking so pleased to see us.'

I knew what she meant. Every time I had opened a door, peered behind a pile of rubbish or looked into a dark corner I had been convinced that I would see Emily there.

'Let's try the vegetable garden,' said Patsy suddenly. 'She might be somewhere in there.' We both knew that she loved the walled garden because it was sheltered and warm and yet full of shady spots.

As we walked into the walled garden we both heard it at the same moment: a faint yet unmistakeably plaintive miaowing that was coming from the direction of the greenhouse.

We ran along the broad, hard dusty paths that lay between the ornamental brickwork which bordered the flower and vegetable beds, towards the greenhouse. Patsy got there first and pulled open the door. It creaked and grated and protested for its hinges needed oiling and the door had slipped an inch or so and was scraping on the flagstones which made up the floor.

Emily, who was sitting on a pile of old thick, brown, paper, compost sacks piled in a corner of the greenhouse, stretched a leg when she saw us and miaowed even more loudly than before. It was a miaow of pleasure and protest: pleasure at seeing us and protest at the fact that she had spent the night locked in. Judging by the indentation made on the sacks she had spent the night sleeping in that very same place.

Patsy went over to her and picked her up. Emily snuggled against her chest and purred loudly, rubbing her head against Patsy's shirt. I stroked her neck and she held her head so that I could tickle her under her chin. She purred even more loudly.

'How on earth do you think she got locked in?' asked Patsy.
'I shut the door yesterday evening,' I said guiltily. 'But I didn't see her in here then.' I looked around and then found another kitten shaped indentation on a pile of straw underneath a length of wooden staging that ran the whole length of the greenhouse. Emily must have been sleeping under there out of the sun and out of sight when I had gone out to the vegetable garden to water the plants and shut up the greenhouse.

'I'm sorry, Emily!' I said. She purred at me and reached out with a white paw to touch my arm. It was as though she was telling me that everything was all right and that she forgave me.

'Let's get you back to the house,' murmured Patsy to Emily. 'I bet you're hungry.'

'I bet she is!' I agreed.

I suddenly realised that I was hungry too. We'd been searching for Emily for over an hour and I hadn't yet had any breakfast. I felt as happy as I had felt sad an hour or so earlier.

*   *   *

Our new set of paying guests arrived that morning and by the time I arrived back from the morning surgery they were settled into the flat and had spread themselves over much of the courtyard too.

Mr and Mrs Onions ('pronounced oh-ny-ans' insisted Mr Onions the moment we met) had driven from London in their BMW motor car, and although they had only booked in for a week's holiday they seemed to have brought enough to last them three months. Patsy said that she'd been in the kitchen when they had arrived and she had seen Mr Onions carry at least eight suitcases up the spiral staircase to the flat. She said that the back of the car as well as the boot had been filled with luggage and that they had carried their largest cases on their roof rack. Diving equipment, golf clubs, riding boots and capes and tennis racquets in profusion were stacked neatly against the walls at the entrance to the courtyard.

When Mr Onions came to knock on the back door Patsy and I were just finishing a quick salad lunch before going out to spend the afternoon in the garden.

'Nice place you've got,' said Mr Onions. 'We've got friends in Cornwall who've got a house rather similar to this.' He paused and looked around critically at the peeling paint and the cracks in the mortar on the outside of the house. 'Of course,' he added, 'their house is in much better condition.' He looked around again and turned to his wife. 'Much better, isn't it?'

'Oh definitely,' agreed Mrs Onions.

Mr Onions, who was rather plump faced and portly was wearing a beige safari suit with a cream shirt and a paisley muffler, and looked as though he was in his late twenties. His wife, who was as thin as a stick insect was wearing a spotless white dress with a plunging neckline and no back, and looked a few years younger. She was clearly not wearing a bra and yet her breasts seemed suspended in mid air. I suspected the influence of silicone.

'Well, I hope you have a nice stay here,' I said, after what had threatened to be an embarrassing silence.

'Would you like to come in for a cup of tea?' asked Patsy.

'That's very kind of you,' smiled Mrs Onions sweetly. She didn't wait to see what her husband said but stepped past me into the kitchen. She wore white patent leather shoes with the highest heels I'd ever seen and they click clacked noisily on our floor. Mr Onions followed her quickly as though half afraid that we might change our minds. He saw Sophie asleep on a cushion on one of our chairs. Emily, always the nervous kitten, who had spent the morning staying as close to Patsy as she could, had run out of the kitchen into the hall and then upstairs the moment she had heard voices outside the back door.

'Oh,' he said. 'A cat.'

'That's Sophie,' I said.

'I don't like cats very much,' said Mr Onions. 'They bring on my asthma.'

'Oh, I'm sorry to hear that.' I said.

Sophie leapt down off the chair and walked over to Mr Onions. She began to brush against his legs. He recoiled as though she was a cobra.

'I'll put her outside,' I said. I didn't really like doing it since it was more Sophie's kitchen than Mr Onions' but I felt my responsibility as a landlord. I picked Sophie up and slipped her through the door into the hall. Then I shut the door.

'Earl Grey tea with lemon, please,' said Mrs Onions as Patsy put the kettle on. 'You have got that, haven't you?'

Patsy blushed. 'I'm afraid we've only got this,' she said, holding up a pack of a well-known proprietary brand of tea. She looked at me and then back at Mrs Onions. 'And I'm afraid I don't have any lemon.'

'Oh,' said Mrs Onions, looking rather shocked. 'We always keep at least half a dozen kinds of tea, don't we Simon?'

Mr Onions agreed that they did. 'I expect it's difficult to get much variety out here,' he said. 'Though you could always have groceries brought in specially.'

'Our friends in Cornwall have all their groceries posted down from Harrods,' said Mrs Onions. 'They say it's the only way they can live down there.'

'Will ordinary tea be all right?' asked Patsy. She sounded rather sad and embarrassed and I felt angry with the Onions.

'Oh yes, it'll do for now,' said Mrs Onions, somehow managing to sound even more patronising than she had before.

'Did you have a good drive down?' I asked Mr Onions.

'Very good,' replied our guest. 'Three hours twenty minutes.'

'That's very good,' I agreed.

'I've got the new 3 lire fuel-injected model,' said Mr Onions. 'I like to change my car every two years but I always stick with BMW.' He raised an eyebrow. 'What do you drive?'

'A Morris Minor,' I said. 'Convertible.' I added.

Mr Onions did not seem impressed by this. 'I suppose you find that convenient for the lanes,' he said.

'It's really all I can afford,' I said. 'But yes it is very convenient.'

'Have you got anywhere we can store our things?' asked Mr Onions. 'We've got some rather valuable sporting equipment out there and there isn't room in the flat.' He looked at me and smiled but it wasn't really a smile. 'It's rather smaller than we expected.'

'You can put it into one of the barns,' I said. 'I'll clear

194

out some space for you.'

'Is it secure?'

'Oh yes.' I said. 'I should think so.'

'Simon has just bought some new golf clubs,' said Mrs Onions. 'They cost over £300.'

'Gosh.' I said. 'That seems a lot. I didn't think golf clubs cost that much!' I frowned. 'In fact I'm sure I saw some in a shop in Barnstaple that were much less than that.'

'Oh you can buy cheap ones,' said Mrs Onions. 'But these have rather fancy shafts and they're endorsed.' She mentioned the name of a golfer who had apparently just won a major trophy.

'Ah.' I said, not really understanding how that could make a set of golf clubs worth so much more.

'Tea's ready,' said Patsy. She handed Mr and Mrs Onions mugs of tea. 'Do either of you take sugar?'

Mrs Onions looked at the mug she had been handed and was now holding in two immaculately manicured hands. 'Good heavens!' she said. 'I don't think I've ever drunk tea out of anything quite like this before.' She giggled nervously. 'I don't think I can hold it,' she said. Her husband reached across, took the mug from her and put it down on the kitchen table. He then took a sip from his mug, grimaced and put it down too.

'Perhaps you'd be kind enough to show us where we can store our things, then?' said Mr Onions, standing up. 'I don't like leaving them out in the open longer than necessary.'

'It'll be quite safe!' said Patsy. 'We don't have any thieves around here.'

Mr Onions looked at her pityingly. 'There are thieves everywhere,' he said severely.

I followed the two of them outside and then found them a place in one of the stables where they could store their sporting equipment. Mr Onions insisted that the stable be locked so I had to drive down to Peter Marshall's shop to buy a padlock and chain.

* * *

We spent the rest of the day in the garden.

First, we weeded the strawberries, the lettuce and the other

195

crops we'd sown. Then we continued clearing away the brambles and nettles, though for this we had to go indoors and change into thicker clothes. We were both soon soaked with sweat. I lit a huge bonfire and the heat and smoke from that made us even hotter.

When the thunderstorm came at a few minutes after five o'clock we were, I think, both secretly pleased. Apart from cooling us down, it also gave us a good excuse to stop. We had only been gardening for about three hours but we were both absolutely exhausted. We went into the house and slumped onto chairs in the kitchen. Patsy had made a pitcher of orange juice and we emptied it completely in just a few minutes. I was leaning back on my chair, with my bare feet resting on the edge of the table when suddenly my chair slipped and I crashed backwards into the wall.

'Are you all right?' cried Patsy, rushing over to help me up.

'I'm fine!' I said. I looked around. 'But the wall isn't!' I said, extricating my elbow from the hole it had made in what we had both thought was a solid wall.

We both looked at the hole.

The wall that my elbow had penetrated was merely a sheet of hardboard that had been covered in wallpaper and then painted white to match the rest of the kitchen.

'I wonder what's behind it?' said Patsy. 'What do you think they covered up?'

'It's probably just an alcove.' I said. I poked my fingers into the hole I'd made and could feel nothing but space. I looked around the kitchen, could see nothing useful and slipped outside into the courtyard. Moments later I returned with a short pea stick I'd found. I poked the cane through the hole, expecting to reach a solid wall within a few inches. But the cane just kept on disappearing. 'There's an enormous hole!' I said, astonished.

'Let's see what's there!' said Patsy, excitedly.

I looked at the hardboard wall and then at the rest of the kitchen. We still hadn't decorated the kitchen so it didn't really matter very much if we made a mess. And once we had decorated we would never find out what was hidden behind the hardboard partition wall.

'O.K!' I said. I poked a couple of fingers through the existing hole and pulled. A huge piece of thin hardboard came away in my hand and I could see that it had been nailed onto a wooden frame. It took no more than two or three minutes to strip away enough of the hardboard to make a hole big enough to climb through. Patsy handed me the torch that she'd fetched from a cupboard by the back door and I crept through the hole into a large alcove.

'What's there?' called Patsy, peering through the hole behind me.

'An oven!' I said. 'A huge old oven.'

Patsy climbed through the hole in the hardboard and joined me.

'It's an Aga!' she said.

We gazed in astonishment at the huge old stove that had been boarded up. It was covered in dust and there were massive spider's webs hanging all around it.

'Do you think it will work?' I asked Patsy, rather doubtfully.

'Of course it will!' said Patsy without a moment's hesitation. 'There's isn't anything not to work. They're wonderful!' She sounded really excited and put an arm around my waist and hugged me. She looked up at me and her eyes were sparkling. 'You just wait!' she said, laughing. 'My mum's got one of these and I learnt to cook on it. You wait until you taste my bread and my rock buns!'

I hugged her back, brushed a wisp of hair away from her face and then lowered my head and kissed her softly on the lips. 'Have I told you yet today how much I love you?'

'Yes!' nodded Patsy. 'But I don't mind you telling me again.'

*   *   *

It took me less than half an hour to rip down the rest of the partition which had separated the stove from the rest of the kitchen. I piled up the broken pieces of hardboard in the courtyard and stacked the wooden laths in a corner of one of the stables where I had started to store bits and pieces of useful fire wood.

When we had bought Bilbury Grange I had been surprised at the amount of junk that had been stored in the barns, stables and outhouses. Much of it we had burned or thrown out. I had filled a skip with old chimney pots, unsorted lengths of wire, leaky wellington boots, bald tractor tyres, pieces of broken sewer pipe, neatly tied bundles of newspapers and magazines, empty paint cans, wooden apple boxes, lengths of half perished rubber hose, empty fertiliser and feed bags, panes of glass and empty wine bottles. But now those same barns, stables and outhouses were groaning again with our own variety of rubbish. When the roofers had taken off the old worm-ridden battens and replaced them with new, pressure treated timbers I had begun to throw the old battens onto our constantly burning bonfire but Thumper had stopped me. He had pointed out that if we broke up the battens into short, two foot lengths and then stored the short pieces of dry wood in an outhouse they would make excellent fire-lighting fodder. I had learned that in the country everything – however worthless it may seem to be – has its use. Old chimney pots can be used to force rhubarb. An old and rather rusty water tank made an excellent garden incinerator. Old seed sacks can be used to store potatoes. Leaky garden hose can be used to water plants in several parts of the garden at once and old newspapers can be converted into compost.

Even I could not think of a use for broken pieces of hardboard. But the wooden framework to which they had been nailed clearly were worth keeping. With nine working fire places Bilbury Grange was going to need a lot of fuel to keep it warm in winter.

By the time I had finished clearing away the useless broken hardboard and storing the useful wooden laths Patsy had finished removing most of the cobwebs and the worst of the dust and our new, enlarged kitchen had begun to look much more respectable.

Patsy said that she wanted to give the Aga a final clean so I said I would go upstairs and start running a couple of baths full of hot water. My clothes were filthy dirty so I stripped in the kitchen and put my jeans, shirt, socks and underpants straight into the washing machine. I left my shoes standing by the back door and tiptoed upstairs naked.

The twin cast iron baths in the bathroom next to our bedroom were both huge and they were fed by massive brass taps through which water gushed at a rate of several gallons a minute. These were no ordinary taps. These taps were well over an inch across at the point where the water came out. Even on a warm day water from the cold tap was icy. It would, I suppose, have been nice if water from the hot tap had poured out amidst scalding clouds of steam. But, rather disappointingly, it didn't. Our hot water was provided by an electric immersion heater which struggled to cope with the huge hot water tank. As I waited for the two baths to fill I wondered if our newly discovered Aga could be plumbed into the hot water system.

I went to fetch two towels from the airing cupboard above the hot water tank on the landing but decided that if I waited until Patsy came up stairs the towels would stay warmer for longer. I love drying myself on a new fluffy, warm towel. It is, I think, my favourite luxury.

A couple of minutes later, I turned off the four taps and clambered into one of the baths. I'd done a lot of work and every muscle in my body seemed to ache. A shower may be the most efficient, refreshing and hygienic way to cleanse the human body, but a hot bath is much, much more than a way of washing off the dirt. A hot bath is a chance to return to the womb for a few minutes.

I was floating on my back in the bath relaxing in the warm water, with just my face and my toes above water, when I heard a muffled shout from somewhere below me. With a splash I lowered my body and raised my head. I shook the water from my ears and listened again. I could hear Patsy calling my name. I shouted back to ask her what the trouble was but heard her shout get louder as she came closer. Moments later she burst into the bathroom. She had clearly finished cleaning the Aga for she too had taken off most, but not quite all, of her clothes.

'There's a ... phone call ... for you!' she said, rather out of breath through having run up the stairs.

'Oh damn!' I said, rather uncharitably. 'What's wrong?' I had assumed that the caller was a patient and that I would have to abandon my bath.

'It isn't a patient,' said Patsy. 'It's a doctor.'

'A doctor?' I frowned. I couldn't think why a doctor should be ringing me at home.

199

'He said his name was Dr Robinson,' said Patsy. 'He said you'd know what it was about.'

I racked my brains trying to remember who Dr Robinson was. And then I remembered that Dr Robinson was the senior partner in the practice in the Midlands.

'It's the job!' I cried, leaping out of the bath onto the cold linoleum. Apart from the two baths, a wooden towel rail and a single, blue painted wooden chair, the bathroom was empty. There were lace curtains hanging over the windows on a wire and the floor was covered in a thin, cracked layer of green and blue patterned linoleum but that was about it. I instinctively jumped about as my feet hit the cold floor. Drops of water flew in all directions, leaving puddles everywhere. I looked around for a towel but couldn't see one and then remembered that I hadn't fetched them from the airing cupboard.

'The job in the Midlands?' asked Patsy, following me as I headed for the bathroom door, leaving clear wet footprints on the floor.

'Yes!' I cried, over my shoulder. In my heart I didn't really want thejob. I didn't want even to think about leaving Bilbury. But I didn't seem to have a lot of alternative employment possibilities to contemplate. Still naked and dripping I hurried down the stairs and into the reception room where our old fashioned black Bakelite telephone sat in solitary splendour on an upturned packing case. I could hear Patsy running along the landing above me and wondered where she had gone.

I picked up the telephone receiver. 'I'm sorry to have kept you,' I apologised, hoping that the caller hadn't got fed up and cut the connection.

'Oh, hello,' murmured Dr Robinson. He told me his name. He had a distinctive public school drawl which I found vaguely annoying.

'I was in the bath,' I explained, still rather breathless. I half turned my head as I heard Patsy coming down the stairs, looked up and saw that she was carrying a bath towel in her hand. She saw me and suddenly started to giggle. I looked up at her and raised an eyebrow. I didn't see why she was giggling. I was shivering.

'We'd like you to come for an interview,'said Dr Robinson

'On Wednesday at noon.'

'Oh!' I said, surprised. 'Thank you.'

'You do have a wife, don't you?' He made the word 'wife' sound like a possession. A chromium plated, deluxe accessory.

'Oh yes.' I replied. My beautiful young wife was sitting on the stairs above me dressed only in her very revealing underwear. She was laughing so much that she had to stuff a corner of the towel into her mouth. I still didn't know why she was laughing but it was infectious and I was having difficulty in keeping a straight face.

'Can you bring her with you? We'd like to meet her. There isn't any need for her to dress up in anything formal. Just ask her to come as she is.'

'Certainly,' I agreed. I had to bite the inside of my cheek quite hard to stop myself from giggling. I wondered if Dr Robinson would have been so keen to meet us both if he had been able to see us at that moment. I just managed to stop myself laughing for long enough to say 'goodbye' and to remember to thank Dr Robinson for the invitation. The moment I put the telephone receiver down I burst out laughing.

When she saw that I had finished on the telephone Patsy pulled the towel out of her mouth and rushed down to throw it around my shoulders.

'I'm sorry!' she apologised, controlling herself for an instant. 'But you looked so funny standing there in the nude talking so seriously on the telephone.' She stood in front of me like a naughty school girl and then burst out laughing again.

'We've got an interview,' I told her. 'On Wednesday.' I paused. 'Dr Robinson says there's isn't any need for you to dress up. You can come as you are.' Patsy looked down at herself and the giggling got so bad that we both had to sit down on the floor.

It was several minutes before we climbed back up the stairs to the bathroom and by then the water in our twin baths had gone quite unpleasantly tepid. Washing ourselves in cool water soon put a temporary stop to our jolly mood.

*　⹊　*

CHAPTER EIGHTEEN

Mr Yardley had a broken nose.

'What on earth happened to you?' I asked him, carefully examining his fractured and misshapen proboscis. There was dried blood all over him; on his face, on his shirt and on his jacket.

Mr Yardley looked embarrassed and clearly didn't want to tell me.

'Ith werry dithiculk do breeth,' he told me. 'Cad you do somefink adoud id?'

I told him I would have to arrange for him to see someone at the hospital. 'Your nose needs surgery,' I told him. 'But the doctors at the hospital will want to know how you did it.'

'I hid id,' said Mr Yardley suddenly.

I stared at him for a moment. '*You* hit it?'

He nodded.

'Why?'

'Do make id dweed.'

I decided that although, on the surface, the conversation seemed to be taking a distinctly surrealistic turn there was a certain almost acceptable logic in it all. After all, 'To make it bleed.' seemed as sensible an answer as one could expect to the question: 'Why did you hit yourself on the nose?'

'I didn'd mead do hid id thad hard,' explained Mr Yardley, clearly noticing my surprise. 'I didn'd thing id would dreak.'

'No,' I agreed. 'Of course not.' I stared at him for a few moments. 'But why,' I asked him slowly, 'did you want to make it bleed?'

Mr Yardley looked hurt as well as puzzled. 'I didn'd wand

do dake dose dills you dave me,' he explained. 'Bud you said thad if I made id dweed thad would brink de pressure down.'

'Why didn't you want to take the pills I gave you?' I asked him.

'You said dey could addect my sex life,' replied Mr Yardley instantly and rather indignantly.

I nodded. 'But it's a fairly uncommon side effect,' I said. 'It doesn't happen to everyone.' I looked at him in amazement. He did not look like a man to whom an active sex life was a vital ingredient of life. 'Did it affect you?' I asked him.

He shook his head firmly. 'Oh do,' he said. He wet his lower lip with a tongue which was covered in a thick brown fur and which looked as if it needed Hoovering. 'Bud I didn't wand do dake thad risk.'

I resisted the instinctive temptation to recoil, raised a questioning eyebrow and waited.

'Id's twendy dree years since I had,' he paused and winked, 'you know.' He winked again to make sure that I understood and then wet his upper lip. 'Bud you neder know when id's going do be your luddy day do you?'

I just stared at him. 'So you hit yourself on the nose?'

He nodded.

'What with?'

'A dlick.'

'You hit yourself on the nose with a brick to make yourself bleed so that your blood pressure would come down?'

He smiled at me, rather proudly.

'And you didn't want to take the blood pressure pills I prescribed because even though you haven't had sex for twenty three years you were worried that they might make you impotent?'

Mr Yardley smiled. 'Thad's id!' He nodded, clearly pleased that I understood.

I wasn't so sure that I did understand, but I knew that I would enjoy writing the referral letter which I would have to give Mr Yardley to take with him to the hospital.

*   *   *

'I really don't want to leave Bilbury,' I explained to Dr Brownlow. 'Neither of us do. But things are looking pretty

203

glum. It looks as if Sherlock has got this fellow Perkins in his pocket.'

Dr Brownlow was sitting in his greenhouse tending to his tomato plants and I don't think I had ever seen him look quite so miserable.

'I feel really bad,' he said. 'If I'd known all this was going to happen I wouldn't have dreamt of offering you the practice.'

'Oh, please don't think that!' I said. 'If you hadn't I probably wouldn't have had the nerve to ask Patsy to marry me and I certainly wouldn't have bought Bilbury Grange.' I looked straight at him. 'I've got no regrets,' I told him. 'Nor has Patsy.' It was true, too. Neither of us had any regrets. We had shared a dream and we had, for a few magical months, lived our dream.

'But if you have to leave you'll have to sell up,' Dr Brownlow pointed out.

'I know. But at least we had a try ... ' I shrugged and tried to sound as if it didn't really matter too much, but it did, and I don't think I hid it very well. I had hesitated about telling Dr Brownlow the truth about what was happening in the village largely because I knew that he would feel guilty, as if it was somehow his fault, but now I could no longer keep the secret from him. I had to tell him that I was going up to the Midlands for a job interview at another practice. Apart from it being the courteous thing to do (I didn't want him to find out from someone else) I could only go if he would look after the patients for me for the day.

'I feel sorry for you and I feel sorry for the villagers,' said Dr Brownlow. 'And if the truth be known I feel sorry for myself too.'

I looked at him.

'I've heard these rumours about expanding the village,' he told me. 'I hoped they weren't true.' He shrugged. 'If that fellow Sherlock gets his way ... ' He shook his head.

'The new houses shouldn't interfere too much with you,' I told him. 'They're planning to build on the other side of the village.'

'They'll put me out of business,' said Dr Brownlow firmly. 'If they build all those new houses they'll need more water. And they're bound to put a compulsory purchase order on my underground supply. It would provide the whole village with water.'

We neither of us spoke for a few moments.

'I'm sorry,' I said at last. 'I hadn't even thought of that.'

Dr Brownlow shrugged. 'If I was younger I'd fight them,' he said. 'But ... ' He waved a hand around weakly and left the sentence unfinished. He put down his watering can. 'It's you and Patsy I really feel sorry for.'

'Don't,' I said. 'We'll survive.'

'I know you will.'

'I don't want to run away,' I said. 'But I've got to think about looking after Patsy.' I swallowed. 'If I agree to stay the village will be ruined and I don't think I'll be able to live with myself. So that's out. And if I oppose the new plans to expand the village they'll close down the practice and I'll be out of a job.' I shrugged and tried to laugh. 'It isn't a great choice ... '

'I know,' said Dr Brownlow softly. He reached out and touched the back of my hand. 'Go up to Birmingham or wherever it is on Wednesday,' he said. 'Of course, I'll look after the practice for you.'

'Thank you.'

'And good luck,' said Dr Brownlow. He looked me directly in the eye. 'I really mean that,' he said. 'I'm sad that you can't stay here in Bilbury. But I do wish you well.'

I could feel tears forming in my eyes and I had to leave him quickly. I didn't even manage to say 'thank you.'

*   *   *

When I got back home Patsy had lit the Aga. The heat from it hit me as I walked into the house.

'Phew!' I said, taking off my jacket and tie and hanging them over the back of a chair. 'Isn't it a bit early for this?'

'I wanted to see if it worked properly,' Patsy explained.

'Does it?'

She nodded. 'It's brilliant!' she told me. 'And it does heat our hot water.' She crossed the kitchen to the sink and turned on the hot tap. 'Look!' There was a rumbling noise from somewhere else in the house and then, in a great rush, steam and boiling hot water burst out of the tap and splashed down into the sink. I had to dilute an inch of hot water with six inches of cold before I could bear to dip my hands into the sink to wash them.

'No more tepid baths?'

'No more tepid baths!'

'Does the oven work?'

'Ovens!' said Patsy, correcting me. 'There are two of them. And, yes, they both work.' She waved a hand towards the table. 'Sit down.'

I sat down and she brought me a wonderful piping hot potato and vegetable pie that she had made. For pudding she had prepared a gooseberry pie. When I told her that I hadn't ever eaten better cooking I wasn't exaggerating. I couldn't remember ever seeing Patsy look so pleased.

'Aren't you lucky!' she said, smiling. 'Some women get turned on by diamonds. Some want fur coats. All you have to give me to make me happy is an Aga cooker.'

I was delighted to see her so happy, but I couldn't forget the fact that in two days we were driving up to the Midlands and that if I got the job I had applied for the Aga would be just another Bilbury memory.

*   *   *

I went outside afterwards, intending to cut the lawns. But the young swallows were still sitting in their nest in the stable where I kept the mower. I didn't want to frighten them by starting up the mower so I left it where it was. The grass would have to wait a while. I cared far more about the swallows than about having neatly manicured lawns.

*   *   *

At eight o'clock that evening Patsy and I attended the meeting in the Bilbury Village Hall to discuss Mr Sherlock's proposed development in the village.

Ever since the proposal had become public knowledge conversation in the village shop and the Duck and Puddle had centred around little else. When Patsy and I arrived at five to eight the hall was bursting at the seams, and from the atmosphere in the hall it was clear that everyone in the village had strong views about the proposal. I could see Thumper and Anne, Dr Brownlow, Peter Marshall, Miss Johnson, Patsy's father Mr Kennett, Gilly from the Duck and Puddle and Kay the district nurse.

On the stage at the far end of the village hall a man and a woman sat on folding wooden chairs behind a wooden trestle table with a rather murky carafe of water and a single grubby looking glass in front of them.

The woman was Miss Turner, a retired school mistress and sportswoman who, despite the fact that she neither lived in nor had any great contact with the village, was now our official representative on the county council. She was well into her seventies; she wore a grey tweed suit, and was as tall and as rigid in her thinking as she was in her posture. More importantly, she was also a member of the planning committee which seemed enthusiastic about Mr Sherlock's proposals. I suspected that she was keen on the new eighteen hole golf course he was planning.

The man was Mr Rutter, a rotund and likeable sheep farmer who owned fifty or sixty acres of land and rented another couple of hundred acres in and around the village. Mr Rutter, the father of five beautiful teenage daughters, was chairman of our local parish council. He wore, as he always did, the greasy peaked flat cap that he wore whatever the weather and almost wherever he was. I had once visited at home when he was suffering from a bad back during the lambing season and I'd found him in bed still wearing his cap. The only time I had seen him without it he had been in church at the funeral of an old friend.

Mr Rutter began the meeting by banging his fist on the table and very nearly upsetting the water carafe.

'You all know why you're here,' he said gruffly. 'It's this development they're planning.' Mr Rutter didn't believe in beating about the bush and although his honest and straightforward manner meant that he had no chance of ever succeeding in big time local politics he was immensely popular among the villagers. 'This fellow Sherlock wants to build a housing estate and holiday homes in the village. We have to decide whether or not we want it. I think we should have a vote.'

'Oh, just one moment!' interrupted Miss Turner, who sounded quite dismayed. 'Don't you think we should discuss the issue first?'

'What for?' demanded Mr Rutter, with a frown.

'To acquaint the people with the facts!' replied Miss Turner. She had an unfortunately squeaky voice which made her something of a laughing stock in the village and she had attained her high political office largely through apathy as no one had ever bothered to stand against her.

'Let's have a vote!' insisted Mr Rutter, who clearly wanted to dispense with the formalities as speedily as possible.

'We can't possibly have a vote until the people have heard the facts!' insisted Miss Turner.

'The facts are simple,' said Mr Rutter, banging his right fist into the palm of his left hand. 'Fact one: this fellow Sherlock wants to build his damned houses all over our village. Fact two: we don't want him here.' He stared out at the audience in the village hall as his words were greeted with great cheers of approval and support.

'That's quite outrageous!' said Miss Turner who had turned rather pale. 'The planning committee considered the economic effects of Mr Sherlock's proposals at considerable length and we came to the clear conclusion that his proposals were essential to the future prosperity of the area.' She stood up, fastened her jacket and cleared her throat. 'There is no doubt that if these plans go ahead the nature of Bilbury will change,' she said. 'But the village will benefit enormously ... '

Mr Rutter, who had been listening carefully, shook his head violently.

'Yes it will!' insisted Miss Turner. 'And it would be foolish to deny it.' She raised her left hand, and with her right hand took hold of her little finger. 'First and most important,' she said, 'the village will become far more prosperous. There will be more employment and more money coming into the village.'

'We don't want their bloody money!' shouted someone out of the audience. I couldn't see who it was but the comment was received with an approving cheer.

'You may not want their money but some people in the village probably need it,' said Mrs Turner, blustering on regardless. She paused and leant forwards with her hands resting on the trestle table. 'Most of you rely on two sources of income: farming and tourism. Making a living out of both of these is getting harder and harder.'

There were a few isolated murmurs of approval.

'Second,' said Miss Turner, taking hold of another finger, 'to all that you have to add the fact that if Sherlock builds new homes then there will be better facilities. There will probably be a decent, regular bus service into Barnstaple and maybe into Ilfracombe as well instead of the twice a week service you've got now. There will be more shops and there will be a new petrol station built on the Combe Martin road. There will also be a new surgery.'

Mr Rutter stood up and interrupted her.

She paused and lifted her head a fraction higher. The cords in her neck stood out like hawsers. 'It is of paramount importance that the villagers be acquainted with all the facts if they are to make an informed decision.'

'Balderdash!' said Mr Rutter. I had never heard anyone say 'balderdash' before in real life. He stood up. 'Let's have a vote about whether or not we want to have to listen to any more of Miss Turner's facts.' He turned and glowered at her. 'Do you have any objection to that?' He put a lot of emphasis on the word 'that'. There was another roar of approval from the villagers who took a certain simple pride in their capacity for bias and prejudice.

Miss Turner, who could hardly object to such a straightforward example of democracy in action, murmured something inaudible, pursed her lips as though she had mistakenly put a slice of lemon in her mouth and shook her head.

'Right!' said Mr Rutter. 'Hands up all those who are opposed to this fellow Sherlock's plan to build all over Bilbury and don't want to hear any more of Miss Turner's facts.' He looked around, with ill concealed delight, at the forest of hands which filled the hall. 'Right. And now – hands up anyone who doesn't realise what a bloody disgrace the plans are and wants to hear more from Miss Turner.' This time not a single hand was raised.

'There you are!' said Mr Rutter. 'Now are you satisfied?'

Miss Turner, who had turned bright red, did not say anything but, instead, chose to take a close interest in the village hall ceiling.

'So now we can get down to the real business of the evening,' said Mr Rutter. 'Which is – how are we going to stop this bugger Sherlock from ruining our village?' He looked down into the audience, saw someone who brought a smile of recognition to his face, pointed and called him up onto the stage. With great reluctance, and a helping heave from a burly farmer whose name I couldn't remember but whose capacious brown corduroy trousers hid, I remembered, a fine collection of ripe haemorrhoids, Dr Brownlow clambered up to join him.

'I've invited Dr Brownlow onto the stage this evening because you all know him . . . ,' began Mr Rutter.

' . . . he delivered most of us!' shouted an anonymous male voice in the crowd.

' . . . and probably wishes he hadn't!' said Mr Rutter, instantly, holding up a hand to stifle any further heckling. 'And because I know he's got something important to say.'

Dr Brownlow stood up and faced the audience. For a moment he said nothing, though his silence was, I felt sure, either inspired by emotion or by a determination to speak only when he knew what he was going to say. It certainly was not inspired by shyness. When he did speak his voice was low but the atmosphere in the village hall was electric and he could be heard easily. The people of Bilbury respected and trusted him and very much wanted to hear what he had to say.

'I am totally opposed to Sherlock's plans,' he said to loud and predictable cheers. 'But you have to understand that if we reject the Sherlock building project then there will be some pretty awesome consequences. For one thing Bilbury will no longer have a doctor of its own.'

This clearly came of something of a surprise to many and there were loud cries of 'Why?' from around the floor. 'I'm going to let my successor answer that,' said Dr Brownlow, holding up a hand.

He beckoned to me to go up and join him on the stage. I didn't want to go but the way things stood I knew that I really didn't have much option. Patsy gave my hand a squeeze and I threaded my way through the villagers and climbed up onto the stage. My heart was beating so loudly by the time I reached Dr Brownlow's side that I felt sure that everyone must be able to hear it.

I explained what I knew.

I told the villagers that if I agreed to go and work in the new surgery that Mr Sherlock planned to build then the village would continue to have its own medical practice, but if the villagers successfully opposed plans for the new development then Bilbury would lose its doctor and the practice which Dr Brownlow had founded would be closed.

This news was received by the audience in silence.

After a moment or two Mr Rutter turned to me. 'May I ask you, doctor,' he began, speaking very quietly, 'about your own personal feelings. You have a considerable interest in the Sherlock plans – probably as great as any of us here even though you're a newcomer to the village – so what do you think?'

I didn't need to think about my reply.

'I think we should oppose the Sherlock plans,' I said firmly. 'If we allow him to go ahead and build all over Softly's Bottom and Bluebell Wood then the village of Bilbury will be ruined for ever. It will never, ever be the same again. But if we managed to stop Sherlock's plans then the village will stay the same, apart from the fact that it will lose its surgery and the villagers will have to travel into Barnstaple for medical attention.' I paused. 'That will be sad and it will be inconvenient but it won't ruin Bilbury.' I said. 'And that need not necessarily be a permanent problem,' I added. 'It is possible that at some future time it will be possible to re-open the surgery.' I paused again for a moment for something had just occurred to me. 'Under the Health Service regulations,' I said, 'the practice in Barnstaple which takes over Bilbury will be responsible for providing night time and emergency cover. Villagers will still be entitled to call out a doctor if they need help and can't get into the surgery. It will be up to people in the village to decide how often they need to call a doctor out.'

'So,' said Mr Rutter who had understood exactly what I was getting at, 'if the practice in Barnstaple finds that it gets called out a great deal they may decide that they no longer want to be responsible for us?'

'Exactly,' I agreed. 'In which case Bilbury will probably

get its doctor back. Or at the very least the practice in Barnstaple will start to do surgeries out here.' I looked around. 'Maybe here in the village hall. Or in the Duck and Puddle.'

'Doctor, can I ask you what you've decided to do?' asked Mr Rutter.

'I've told Mr Sherlock that I will have nothing to do with his plans,' I said. 'I will not work in his new surgery.'

'Even though that means putting yourself out of a job?'

I nodded.

'Thank you doctor! That's all good enough for me,' said Mr Rutter. 'Sit yourself down.' He pointed to a spare chair at the back of the stage. I sat down. 'No,' he said, 'Bring it over here.' He waved me forwards to join him, Miss Turner and Dr Brownlow at the table. Dr Brownlow had already found a chair of his own. He winked at me as I sat down beside him.

'So,' said Mr Rutter, rubbing his hands together, 'now all we've got to do is make it clear to the authorities that we don't want that fellow Sherlock bringing his damned bulldozers and his bricklayers into Bilbury.'

Peter Marshall wanted us to dump tractor loads of manure on the council office steps in Barnstaple. Thumper thought we should simply park old vehicles around the village to create a barricade. And Gilly from the pub suggested that we withhold our rates until the council agreed to reject Sherlock's plans. Mr Rutter carefully wrote down all these suggestions on the back of a seed catalogue. Miss Turner just sat and looked cross, something at which she seemed to have had a lot of practice.

But while I had been speaking I had an idea which I thought would work quite well without any of us having to break the law. But a public meeting in the village hall wasn't the place to share my thoughts and so for the time being I kept them to myself.

*   *   *

212

CHAPTER NINETEEN

We left home at seven on the morning we were due to be interviewed for the job in the Midlands. (Theoretically I was the one who was going to be interviewed, but my conversation with the senior partner had made it pretty clear that my wife would be interviewed too).

We were both dressed for the occasion in our Sunday best.

I wore a woollen shirt with a faint red and brown check woven into the material, my faithful old sports jacket, best grey flannel trousers (I had put a little shoe polish onto the leather elbow patches on the sleeves of the jacket) and my old medical school tie (a blue, grey and yellow concoction which was the only tie I had which did not have any stains on it). Patsy wore her new, white dress – the one which she had converted from the old wedding gown. Because it was chilly she also wore a white cardigan which had two small patch pockets on the front and which was fastened with small pearl coloured buttons. On her feet she wore pretty white sandals and around her neck she wore, as she always did, a simple gold locket which I had given to her on our wedding day. Patsy brought with her a small box of Bilbury Grange strawberries and a bag of her home made rock buns to eat on the journey.

We were both very nervous.

I had never been to a proper job interview before. When I had accepted the job as assistant to Dr Brownlow I had been interviewed by telephone and the whole thing had taken just a few seconds. And Patsy, I discovered, had never been outside North Devon before.

We drove westwards from Bilbury to Lynton and then took

the coast road through Porlock and Dunster before turning inland and heading through Bridgwater towards Weston-super-Mare. The traffic was light, and although our Morris Minor only had a rather small engine, which meant that it had seemed to take for ever to climb up the long, steep, Countisbury Hill out of Lynmouth, it seemed to love the twisting, turning lanes along which our journey took us.

Just before Bristol we stopped for breakfast at a roadside cafe where a jovial man in a red plaid shirt and dark green trousers served us both with plates full of scrambled eggs and mushrooms. We ate with great pleasure and followed it with plenty of fresh toast and marmalade. We washed it all down with huge mugs of tea. After breakfast I put the hood down and we drove on past Bristol, through Gloucester, where we filled up the car with petrol at a garage where a small, wizened man in a freshly starched white coat served us and told us that it was going to rain and that we should put our hood up, through Cheltenham, where we got lost and drove twice down the main street, and then through Evesham, where we each ate one of Patsy's rock buns.

Our journey had taken us through some of England's most beautiful scenery: rolling hills, fields full of ripening crops and hedgerows studded with huge oaks, sycamore and elm and dotted with dancing, scarlet poppies and massive, purple foxgloves. Patsy who had no idea what to expect had been more than pleasantly surprised by it all.

But after Leamington Spa the view from the Morris changed dramatically.

Instead of fields and hedgerows the road was lined with houses, shops and factories. Instead of cows and sheep, grazing in meadows which were yellow with buttercups, we were surrounded by pedestrians scurrying about their business and by businessmen hurrying to work. Instead of being fresh and clean, the air we breathed in became heavy with car exhaust fumes and factory smoke. For the first time we found ourselves sitting in long lines of slow moving traffic. Patsy had never seen anything like it. Even in Barnstaple, the biggest town in North Devon, traffic jams usually only happen in the height of summer and then usually consist of little more than half a dozen cars, a tractor and either a car towing a caravan or a coach full of holiday-makers. Eventually we stopped and put up the hood in a vain attempt to shut out some of the dirt and the noise.

'What's the name of this town?' asked Patsy, as we drove on and on along endless roads which seemed to have no beginnings, no ends and no names.

I had to confess that I didn't know. I knew only that we had now entered the industrial Midlands and were still heading for, and getting ever closer to, Mettleham.

In Devon the towns and villages are clearly separated from one another by fields and acres of green land. Here in the industrial wastelands there were no such natural separations. The villages had all grown into towns and the towns had all grown into one another.

Mettleham was a typical, small town. It had developed around a single coal mine in the nineteenth century, and in the twentieth century had grown around a car factory. The mine now employed no more than a couple of hundred men, but the car factory had continued to grow and had spawned a huge number of smaller but dependent factories where skilled workmen made tyres, lighting equipment, car seats and all the other bits and pieces which the big factory needed. Nearly everyone in Mettleham was dependent upon the car industry for their weekly pay packets, monthly salary cheques or twice yearly dividends.

The high street had its own branches of all the big stores and was undistinguishable from all the other high streets in the area.

There was a statue of a long forgotten local hero sitting proudly on a horse in front of a sooty library; an ugly local council building in sixties block, steel and glass style and a small extravagantly gated park with neat but strangely subdued flower beds, tarmacadam paths and a long list of forbidden activities pasted up on a series of huge boards.

Apart from these inevitable and essential ingredients the town seemed to have dedicated itself to the internal combustion engine in general and to the motor car in particular. Every lamp post was decorated with instructions, exhortations and threats; every pavement was decorated with parking meters and the air was blue with carbon monoxide and the

expletives of motorists. Pedestrians were prevented from inter-
fering with the flow of the traffic by miles of grey steel tubing.

With helpful advice from a woman with a pushchair containing a fractious child we arrived at our target, the Mettleham Health Centre, at fifteen minutes to twelve. The original
building had been a fairly ordinary Victorian terraced house
but an ugly two storey extension in concrete had been added
where a garage or conservatory had once been. There was
a brass plate attached to a wooden board beside the front
door to the house.

I parked the Morris in a small space between a huge Volvo
and a Rover, but before I had chance to turn off the engine
a woman in a white coat came hurrying out of the front door.
She had blue hair and wore the largest pair of spectacles I
had ever seen. She had a row of pens in her top pocket and
carried another pen in her hand. I wound down my window
as she approached.

'You can't park there!' she said. 'Can't you read?' She
pointed to a huge red and white sign fastened to the wall
which said 'DOCTORS ONLY'.

'I am a doctor,' I explained.

The woman in the white coat glowered at me. 'You're not
one of our doctors,' she said firmly. She had a large wart
an inch to the right of her mouth and a thin but clearly visible
moustache.

'No,' I agreed. 'I've come for an interview. We've just driven
up from Devon.'

'Well you can't park here,' snapped the receptionist. 'Dr
Evans will be here in a minute and you're in his space.'

'Where can I park?' I asked.

'Anywhere but here,' she said. She waved a hand at me,
indicating that I should reverse out of the space in which
I had parked, and that I should do so as quickly as possible.
Wearily, I put the car into reverse, backed out of the tiny
car park and, with difficulty, out into the never ending stream
of traffic. A lorry driver banged his fist on his horn and an
elderly woman in steel rimmed spectacles and a Hillman Minx
mouthed what seemed like obscenities at me. Only when I
had gone did the woman in the white coat turn and disappear
back into the building.

As I drove out I saw a second Volvo turn into the car park and sweep into the space I had just vacated.

'She wasn't very nice,' said Patsy. She reached out and put her hand on my arm. I looked across at her. She looked as frightened and as out of place as I felt. Not for the first time since we had left Devon I began to wonder if I had been hasty in turning down the job that Sherlock had offered me.

'No,' I agreed. 'She wasn't.'

It took us twenty minutes to find a parking space in a multi-storey car park and ten minutes to walk back to the Health Centre.

'I've come for an interview,' I told the receptionist who eventually answered my knock on the small hatch in the waiting room. She was in her early twenties and underneath her white coat, which was unfastened, she wore a tight, lemon coloured sweater with a polo neck. Her hair was puffed up making her head look twice as big as it was, and was held in place with so much lacquer that it looked solid. She sat in a cloud of sickly, cheap perfume which wafted out through the hatch and made me start to wheeze. There was no sign of the receptionist who had thrown us out of the car park. I told her my name.

'You're very late,' she said, looking at a large appointments book which lay before her and finding my name with the aid of a long and lethal looking finger nail that might, in some circumstances, have been classified as a dangerous weapon.

'Fifteen minutes,' I said. 'We couldn't find anywhere to park.'

'The doctors are in a meeting,' said the receptionist. 'I'll check if they'll still see you.' She gave me what I suppose she might have thought was a smile and then shut the hatch firmly in my face. I turned back to Patsy, who was standing behind me, and smiled to try and reassure her. I don't think I had ever felt quite so uncomfortable and ill at ease. Patsy came closer and reached out for my hand. I held it tightly and looked around. The waiting room was in the new part of the house and it was painted all in white. There was a large, wooden table in the middle of the room which was piled high with magazines. Someone had neatly arranged them into categories. Around the walls stood uncomfortable look-ing metal chairs which, I noticed with some surprise, were fastened to the floor with chains.

I was about to suggest to Patsy that we might as well sit down when the hatch doors flew open and the receptionist's head appeared. 'The doctors will see you now,' she said.

Patsy and I started to walk towards the door.

'Just you,' said the receptionist, nodding towards me. 'Mrs Jackson will be here in a few minutes for your wife.'

I looked at Patsy. I didn't want to leave her alone.

'It's O.K!' she whispered. She squeezed my hand, kissed me on the cheek and then moved away from the door and sat down. 'Really,' she said.

'Where do I go?' I asked the receptionist.

'Dr Robinson's room,' said the receptionist. 'Turn right and it's second on your left.'

I thanked her and went off in search of my future.

* * *

There were three of them in the room, which was surpris-ingly spacious and had, presumably, once been the living room when the building had been used as a house. Although it was blocked up, there was still a large fireplace on one wall. On either side of the fireplace there were alcoves which were lined with bookshelves. Most of the shelves were piled high with journals and decorated with ornaments rather than stacked with books. There were three large and rather gloomy oil paintings hanging from the picture rail.

Dr Robinson, the senior partner to whom I had spoken on the telephone, looked to be the eldest of the three doctors and sat behind a large oak desk with his back to the window. He was tall, balding, about fifty five and despite the heat wore a dark green heavy tweed three piece suit. He wore it with a pale green woollen shirt and a dark green paisley tie. He wore heavy brown country brogue walking shoes. It was Dr Robinson who spoke first and who introduced me to his two partners, the other two thirds of the interview panel.

Dr Jackson, whose wife had been deputed to collect Patsy, was in his early forties and looked a jovial sort of fellow. He had a full head of tight curly hair which was going grey and wore a neatly trimmed beard which was darker in colour. He sat in a leather easy chair in shirt sleeves with his suit jacket draped over the back of the chair behind his head. The third member of the inquisitorial panel was Dr Evans. He looked to be no more than four or five years older than me. He sat in the second easy chair and looked very serious. He was balding and wore blue rimmed spectacles and a pale brown silk suit. I don't know why butI1 took an instinctive dislike to him. He had cold, cruel eyes and seemed to have an arrogance about him which I found strangely disturbing rather than just annoying.

'Tell us about yourself,' said Dr Robinson, when he had introduced his colleagues and we had all shaken hands. He hooked his thumbs into his waistcoat pockets and leant back in his chair.

I told him how I had started work for Dr Brownlow, about Bilbury and about Patsy and explained why I had to leave Bilbury.

'Have you ever practised in this sort of area?' asked Dr Evans, when I had finished.

'No,' I confessed.

'How do you think you'll like it?'

I said that I thought in any practice the people were probably more important than the surroundings. This seemed to go down quite well.

After talking together for between half and three quarters of an hour Dr Robinson unhooked his thumbs, looked at his watch, a large, old fashioned thing which he hauled out of his waist coat pocket with the aid of a silver chain, and announced that it seemed to him to be a good time for us to go and get some lunch.

'Are you hungry?' he asked me.

I said I was and then suddenly remembered that I had forgotten to tell him that Patsy and I did not eat meat. The whole interview had rather startled me for no one had seemed interested in my medical knowledge, and the conversation had largely centred around politics and sport.

We drove in a convoy of four cars from the Health Centre to Dr Robinson's home which was situated in what was clearly one of the most expensive areas of the town. The house was surrounded by about an acre of gardens and looked as though it had probably been built in the 1930s. As we parked our cars in the driveway I could see a swimming pool in the garden at the back of the house. Dr Robinson went to the front door, opened it and waved me through. The other two partners followed me and Dr Robinson brought up the rear.

Patsy and the doctors' three wives were already there and were sitting in the living room sipping sherries and nibbling small cheese biscuits. Dr Robinson's wife was plump but definitely not jolly. She had neatly permed grey hair, cold eyes and lips that turned downwards at the corners. She wore a pink and grey checked suit with a white blouse which was buttoned up to the neck and fastened with a brooch in the shape of a butterfly. Dr Jackson's wife, was about ten years younger than her husband, tall, slim and quite pretty. She had long brown hair that looked as if it got brushed a lot and wore a very short black dress that had virtually no back to it. Dr Evans' wife, who was dressed in the uniform of either a midwife or a district nurse (I wasn't sure which) was short, plumpish and looked as sour and as unpleasant as her husband.

Dr Robinson introduced me to the three wives and his wife then introduced Patsy to the three doctors. We then all sat around making polite, dull but safe conversation about the weather, the state of the nation and the soaring cost of private education. It seemed that the two younger partners both had children at private schools while Dr Robinson's children were now grown up and graduated from university. After a quarter of an hour a round, homely looking woman dressed in a flowered pinafore came in and told us that lunch was ready. This, Mrs Robinson told Patsy and I, was Mrs Yates, her daily help without whom her life would be unbearable.

Lunch was something of a disaster, though this was entirely our fault. Neither Patsy nor I had dared to explain to either our host or our hostess that we were vegetarians and so we had to try to hide the fact that when we had finished eating our plates were still very nearly as full as they had been when we had started. We both discovered that it is not easy to hide thick slices of roast pork with a few peas and a brussels sprout. I would have gladly eaten more of the vegetables I was given but I needed them to help hide the pork.

Afterwards all six of us retired to the living room again where Mrs Yates served coffee and Mrs Robinson offered us chocolates out of an expensive looking box. After twenty minutes of insignificant chatter, which seemed largely to centre upon the iniquities of the tax system, the comparative advantages of supermarket versus delicatessen shopping and the soaring cost of private education, Dr Robinson hauled his watch out of his waistcoat pocket and announced that he had an ante natal clinic to attend.

The interview was over.

* * *

'How do you think it went?' asked Patsy, as we queued to get out of Mettleham. I could hardly see the lorry in front of us for the clouds of smoke that were belching out of its exhaust pipe.

I didn't answer straight away. 'I don't know,' I said eventually. I looked at her and shrugged. 'I really haven't the faintest idea.'

The truth was that I had found it all deeply depressing. No one had asked me anything about my hopes and fears for general practice in the last quarter of the twentieth century. None of the partners had shared their own ambitions with me. If they had opened up their hearts and at least confessed to having one or two prejudices I might not have agreed with them but at least I would have known where I stood with them. I know that I could have asked them questions, but somehow it hadn't seemed right to do that. Being thrown out of the car park and then kept standing in the waiting room had made me very conscious of the fact that I was applying for a job.

'Can I say something?' asked Patsy.

'Of course!'

'You won't be cross?'

'No!'

'I didn't think any of them were very nice people,' she said, hesitantly.

'No.' I agreed. 'I thought they were awful.'

'Mrs Jackson told me that if you got the job I would have

to smarten you up a bit,' said Patsy.

I turned and looked at her. 'When did she say that?'

'When you were talking to her husband and Dr Robinson after lunch.'

'What did you say?'

'I didn't know what to say,' said Patsy.

'But what on earth *did* you say?'

'I think I muttered something about doing my best.' said Patsy. She looked very unhappy.

'What a cheek!' I said. I looked down. Patsy had made a good job of mending my trousers and I could still smell the polish I had put on the elbow patches on my jacket. I couldn't understand how wearing a suit could make me a better doctor.

A car driver somewhere behind us started banging on his horn and within a couple of seconds half a dozen other drivers were doing the same thing. I looked in front of us. The lorry had moved forwards a couple of yards. I put the car into gear and edged forwards.

'Mrs Evans wanted to know whether I had any medical training,' said Patsy. 'She said that doctors wives needed an understanding of medicine in order to support their husbands properly.'

I turned my head. Patsy was crying. I slipped the car out of gear, put on the handbrake and put my arms around her. 'Hey! Come on now!' I said. 'Don't let them get to you.'

'I'm sorry,' she said. 'I think I let you down.'

'Don't be silly,' I murmured. 'You could never let me down.'

I felt a strong desire to turn round, drive back and tell them all what I thought of them.

'I wish we didn't have to leave Bilbury,' said Patsy.

'I know.' I said. A driver behind tooted his horn again. I looked forwards, through the windscreen. The lorry had moved on another couple of yards.

'All the wives seemed to care about was school fees and shopping,' said Patsy.

'The men were almost as bad,' I said. 'But they were interested in cars, golf and income tax as well.'

The driver behind tooted again. Through the back window of the Morris I could see him waving a small number of fingers at me. I waved back at him. I looked at my watch. It was not quite three o'clock.

'Are you hungry?'

Patsy looked at me. 'I'm starving.'

'So am I. Why don't we stop at the next shop we see, buy some bread and cheese and a bottle of something cheap and fizzy and have a picnic as soon as we get out of all this traffic?'

'Yes!' said Patsy, delightedly.

'It's a pity to waste the whole day,' I said. 'Have we got any of your buns left?'

'Oh, yes! I packed a large bagful and we've only eaten a couple.' She reached over into the back of the car and found the brown paper bag. It was one of Peter Marshall's stout grocery bags from the village shop. 'There are the strawberries as well!'

Suddenly, the day didn't seem quite so miserable.

*   *   *

When we got back to Bilbury I dropped Patsy at The Grange and stayed just long enough to peep cautiously into the stable where our family of swallows were nesting. The two young swallows had now clambered out of the nest and were standing on the edge of one of the beams. As we watched, first one and then the other jumped off the beam out into the unknown, swooped and dived around with only the slightest uncertainty and then landed back on their beam where they rested, slightly wobbly, rather like trapeze artists who had successfully accomplished a difficult manoeuvre. They seemed to be waiting for applause so Patsy and I, both as excited as young parents, murmured words of appreciation before we backed quietly away from the stable. How could we possibly have dreamt of moving away from the country?

While Patsy went into the house I got back into the car because although it was late I wanted to visit two patients, Miss Phillips and Mrs Blossom, at their homes.

I was truly delighted to find them both looking far happier and considerably more content than they had been when I had seen them last. Although it was clearly going to take some time before either of them made anything close to a real recovery, the gentle withdrawal programme I had devised

223

seemed to be working.

Mrs Blossom was out of bed and was sitting watching television. She looked considerably brighter and more alert than she had the last time I had seen her.

'Hello,' she said.

Her father looked at me with pride, like a father whose baby has just spoken its first word. 'She's a lot better than she was,' he said. He seemed genuinely relieved.

'How do *you* feel?' I asked her.

Mrs Blossom licked her lips which were dry and cracked. 'I wish I'd never started taking them,' she told me. She rubbed at her left forearm with her right hand. 'My skin is very dry,' she told me. 'Could that be the pills?'

I nodded. 'It could.' I remembered that Miss Phillips had complained of something similar.

'I won't ever moan again,' said Mrs Blossom. 'I didn't know how lucky I was before.' She licked her lips and smiled at me. 'Do you think I'll get better?'

'Yes,' I said. 'Yes, I do.'

I was, however, still appalled at the way that the drug company making Angipax was encouraging doctors to prescribe the drug for long periods to unsuspecting patients, and at the way that doctors were handing out the drug unquestioningly.

Miss Phillips was much better too. She had spent the day in the garden and was anxious to tell me everything she had done.

Although it was nearly dark we went outside and walked around and inspected her vegetable patch and her flower garden.

In her vegetable patch she had runner beans, carrots, beetroot, swede, potatoes, radishes, lettuce, tomatoes, peas and, something I had never before seen in a garden, petit pois, tiny little peas that tasted sweeter than any I'd ever tasted before. She was also growing peas called mange tout that Miss Phillips told me could be eaten complete with their pods.

In her flower patch she specialised in natural, wild Exmoor plants such as gorse, heather, red campion, sweet violets, huge armies of foxglove, cranesbill and silver ragwort. Underneath a small tree grew yellow pimpernel, wood sorrel, nightshade and a dozen different types of fern. By a small stream down one side of the garden grew orange montbretia, marsh ragwort and yellow flag. As she walked with me around the garden she pointed out each plant and talked to it by name, offering each one comfort and encouragement in the cool of the summer evening.

'Do you like flowers?' she asked me.

I smiled and nodded. 'But I'm afraid I don't know very much about them.'

'Miss Tweedsmuir and I would be delighted to teach you anything you'd like to know,' said Miss Phillips. 'We both love flowers.'

'I'd love to learn more,' I said. 'Ever since you found that red helleborine in our beech wood my enthusiasm has been growing. Just how rare is that orchid, by the way?'

'Oh, very!' said Miss Phillips. 'Very rare indeed.'

'Am I right in thinking that if a plant like that was found on land that was earmarked for building the authorities would have to withhold planning permission?'

'I'm sure they would,' said Miss Phillips. 'When a clump of military orchids or orchis militaris were found in the path of a motorway two years ago the contractors had to go round them.'

She held her head on one side and looked at me as though she'd read my mind. 'I'm afraid that was the first thing Miss Tweedsmuir and I thought of,' said Miss Phillips. 'We know Bluebell Wood very well and there aren't any protected species of anything in there.'

'No red helleborine?'

'No,' said Miss Phillips. 'The woodland is very similar to yours, beech trees and lots of shade, but there aren't any red helleborine plants there.'

'That's a pity,' I said.

'It certainly is,' said Miss Phillips. 'A clump of cephalanthera rubra growing in Bluebell Wood would have stopped Mr Sherlock's bulldozers for good.'

On the way home I stopped at a public call box and rang Thumper.

*   *   *

225

CHAPTER TWENTY

When we arrived back from Mettleham we were much more cheerful than when we had left. The long drive south had made us both tired, but we had enjoyed a glorious picnic in a field just outside Cheltenham and somehow, after that, the day had seemed much brighter.

'There must be other jobs,' I had said to Patsy, as we drove very slowly up Porlock Hill in the early evening. A hare sat up in the middle of the road washing its face. It looked directly at us as we approached and then carried on with its evening ablutions. Just as I was about to put my foot on the brake the hare stopped washing and darted off up the road at top speed. We had both laughed and Patsy rested her head on my shoulder as the Morris Minor struggled up the hill in first gear.

'Something will turn up,' Patsy murmured. 'And if not it doesn't matter as long as we have each other.'

'And as long as we don't have to move to Mettleham,' I added.

It wasn't Mettleham that I particularly disliked (though I confess I hadn't been too keen on it), but the people we'd met. I had meant every word when I had told Dr Robinson and his colleagues that it was the people who were more important than the place.

I had gone to bed late, determined to spend the next day looking through the situations vacant section of the British Medical Journal. It may have been because they had missed us, or because they knew that we had a trying day, but Ben, Emily and Sophie spent most of the night sleeping on our bed.

I was woken up the next morning at a quarter past seven by the ringing of the telephone. It was a woman from London who was staying in Bilbury and wanted to know what time the surgery started. She said she had run out of pills and wanted me to prescribe some more for her. It wasn't worth trying to go back to sleep and so I slipped out of bed and peeped through the curtains to see what the weather was like. It was gloriously sunny; the garden at Bilbury Grange looked spectacularly beautiful and everywhere I looked there were flowers in bloom. My eye was attracted by a movement just below the window and I watched with amusement as Sophie, who had risen early, hurried across the lawn with her head held high and a very aloof look on her face. Behind her, protecting some unseen nest, marched two huge and belligerent looking magpies. I glanced behind me and was glad for Sophie's sake that Emily was still asleep on the bed.

We breakfasted on toast and coffee after Patsy and I checked that the lambs were all right.

'You were late getting in last night,' said Patsy.

'I know,' I said. 'You were asleep.'

'I rang Miss Phillips but she said you'd left,' said Patsy. 'I tried to stay awake but I was exhausted.'

'I went for a walk with Thumper.'

'A walk! It must have been nearly midnight!'

'It was.'

Patsy looked at me and frowned. 'What's going on?' she asked. 'What were you doing?'

'Just a bit of gardening,' I said and kissed her goodbye.

Outside in the front driveway I had just lowered the hood of the Morris Minor to take full advantage of the summer sunshine when I heard a car approaching from behind me. I turned and saw our visitors approaching in their smart German car.

Mr Onions stopped his car no more than a yard away from me and pressed a button. His window hummed downwards smoothly. He waited until the window had disappeared down into the door, smiled at me and held out a hand. 'I'm glad I caught you,' he said. The smile didn't look so much like a smile as an opportunity to display his expensively capped teeth. His hair was neatly combed and freshly washed and he wore a lime green suit and a multi coloured shirt with the collar folded over the suit jacket collar. His handshake was limp and his palm felt soft and clammy. I noticed that he wore a loose gold chain around his right wrist. He looked down. 'That's a rather nice bag!'

I was carrying the Gladstone bag that had been repaired in Barnstaple. I followed his glance downwards. 'Yes.' I agreed. 'It is nice isn't it?' The cobbler had done an excellent job and I was extremely proud of the bag. It was, in truth, rather too small for all the things I had to carry but I liked it so much that I put up with that and kept some of the bulkier items in another bag in the boot of the car.

I had taken a rather strong dislike to Mr Onions and for some odd reason I didn't trust him. I felt myself instinctively taking a firmer hold on the bag as though afraid that he might somehow try to take it from me.

'Have you got a moment?' he asked.

I admitted that I had.

'It's about the books in the flat,' said Mr Onions. 'Could I buy them from you?'

For a few seconds I couldn't think what he meant. Then I remembered. When Patsy had bought her tin bath and contents at a recent auction (the same tin bath that had contained the Gladstone bag I was carrying) the bath had contained a few books. Because most were still wrapped in their colourful paper jackets and looked rather bright, and because we still didn't have any bookshelves of our own in Bilbury Grange, Patsy had put them into the flat, standing them up on the mantlepiece and using them to hide a rough patch on the wall.

'I don't know,' I said. I had never bothered even to look at the books. I had no idea what they were.

'I'll pay you ten pounds for them,' said Mr Onions. He smiled again. 'My wife started reading one in bed at night and I'm reading another and there are several there we both like the look of.' His wife, who was sitting beside him, and who had not said a word turned her head slightly and almost smiled. She wore a white tank top and a tight and rather short white skirt and had a broad brimmed sun hat on her head. She wore dark glasses with heavy black frames.

Alarm bells had started to ring in my head. Ten pounds seemed an awful lot of money to pay for a row of old, second-hand books. Above us and slightly to our right I noticed our family of swallows sitting together on a telephone wire. Suddenly and noiselessly a sparrowhawk swooped out of the sky heading for one of the baby swallows. Instantly it was surrounded not just by the parents of the baby swallow but by a dozen other swallows which I hadn't even noticed. The sparrowhawk flapped its wings angrily and then headed off over the fields, followed by a crowd of swallows. I watched them shoo it away until they felt it had learnt its lesson.

'I'll need to have a look,' I said. 'Do you mind if I pop into the flat this afternoon?'

'Of course not!' said Mr Onions, giving me another chance to view his dentist's handiwork. 'By the way, I hear you sell strawberries. Do you have any we can buy from you?'

'Oh just help yourself!' I said, generously. 'The strawberry bed is in the walled garden.'

'Very kind of you,' said Mr Onions. He gave me what looked like a last flash of expensively capped and polished teeth and then paused and nodded towards the lowered hood of the Morris.

'You ought to get a car with air conditioning,' he said, nodding towards a complicated looking device on his dashboard. 'Then you wouldn't need to bother with a hood that came down.'

'I like a convertible!' I said.

'All those flies and all that wind?' said Mr Onions, pulling a face and shaking his head. Then he pressed a button and his window hummed upwards. He put his foot down on the accelerator and sped off down the drive, narrowly missing Sophie who darted out of the shrubbery in front of him.

I really didn't like Mr Onions one little bit.

*   *   *

I was surprised when Miss Johnson told me that there was a telephone call for me from a Dr Robinson in Mettleham. I had expected him to write rather than to telephone to tell me that I had not been successful in my application for the job.

'Did you get back to Devon safely?' asked Dr Robinson. 'It must have been a long day for you.' I could envisage both him and his office as he spoke.

I told him that we had arrived home without mishap and thanked him and his wife for their hospitality. Patsy and I had agreed that she would telephone a florist in Barnstaple to arrange for a courtesy 'thank you' bunch of flowers to be delivered to Mrs Robinson.

'We very much enjoyed meeting you both,' said Dr Robinson. 'We had a partners' meeting yesterday evening and decided unanimously that we would very much like to accept you as our new junior partner.'

This was not at all what I expected to hear, and when my mouth opened to reply my brain still hadn't decided what to say. The end result was an almost inaudible and certainly incomprehensible mumble.

'I'm sorry ... ' said Dr Robinson, 'I'm afraid I didn't quite catch what you said.'

'That's very kind of you,' I managed to stutter. 'And I'm honoured that you should have chosen me...'

'Well, to be perfectly honest you didn't have an awful lot of competition,' said Dr Robinson, adopting his best and most confidential bedside manner voice.

'We'd like you to come on a six months trial contract to start with. We'll arrange rented accommodation for you in the town during your probationary period which will give you a chance to look around to see what's available on the housing market.'

I tried to interrupt him, to tell him as politely as I could that I didn't want his job, but he was in full flow now and without being rude I just couldn't get a word in. I really didn't want anything more to do with him or his practice, and I certainly didn't want to work with him. I knew that Patsy didn't want to move to Mettleham either.

'As the junior partner you will be responsible for the weekend emergency rota and we'd also expect you to be on call for the practice on alternate nights,' continued Dr Robinson. 'I'm sure you'll agree that the arrangement is a fair one.'

I was by now finding it slightly difficult not to laugh. In addition to expecting me to be on call every weekend Dr

Robinson and his two partners were expecting me to be on call every other night – which meant that they would each be on call less than one night a week.

'It's very good of you, but ... ' I began.

'To begin with you will receive ten per cent of the net practice profits,' continued Dr Robinson. 'Your share will go up by one per cent every year until you reach parity with the rest of us.'

I was glad I didn't want the job and relieved that I didn't need it. His terms were getting more and more outrageous by the minute. I opened my mouth to speak but Dr Robinson hadn't finished yet.

'You will, of course, expect to buy your share of the practice premises,' said Dr Robinson. 'But we realise that you may have difficulty in raising the sort of money involved. We will arrange for a surveyor to work out your liability and then we will make deductions from your income over the next ten years, charging you interest at five per cent over base rate.'

'It's very kind of you ... ' I began.

'Not at all,' said Dr Robinson. 'We want you and Patricia to feel welcome here in Mettleham.'

'Patsy.' I said firmly. 'My wife's name is Patsy.'

'We think Patricia is more suitable for a doctor's wife,' said Dr Robinson, rather starchily. 'We'd like you to start on the first of next month. Is that convenient?'

'I'm sorry,' I said sharply, relieved to have a chance to speak. 'But Patsy and I won't be coming to Mettleham at all.'

'I beg your pardon?' said Dr Robinson. He sounded shocked and outraged. 'What do you mean 'you won't be coming'?'

'We talked it over and I'm afraid we decided that we wouldn't be happy in Mettleham,' I told him.

'Oh.' said Dr Robinson. 'Well in that case I can offer you a starting salary of 12% of the net practice profits and we'll charge you interest on your loan at three per cent over base rate.'

'That's very kind of you,' I said. 'But I'm afraid it really isn't a question of money. It's just that neither Patsy nor I think that we would be happy in Mettleham.'

There was a long pause while this sank in. 'Well!' said Dr Robinson. 'I do think you've got a cheek. What do you think you were playing at? We're all very busy people. We don't have time to waste you know!'

I was tempted to explain to him that, just as he and his partners had been interviewing us, we had been interviewing them, and that they had failed miserably. But I didn't. I did, however, point out that I had gone to Mettleham because I was seriously interested in taking the job if it was offered to me. However, Dr Robinson did not seem very interested in anything I had to say.

'I think your behaviour is quite outrageous!' he said. And he repeated the last two words to emphasise them.

'I'm sorry you feel like that,' I said.

But Dr Robinson wasn't listening. He was threatening to report me to the General Medical Council and the British Medical Association, though what for I couldn't begin to imagine. I gently put the telephone receiver back onto its base. I couldn't help thinking that I could do quite well without people like Mr Onions and Dr Robinson in my life.

*   *   *

When I'd put the phone down I telephoned Miss Phillips.

'Would you do me a favour?'

'Of course!'

'Would you pop out to Bluebell Wood one more time and check to make sure that there aren't any protected species growing there? It's the only chance the village has got.'

'We have checked it very thoroughly,' said Miss Phillips. 'But if you'd like us to we'll go there again.'

'I'd be grateful,' I said. 'You never know. Something might have grown since you were last there.'

*   *   *

There were eleven books on the mantlepiece.

'Can you remember how many there were?' I asked Patsy, who'd come across to the coach-house flat with me as soon as we had eaten our lunch after I'd got back home at lunch-time. We wanted to look at the books that Mr Onions had asked if he could buy.

232

'I can't remember how many there were but I know they're all there,' said Patsy. 'They just fitted on the mantlepiece between those two pieces of stone.' She had used two large and rather colourful stones out of the garden as bookends.

I immediately thought that was rather odd, but I couldn't think why. I picked out one of the books at random and examined it. The jacket and the book were both in surprisingly good condition. The book was a historical romance and the cover showed a stunning brunette in the arms of a rakish looking fellow dressed in an officer's uniform. I had never heard of the author. I didn't know much about books but it seemed unlikely that this one was valuable. I carefully worked my way through the rest of the books but could not see any which seeed likely to be worth much money. Most of the books, and all of the ones which still had jackets, were novels. There were just two non fiction books, one about trains and a large one about gardening.

'Do you think we should let him buy them?' asked Patsy thoughtfully. 'Ten pounds seems quite a lot. It's twenty times as much as I paid for the whole tin bath.' She replaced one of the books which she had been examining. 'It would mean that we bought your Gladstone bag, got it repaired for nothing and still made a profit!'

I thought about it for a moment and I suddenly realised what was odd about what Mr Onions had said. He had said that he wanted to buy the books because his wife was reading one of them in bed at night and that he was reading another. And yet Patsy had confirmed that all the books were still in the same place. It seemed strange and extremely unlikely that they should put the books back onto the mantlepiece every morning. 'No,' I said. 'I don't think we should.'

When we had finished in the flat we went round to the vegetable garden. At once both of us noticed that someone had been picking strawberries. There was hardly a strawberry in sight. Someone must have picked at least ten or fifteen pounds of them. Even worse when they had put the netting back they hadn't made it taut and the magpies who had landed on it had been able to reach through and peck at the few fruits which were left. I'd seen them do that before. Normally we stretched the netting across the strawberry bed about two or three feet above the plants, keeping it in place with pea sticks and allowing the excess netting to hang down at the sides. It proved a very attractive bird barrier. But if the netting wasn't stretched tightly enough the birds landed on it in a group and weighed it down so that they could feed through the holes in the netting.

'Who on earth has done that?' asked Patsy crossly.

'It was the Onions,' I sighed. 'I'm sorry. It was my fault.' I explained that I had told Mr Onions that he could help himself to a few strawberries. I hadn't imagined that he would take everything we had.

We walked rather miserably back through the courtyard and into the kitchen. One of us would have to speak to Peter Marshall and tell him that there wouldn't be any more strawberries for a few days.

'Oh, I forgot!' said Patsy, as we got back to the house. 'There was a letter for you this morning.'

Our local postman had a large rural round and usually delivered the mail just before lunch. Not that we received much mail. Most of what we did get was bills. (Though the Sunday News had started sending me fairly huge amounts of mail in one of their vans).

Patsy reached behind the kettle and produced a long white envelope which was post marked London. I stared at for a moment before opening it. I didn't like getting letters from London. The envelope felt heavy and expensive.

'I wonder who its from?' I asked.

'I've got no idea,' said Patsy. 'Why don't you open it? Maybe you've won some money on the premium bonds!' She filled the kettle with water.

I looked at my watch. 'That'll be a surprise! I haven't got any premium bonds.' Come to that I didn't have any savings at all. I stuck my thumb under the flap, tore open the envelope and pulled out the contents.

'What is it?' asked Patsy a moment or two later. I looked up. She was staring at me with a worried look on her face. She reached out a hand and put it on my arm. 'Is it bad news?'

'No.' I said. 'It isn't bad news at all.' I handed her the letter. A London publisher had written to tell me that he had seen a copy of my article about Angipax. He wanted to know if I would write a book on the subject for his firm.

'They want you to write a book!' said Patsy; having read the first few lines she lowered the letter.

'Maybe!' I felt cautious.

'That's marvellous!'

I said that I agreed with her. She kissed me. I kissed her back. Then Patsy pulled herself away from me for a moment.

'Will they pay you money as well?'

'I suppose so. If they agree to do the book.'

And then, with some reluctance, I realised that it was time for me to go back to the surgery.

* * *

When I got there Miss Johnson was waiting for me. 'Would you ring Miss Phillips,' she said. 'She's rung three times in the last fifteen minutes. She says it's very urgent.'

I picked the telephone up immediately and dialled Miss Phillips' number.

'It's a miracle!' said Miss Phillips, excitedly. 'Miss Tweedsmuir and I found a clump of red helleborine in Bluebell Wood!'

'Wonderful!'

'What shall we do?'

'Telephone the newsdesk on the Sunday News,' I told her. 'And ask to speak to the news editor.' I gave her his name and telephone number. Tell him what you've found and I'm pretty sure that they will send a reporter and a photographer along. Don't tell anyone else yet. Once the photographer and the reporter have been then you can start ringing round as many conservation groups as you can think of.'

'Right!' said Miss Phillips. 'Do you know,' she said. 'I think this is the most wonderful news I've ever had. Miss Tweedsmuir says that we must go to church on Sunday to give thanks. It must be a miracle. We're both sure the flowers weren't there the last time we looked.'

I promised that Patsy and I would go to church with her.

* * *

By the time I got back home the telephone lines around Bilbury had been buzzing, and everyone seemed to know

235

about the discovery of the rare orchid growing in Bluebell Wood.

'It's amazing news!' said Dr Brownlow. 'I spoke to a man in the planning department who says that there's no chance of Sherlock Homes getting their planning permission now.'

'That's wonderful!'

'But I'm still sorry for you,' said Dr Brownlow. 'Really I am. It doesn't seem fair.'

'Don't worry,' I insisted. 'Patsy and I are very happy that Bilbury is going to be saved.'

'I still can't believe it!' said Dr Brownlow. 'Isn't it an amazing piece of luck?'

'Astonishing!' I agreed.

*   *   *

'Did you have a chance to look at those books of yours?' asked Mr Onions that evening. He had called round at the back door as Patsy and I were enjoying a wonderful vegetable hot pot. He held out a crisp, brand new ten pound note.

'I did,' I said. 'But they're my wife's books and there are one or two that she's especially fond of so I'm afraid I can't let you have them.'

Mr Onions looked disappointed but didn't say anything. He reached into his back pocket and pulled out a roll of bank notes. He peeled off another ten pound note.

'What about for £20?'

'No. I'm afraid not.'

He peeled off another note.

'£30?'

I shook my head. He peeled off two more notes.

'£50?'

I felt myself beginning to sweat but shook my head again. I was now certain that Mr Onions didn't want those books just to read them. 'I'm afraid not,' I said. 'My wife doesn't want to sell them.'

Mr Onions stared at me and shrugged. 'Please yourself,' he said and walked away.

*   *   *

236

CHAPTER TWENTY ONE

A few days later Patsy and I went to London.

I had written back to the publisher to tell him that I would very much like to accept his suggestion, and the next day his secretary had telephoned to ask me if I would go up and have lunch with him in London. She said that the firm would pay all my expenses, including a first class rail ticket. She also said that the publisher was keen for me to sign a contract as soon as possible because he wanted to have the book on his list.

'Why don't you come with me?' I said to Patsy. 'You could have a look around while I'm at my meeting – and then we could have tea together.' I knew that Patsy had never been to London before and I thought she might find it exciting.

At first Patsy said she didn't want to go, but then she admitted that it wasn't so much that she didn't want to go as that she didn't think we could afford the railway ticket.

'But it won't cost us anything!' I pointed out. 'The publishers will pay for a first class ticket for me but we can buy two second class tickets for the same price, or even less.'

Patsy looked worried. 'Isn't that fraud?'

'Of course not!' I told her. It took me a few minutes, but eventually I was able to persuade her that there was nothing dishonest in using the publisher's money to pay for two cheaper tickets. Once she had agreed I telephoned the station and reserved two seats for us before she could change her mind.

'What will I do while you're in your meeting?' Patsy asked me.

'You could go shopping.'

'Oh, I don't think so,' said Patsy, shaking her head. 'Not in London.'

'You could see some of the sights. Buckingham Palace. Saint Paul's Cathedral. The Tower of London. Trafalgar Square. That sort of thing.'

'Not without you,' said Patsy. 'Maybe you could show me around it all if there's time after your meeting?'

I smiled. 'We won't get to see much of London in a few hours.'

'That's all right. I don't mind.'

'You could take those books out of the flat to a book dealer.' I suggested. 'To see if any of them really are worth anything.'

'Oh yes!' cried Patsy, excitedly. But then a worried look replaced the momentary thrill. 'But where would I find a book dealer in London?'

'There will probably be one or two near to the offices where I'm meeting the publisher,' I told her.

We got up at five o'clock and drove to Barnstaple station where I parked the car in the almost deserted car park. We then caught the early morning stopping train from Barnstaple to Exeter. Patsy carried a bag filled with salad sandwiches and I carried our books wrapped up in two brown paper parcels tied with string. It was the first time I had been on the train since my very first trip to North Devon nearly a year earlier and I had forgotten what a beautiful journey it was.

At Eggesford they were getting ready for their annual Revels and the whole station was decorated with flowers and brightly coloured bunting.

At Exeter we caught the fast, main line express from the West Country to Paddington Station in London. It was a good thing that we had reserved our seats for the train was bursting with holiday-makers going home and men in suits going up to the City on business. The overhead racks and the narrow spaces between the seats were packed with bulging suitcases, brightly painted tin buckets and wooden handled metal spades, huge raffia work baskets packed with souvenirs for friends and neighbours, and straw hats that would be pushed to the back of a cupboard and never be worn again.

Fathers sat in their shirt sleeves reading their newspapers.

Mothers sat nursing shopping baskets packed to the top with sandwiches wrapped in greaseproof paper or packed in small, air tight plastic boxes, vacuum flasks full of hot tea, and bottles of ready mixed orange squash. Children, gloomy at the prospect of the long journey home and another fifty week wait for the next seaside adventure, scribbled with brightly coloured crayons on colouring books, table tops and each other, hunted underneath the seats for dice and counters lost from board games and fought endlessly and noisily.

Dotted amongst all this colour and noise sat dark-suited, dandruff-shouldered men dourly struggling with tedious looking sheaves of correspondence, pocket calculators and accounts which they took out of their black plastic briefcases. I felt sorry for them as they struggled to concentrate on their work amidst such chaos.

The train stopped just three times; at Taunton, at Westbury and at Reading. We ate our sandwiches between Taunton and Westbury. And then, less than two and a half hours after we had left Exeter, we were in London.

As we left the train at Paddington Station Patsy clutched at my hand and gazed about her in astonishment. Not even the bustle of Mettleham had prepared her for this. Although I had been to London several times before, my last visit had been some time ago and I too felt overwhelmed by it all. The noise, the bustle, the dirt and most of all the fact that everything seemed so enormous.

In Barnstaple the single platform at the railway station is covered by a small glass awning. At Paddington the whole station is covered by a glass roof which could cover half the town of Barnstaple itself. In London everything – crowds, traffic jams and noise – was a hundred times bigger than either of us was used to.

The publisher's office was at an address no more than five minutes walk away from the British Museum, but too far away from Paddington for us to walk in the time we had available (even if we had been confident about finding our way there) and I decided that he wouldn't mind paying for a taxi ride. I wanted Patsy to be able to see as much of London as possible and you don't see much of a city when you travel deep underneath it on an underground train.

We sat together in silence in the back of a black cab and Patsy, sitting on the edge of her seat and staring out of the window like a child outside a toy shop window, held onto my hand as though frightened to be alone for even an instant. 'What's your first impression?' I asked her, as the cab crawled along in one of London's never ending traffic jams.

Patsy turned towards me. 'It's all so dirty!' she whispered, as though worried that the taxi driver might hear her and be offended. I followed her gaze out of the window and stared at the huge, grimy old buildings and the rubbish littered streets. I nodded but had to laugh. This was Patsy's first impression of London, and sadly it wasn't the splendour of the buildings or the buzz and excitement on the streets which she would remember most vividly but the dirt and the rubbish.

'So you don't want to come and live here?'

Patsy looked at me. 'I will if you want to,' she said quietly. But there was horror in her eyes.

'It's all right!' I laughed. I put my arm around her. 'I was joking.' Patsy pretended to be cross with me but looked relieved.

A few moments later the taxi driver stopped outside the British Museum gates.

I had half an hour to spare and so we went for a cup of coffee at a small cafe in a narrow side street. The coffee was strong, thick and served in cups that were about the size of thimbles. We drank it in a dark, tiny, empty room the walls of which were lined with travel posters.

Afterwards, I pointed out two antiquarian bookshops to Patsy and said I'd meet her at a nearby public house called, quite appropriately, The Devon Arms at three o'clock. I asked Patsy if she would be all right by herself. She said she would and wished me good luck.

*   *   *

The publisher's offices were not at all what I had expected. (Although to be honest I don't really know exactly what I had expected. Probably something rather larger and more extravagantly furnished.)

At street level the only sign that the publisher existed was a small rectangular metal plate with the publisher's name printed on it screwed to the wall by the side of a scruffy looking door. Two plastic bags full of rubbish stood to the right of the door and an overflowing metal dustbin stood on the other side. The door was open, and although it was dark inside I could see that the tiny hallway was almost completely blocked with cardboard boxes. From the labels which they bore I assumed that these were full of new books. Abandoned 'free' newspapers were littered around on the floor.

I walked cautiously through the doorway, looked for a moment at a tiny lift at the end of the corridor, decided not to risk it, and started to climb slowly up the stairs.

An advertising agency had the offices on the first floor, a firm of accountants shared the second floor with a financial services consultant and a glamour magazine had the offices on the third floor. A series of small hand printed cardboard notices told me that the publisher I was looking for had offices on the fourth and uppermost floor.

Every door and every wall desperately needed painting. The stairs were uncarpeted and were littered with old newspapers, discarded envelopes, promotional cards which had fallen out of magazines and crumpled cigarette packets.

I knocked on the door to the publisher's office and, in response to a distant cry of 'Come in!' opened the door and entered.

A buxom woman of about forty, dressed in a violet dress and, despite the summer warmth, a grey cardigan, sat behind an old and battered typewriter with her hands clasped in her lap. She wore a pair of old fashioned half moon spectacles and had a single string of pearls around her neck. Her desk was piled high with papers, files and books and manuscripts. Behind her a dark haired girl of about seventeen, dressed in a rather grubby white tee shirt and a pair of torn blue jeans, sat hunched over another small desk licking envelopes. Her desk, too, was piled high with books and papers and files and manuscripts. Two filing cabinets, also piled high with books and papers and manuscripts and files, stood in a corner. The room was smaller than our bathroom at Bilbury Grange. I nervously and hesitantly introduced myself.

'Mr Inchmore is expecting you,' smiled the woman. She had a lovely smile. 'I'll tell him you're here.' She swung around on her chair and knocked on a door to her left. The black haired girl did not look up but just carried on licking her envelopes.

Out of sight there was a crashing noise and a half stifled curse and then a huge mountain of a man burst through the door with a fistful of papers in his left hand and a pair of horn rimmed spectacles in his right. He wore a badly fitting dark grey suit, a blue shirt and a bright red tie. When he saw me he slipped the spectacles into place. I couldn't help noticing that they were repaired in two places with bits of pink sticking plaster.

We shook hands and then he backed into his office and indicated that I should follow him. It wasn't an easy manoeuvre because I had to squeeze through a narrow gap between the chairs occupied by the buxom typist and the teen-age envelope licker.

Mr Inchmore's office was slightly larger than the outer room but, if possible, even more crowded. There were piles of books and papers everywhere. There was not one clear square inch of desk top visible.

'I loved your article about Angipax,' said the publisher. I tried to tip toe around a huge pile of books that had fallen over and which had, presumably, been the source of the crash I had heard. 'I've got a copy here somewhere,' he said. He rummaged around on his desk and, much to my surprise, produced a cutting which I instantly recognised. He handed it to me either for me to look at or, more likely, simply to prove to me that he was not quite as disorganised as he seemed to be.

'Have you ever written a book before?' he asked me.

I shook my head.

'Completely different business to writing newspaper columns,' he said. 'A newspaper piece is like a sprint but a book is more like a marathon.'

I swallowed hard and nodded. I had fallen in love with the idea of writing a book without stopping to realise that I didn't know how to begin, let alone finish the task.

'What I want is a book about the way doctors and drug companies give people pills without really knowing what's going to happen,' said the publisher. 'Lots of names. Tough.

Can you do that?'

'I think so,' I agreed. 'I'll need to do some research, of course . . . '

'Great,' said Mr Inchmore. 'I thought you could.' He fiddled with his spectacles and took them off again. 'I go by instinct,' he told me. He looked at me. 'I think you'll make an author.'

'Thank you,' I said.

'I can't pay you much,' said Mr Inchmore.'Did I suggest a figure in my letter?'

'No.'

'Would £750 be acceptable?'

'£750?.'

'As an advance against royalties, of course. I ought to get you to write an outline,' he said. 'But since you've never written a book before you probably won't be able to write an outline.' He grinned at me broadly. 'Writing an outline is harder than writing a book. To write an outline you've got to know what the book is going to look like when you've finished it.'

I was beginning to get cold feet.

'Just write the damned thing and then I'll show you what's wrong with it and we'll make a book out of it,' said Mr Inchmore with a laugh.

'The drug companies won't like it,' I said. 'Nor will a lot of doctors.' I thought I ought to warn him.

'Don't worry about libel,' said Mr Inchmore.'We'll take out the most dangerous stuff. If you don't put anything dangerous in it to start with it won't be worth publishing!' He squeezed past me to the doorway. 'Norma!' he called.

The buxom woman in the grey cardigan came in. Mr Inchmore introduced us to one another.

'Do one of our standard contracts for the Angipax book, will you?' He said to her. 'Then pop it in the post when it's ready.'

Doris promised to do it right away and then backed out of the room.

'Fancy some lunch?' asked the publisher.

I said that would be very nice.

'Great!' said Mr Inchmore. 'Follow me!'

In the outer office he introduced me to the girl with the black hair whose name was Helena and who had a beautiful face but the worst case of acne I think I had ever seen, borrowed two pounds off Norma and promised to be back within an hour. We then went down to the ground floor via the staircase. 'I never use the lift,' said Mr Inchmore. 'It gets stuck at least once a day.'

We walked around the corner, bought sandwiches at a baker's shop and ate them in a tiny park.

'I bet you thought publishers always took authors to posh lunches in fashionable restaurants,' said Mr Inchmore with a mouthful of beef sandwich.

I muttered something indecisive.

'I can't stand wasting money on restaurants,' he said. 'Food is just fuel. You don't spend a fortune on buying your petrol in a posh looking garage with expensive wall paper, do you?'

I agreed with this, though I didn't really think any comment was expected.

Ten minutes later we shook hands in the street outside Mr Inchmore's office. 'Norma will send you a contract,' he said. 'You send it back with your expenses and then she'll send you a cheque for your advance and your expenses all together.'

'Fine,' I said. 'Thank you very much.'

'I'm looking forward to this one,' said Mr Inchmore, rubbing his hands gleefully. He winked at me and then disappeared into the tiny hallway, squeezed past the boxes full of books and scurried up the stairs back to his office. I looked at my watch. It was a quarter past two.

I walked on along the street towards The Devon Arms to wait for Patsy.

I might not have yet written a book but I almost felt like an author.

*   *   *

Patsy was already waiting for me, sitting on the pavement outside the pub on a wooden bench at a wooden table with a long, cold drink in front of her.

I noticed, with some disappointment, that she had two crudely tied parcels of books sitting on the bench beside her. She was busy reading a magazine she had bought and didn't see me approaching.

'Excuse me,' I said. 'But can I join you?'

Patsy looked up and smiled. 'I'm so pleased to see you! How did you get on?'

'Great!' I told her. 'The publisher is quite a character. He's sending me a contract and he wants me to write the book.' I told her briefly about my meeting with Mr Inchmore.

'That's wonderful!' said Patsy.

'They're paying me £750 in advance,' I told her. 'If the book sells well I'll get even more!'

Patsy looked at me. 'We could nearly live on that!' she whispered.

'Plus, we've got my income from the column, and whatever fruit and vegetables we can sell to Peter Marshall and the rent from the coach-house flat!'

'Does that mean we might be able to stay in Bilbury?' asked Patsy, excitedly.

'Yes!' I told her. 'And how did you get on?' I nodded towards the parcels of books. 'No luck with the bookshops? Maybe we should have accepted Mr Onions' money after all.'

'Oh no we shouldn't!' said Patsy, with a broad smile on her face. 'You were absolutely right!'

I nodded towards the two parcels of books. 'But ... '

'They aren't all there,' said Patsy quickly. 'We brought eleven books with us but there are only ten left now.'

'You managed to sell one?'

Patsy nodded.

'That's wonderful! Which one?'

'Guess!'

'A novel?' I said, thinking I was being clever. Most of the books were novels.

'No.'

I tried to think what alternatives there were.

'The railway book?' I suggested, picking the least unlikely volume.

'No!' said Patsy, triumphantly. 'The one on gardening.'

'Why on earth was that one valuable? How much did they give you?'

'It was apparently a rare first edition by someone called Gertrude Jekyll. A very nice man in a very smart bookshop gave me £75 for it. All in brand new £5 notes!'

'Who on earth is Gertrude Jekyll?' I asked.

'Was,' corrected Patsy. 'She's dead now. She was a famous garden designer and gardening writer. Apparently people who collect gardening books think a lot of her.' She reached into her cardigan pocket and pulled out her purse. 'You'd better have this,' she said, handing it to me. 'I don't like carrying all that money around with me.' She told me that the bookseller had shown her a picture of the book she had sold him in one of his catalogues. It had been priced at £150.

'Brilliant!' I said. I slipped the purse into my inside jacket pocket. 'Where else have you been?'

Patsy looked down at her drink. 'I didn't go anywhere else,' she said quietly. 'I just came straight here when I came out of the book shop.'

'Why?' I asked her. 'Why didn't you go exploring?'

'I was frightened that I'd get lost,' confessed Patsy. 'I don't really like London very much,' she said apologetically. 'But I'm glad I've seen it.'

She paused and took a sip of her drink. She seemed hesitant and so I waited for her to continue. 'I've got some more good news,' she said. 'The man in the bookshop asked me if I went to many auctions. He said he would be keen to see any more old books I found and he gave me a catalogue listing some of the books he's looking for.' She moved a little closer and whispered. 'He said he'd pay hundreds of pounds for some books!'

Patsy went on to tell me that the bookseller had explained that most country house auctions a long way from London were attended only by furniture dealers who often didn't know anything about books. He had told her that if she went to auctions and junk shops she would probably find quite a number of valuable editions and that he would give her half the catalogue price for anything she found in good condition.

'I can't wait!' she whispered excitedly. 'It'll be great fun. We could make a bit more money that way. And we could go together if you're not working as a doctor any more.'

I said I would like that very much indeed.

'What else would you like to see while we're in London?' I asked her.

'I don't know. What is there?'

I told her about the changing of the guard, the shops in the Burlington Arcade, the National Portrait Gallery, the Science Museum, the stores in Knightsbridge and Oxford Street, the parks, Fleet Street, the Bank of England and Piccadilly Circus.

Patsy did not look very impressed. In fact she looked a little sad.

'What's the matter?' I asked her. 'Is there something else you'd rather do?'

'Well . . . ' began Patsy, shyly.

'What is it? Whatever it is we'll do it.'

'No, you'll think I'm silly...'

'I won't. Honestly.'

'You will.'

'I won't.'

'Honestly. Whatever it is you want to do we'll do it.'

'Even if it's silly?'

'However silly it is.'

'I'd like to go home to see the lambs and pick the strawberries. And look in the local newspaper to see what auctions there are. And you could start work on your book.'

I laughed out loud. I couldn't help it. But, as I quickly told Patsy, I wasn't laughing at her. I was laughing because I too couldn't think of anything I would rather have done.

'We're just a pair of country bumpkins,' I told her as we walked hand in hand back towards Paddington Station.

It wasn't as far or as difficult to find as I had feared, and an hour later Patsy and I were sitting beside one another on the train home, with our two parcels of worthless books beside us and Patsy's £75 in crisp, brand new £5 notes tucked safely in my jacket pocket.

As the train pulled out of the station Patsy sighed, tucked her arm in mine and leant her head on my shoulder.

'I'm glad we live in Bilbury,' she murmured.

'So am I,' I whispered back. 'So am I.' I looked down at her and saw that her eyes were closed.

She slept all the way back to Devon.

I didn't know exactly what the future held but I was looking forward to every minute of it.

Also Published by Chilton Designs

THE BILBURY CHRONICLES
Vernon Coleman

The first in a series of novels describing the adventures (and misadventures) of a young doctor who enters general practice as the assistant to an elderly and rather eccentric doctor in North Devon.

When he arrives in Bilbury, a small village on the edge of Exmoor, the young doctor doesn't realise how much he has to learn. And he soon discovers the true extent of his ignorance when he meets his patients.

There's Anne Thwaites who gives birth to her first baby in a field; Thumper Robinson who knows a few tricks that aren't in any textbook and Mike Trickle, a TV quiz show host who causes great excitement when he buys a house in the village.

Then there's elderly Dr Brownlow himself who lives in a house that looks like a castle, drives an old Rolls Royce and patches his stethoscope with a bicycle inner tube repair kit; Frank the inebriate landlord of the Duck and Puddle and Peter who runs the local taxi, delivers the mail and works as the local undertaker.

There's Miss Johnson, the receptionist with a look that can curdle milk; Mrs Wilson the buxom district nurse and Len her husband who is the local policeman with an embarrassing secret.

'A delightful read. I was entranced for hours.'

Miss S, Devon

'I loved this book. Please send two more copies as soon as possible.'

Mrs S, Nottingham

'Wonderful. One of the best novels I've ever read.'

Mr T, Leamington Spa

'I enjoyed 'The Bilbury Chronicles' more than any other book I've read for years. I am very much looking forward to the sequel.

Mrs G. Sunderland

'All your books are wonderful. The only snag is that I love them so much that I won't lend them to anyone because I'm frightened that I won't get them back. However, I do want my friends to share my pleasure so I enclose my cheque for two more copies of 'The Bilbury Chronicles'.'

Mr W. Plymouth

The Bilbury Chronicles by Vernon Coleman
ISBN 0 9503527 5 6   230 pages £12.95

Available post free from Chilton Designs Publishers, Publishing House, Trinity Place, Barnstaple, Devon, EX32 9HJ, England. (overseas customers please enquire about postage rates)

THE VILLAGE CRICKET TOUR
By Vernon Coleman

The story of a team of cricketers who spend two weeks of their summer holidays on a cricket tour of the West Country, and who make up in enthusiasm for what they may lack in skill.

'If anyone ever manages to bottle the essence of village cricket he will very quickly scale the dizzy heights of personal fortune. In the meantime we read and write about it in the pursuit of understanding. Seminal reading here includes de Selincourt and Blunden and should now embrace Vernon Coleman's latest offering, a whimsical piece about the peregrinations of a village team on its summer tour ... all the characters are here, woven together by a raft of anecdotes and reminiscences and a travelogue of some of the most picturesque spots in the south west.'

The Cricketer

'Describes in hilarious fashion the triumphs and disasters of a Midlands team's tour of the West Country and there is not a little of Jerome K.Jerome in Mr Coleman's style.'

Worcester Evening News

'I enjoyed it immensely. He has succeeded in writing a book that will entertain, a book that will amuse and warm the cockles of tired hearts. And what a change it makes from the wearisome cluckings of the current crop of cricket books with their grinding pomposity and, in many cases, their staggering lack of craftsmanship and originality.'

Punch

'A delightful book which also highlights some of the most spectacular scenery in Cornwall and Devon.'

The Cornishman

'Vernon Coleman is obviously a man who has enjoyed his cricket and over the years has committed to memory the many characters he has seen playing the game. He weaves them into the story as he charts the progress of his team's tour of Devon and Cornwall. The tale captures club cricket as everyone imagines it should be.'

Falmouth Packet

'Coleman is a very funny writer. It would be a pity if cricketers were the only people to read this book.'

This England

The Village Cricket Tour by Vernon Coleman
ISBN 0 95035273 X   180pages £12.95

Available post free from Chilton Designs Publishers, Publishing House, Trinity Place, Barnstaple, Devon, EX32 9HJ, England. (overseas customers please enquire about postage rates)

ALICE'S DIARY
The Memoirs of a Cat

Alice is a mixed tabby cat whose first book sparkles with wit and fun and a rare enthusiasm for life. Whether she is describing her relationship with the human beings with whom she shares her life (there are two of them – described as the Upright in Trousers and the Upright who wears a Skirt), her relationships with her many cat friends or her (not always successful) attempts at hunting, no cat lover will fail to find her story enchanting. Most important, every reader will, for the first time, have an insight into what it is really like to be a cat.

Extracts from some of the hundreds of letters received:

'I have just finished reading 'Alice's Diary' and what a delight it was. We have three cats and I can say with all honesty that I could have been reading about them.'

Mrs W. Cheshire

'I have just received my copy of 'Alice's Diary' and really did enjoy every page. I have recommended it to several of my friends.'

Mrs C. London

'Each night I read one month of your diary to my husband and all three of our cats came to listen as well!'

Mrs G. Berkshire

'Please send copies of 'Alice's Diary' to the eleven friends on the accompanying list. It is a wonderful book that will give them all great pleasure.'

Mr R. Lancashire

'A delightful book. I thoroughly enjoyed it.'

Mr W. Midlands

''Alice's Diary' is one of the nicest books I have read. She has wonderful insight. When do we get the next instalment? I can hardly wait. It really is an enchanting book.'

Mrs J. London

Alice's Diary - The Memoirs of a cat
ISBN 0 9503527 1 3   142 pages £9.95

Available post free from Chilton Designs Publishers, Publishing House, Trinity Place, Barnstaple, Devon, EX32 9HJ, England. (overseas customers please enquire about postage rates)

ALICE'S ADVENTURES
The Further Memoirs of a Cat

After the publication of her first book Alice was indundated with fan mail urging her to put pen to paper once more. This result is this, her second volume of memoirs.

No one could have predicted what was to happen to Alice - and many a tear was shed during this, the most eventful year of her life.

'Alice's Adventures' is full of the wry and witty observations which delighted the readers of her first book, 'Alice's Diary', and the wonderful illustrations accurately capture the most poignant moments throughout the year.

'Alice's Adventures' is another must for cat lovers everywhere.

'I didn't think Alice could surpass her first book – but she has. I really loved 'Alice's Adventures'. The saddest moment came when I finished it. When will the next volume be ready?'

Mrs K. Somerset

'We have had cats for 30 years and Alice describes incidents which are so real that we nearly died laughing at them.'

Mrs O. Leeds

'Alice's Adventures' is the loveliest book I have ever read. It captures everything brilliantly. Thinking back over the book I can't help smiling. I have never enjoyed a book as much.'

Mrs H. Edinburgh

'What a wonderful book. It was a real pleasure to read.'

Mr E. Exeter

Alice's Adventures - The Further Memoirs of a cat
ISBN 0 9503527 6 4   133 pages £9.95

Available post free from Chilton Designs Publishers, Publishing House, Trinity Place, Barnstaple, Devon, EX32 9HJ, England. (overseas customers please enquire about postage rates)